Far From Home

To Lorna

With love
Joy

Joy Bounds

Matador
9 Priory Business Park,
Wistow Road, Kibworth Beauchamp,
Leicestershire. LE8 0RX
Tel: (+44) 116 279 2299
Fax: (+44) 116 279 2277
Email: books@troubador.co.uk
Web: www.troubador.co.uk/matador

ISBN 978 1780881 737

British Library Cataloguing in Publication Data.
A catalogue record for this book is available from the British Library.

Typeset in 11pt Aldine401 BT Roman by Troubador Publishing Ltd, Leicester, UK

Matador is an imprint of Troubador Publishing Ltd

Printed and bound in the UK by TJ International, Padstow, Cornwall

To Leif

CHARACTERS

Zabillet (sounds like Zabbiyeh) – mother of Jehanne (Joan of Arc)

Zabillet's family and neighbours

Jacques Darc – her husband
Jacquemin and Yvette – her son and daughter-in-law who live at Vouthon
Pierre (Pierrelot) – her son
Jehanne (Jehanette) – her daughter
Petit-Jean – her son
Guillaumette – Petit-Jean's daughter
(Cathérine – a daughter who dies before the opening of this novel)
Jeanne Baudin – Pierre's wife
Aveline – sister, lives at Burey, near Vaucouleurs
Durand Laxart – husband of Aveline's daughter Marie
Jacques Alain – friend of Durand and of Jehanne

Guillaume – Jehanne's intended husband
Tomas – father of Guillaume
Jean Colin – the husband of the dead Cathérine
Bérenice – Jean Colin's second wife
Curé Frontey – Domremy's priest
Tante Marguerite – neighbour and good friend
Hauviette – daughter of Tante Marguerite
Jean Morel – good friend and a leader in the village of Domremy
Michel Lebuin – a friend of Jehanne's
De Bourlémonts – feudal lords of Domremy, now living some way up the valley
Gérardin d'Épinal – friend of Jehanne, lives in nearby Maxey

Béatrice d'Estellin – friend

Robert de Baudricourt – captain at nearby Vaucouleurs
Bertrand de Poulengy – Jehanne's companion when she leaves
Vaucouleurs
Jean de Metz – Jehanne's companion when she leaves Vaucouleurs
Henri and Cathérine le Royer – people in Vaucouleurs with whom
Jehanne stays

Those with the Dauphin, later King Charles VII, on the Loire

Duke d'Alencon – knight of the court and devotee of Jehanne
Duke Charles d'Orléans – prisoner-of-war long held in England
Bastard d'Orléans – his half-brother, fights alongside Jehanne
La Hire – captain in the French army, fights alongside Jehanne
Jean Pasquerel – priest who accompanies Jehanne
Jean d'Aulon – Jehanne's squire
Louise de Contes – Jehanne's page
Jacques Boucher – Jehanne's host in Orléans
Charlotte Boucher – his daughter
La Trémoïlle – adviser to the King
Bishop of Chartres - adviser to the King

Jehanne's opponents

Duke of Bedford – English regent in France
Philippe of Burgundy – Duke and ally of the English in France
Jean de Luxemburg – ally of Duke of Burgundy. Jehanne was his
prisoner
Bishop Pierre Cauchon – Judge at Jehanne's trial
Jean Massieu – usher at the trial of Jehanne
Martin Ladvenu – a cleric at Jehanne's trial

Others

Nicolas Bailli & Gérard Petit – take evidence about Jehanne for her
    Rouen judges

Richard Moreau – travels to Domremy to tell Zabillet of events in
    Rouen

Guillaume Bouillé – first to investigate the truth of Jehanne's trial
    and verdict

Jean Brehal – Inquisitor, annuls the verdict of Jehanne's trial

Pierre Maugier – Zabillet's counsel in the rehabilitation of Jehanne

Goddams – the English army in France during the 100 years war.

Écorcheurs - marauders

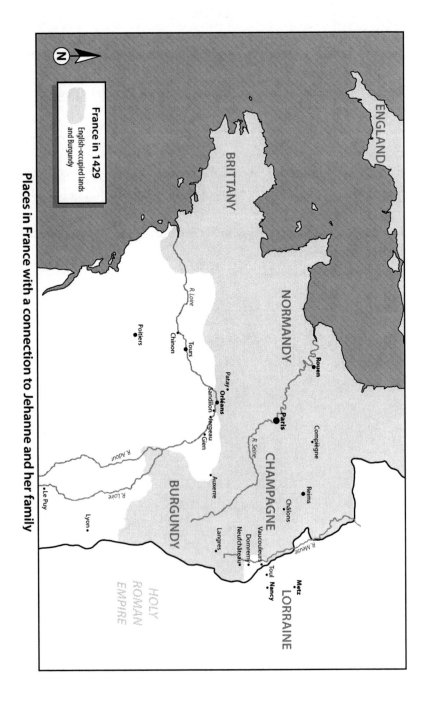

Places in France with a connection to Jehanne and her family

France in 1429

English-occupied lands and Burgundy

ENGLAND

BRITTANY

NORMANDY

CHAMPAGNE

BURGUNDY

LORRAINE

HOLY ROMAN EMPIRE

R. Loire

R. Seine

R. Meuse

R. Adour

R. Loire

Poitiers

Chinon

Tours

Patay

Orléans

Sandillon

Jargeau

Gien

Auxerre

Langres

Neufchâteau

Domrémy

Vaucouleurs

Toul

Nancy

Metz

Rouen

Paris

Compiègne

Reims

Châlons

Lyon

Le Puy

CONVERSATIONS

Zabillet talks with the Chronicler in Orléans

My name is Zabillet in the old Lorraine style, though here they call me Isabelle Romée. I am old. Joints swollen, my very bones cry with pain when I move. Cold and rain create torture in the movement of my limbs. And I am far from home. My mind, so muddled as I weave a slow path through the streets and markets of Orléans, dwells with clarity on the green beauty of my land, where as a young girl I danced to catch the eye of Jacques of Domremy.

From there unfolded the strangest, finest, cruellest story. I will tell you of it, since you ask, but let my heart linger first on the fields, golden under the late autumn sun, and the river, broad and shallow, making its lazy way along the valley; on our little house built on the edge of the village, overlooked by the hills rising behind covered with deep green forest; on the sound of birds and of cows to be milked, and then of babies: Jacquemin, sweet Cathérine, Petit-Jean, kind Pierrelot and Jehanette.

And yet it was a hard life. How could it be otherwise for peasants whose land was not their own, with taxes and levies to be paid before feeding all those mouths? There were long cold winters, snow falling on the fields of Lorraine under the greyest sky. Never quite enough wood for the fire. Never quite enough warm clothes. Never quite enough food.

But there was a calm about it, a rightness, for was this not the experience, throughout time, of all my neighbours, and my dear family and friends? To love and hate the land in equal measure with its whimsical bounty and unpredictable barrenness; to scrape together enough to keep ourselves, and pay the never decreasing taxes to those whose faces and fine clothes we rarely saw; to lend a bit here to a neighbour who had suffered more than their share of deaths amongst the animals, and borrow it back when our grain had become inedible. How calm and serene it looks now, so many years later, a lifestyle lived and enjoyed and suffered over centuries. You will see how, in the course of what I have to tell you, all that was to change.

At the start of my story, France was not the unified country it is now. It had become a fractured land under a mad King; and after his death was ruled through some treaty by the baby King of England, whose regent in France was aided by our neighbours, the traitorous Burgundians. The weak French Dauphin was far away to the south, ignored, powerless, unassertive of his right to be King. France was at war with itself as well as with England. And there were other predators too, lawless brigands we called écorcheurs because they scraped the land clean, burning what was left after they had stolen what they wanted. Yet for all the Dauphin's impotence and distance, we were proud to belong to him, to call ourselves citizens of France, protected by the stubborn French captain at Vaucouleurs just a half-day's walk up the road.

Life in our village and family went on, little touched at first by those events. Our oldest son Jacquemin grew up and married and took on his own house and fields, and Cathérine would have her own sad story. But Jehanette, Petit-Jean and Pierrelot were to become entangled in the tentacles of this war as it tightened its hold on Domremy, and gripped our throats to the destruction of my family.

This story which I must tell of war and great courage and treachery, is one of loss. Though France may celebrate her achievements for centuries to come, it is the story of how I lost my daughter, Jehanne, whom people here call Jeanne d'Arc, and the peace of my family.

Family Life

1427-1429

WINTER 1427

A Betrothal

1

Zabillet did not like the expression on Jacques' face as she hurried to put food on the table. It wasn't that he hated the poor meal – the last of the root vegetables and cabbage, with a few heavily-spiced chunks of pork thrown in, almost the last of the pig slaughtered a few weeks before and beginning to smell foul. He was as used to that as she. Something else was on his mind; she had no idea what it could be. The hearty but unvarying food made her sigh as she chopped up the last of the bread. It would be gruel from now on. Still, she must be glad there was enough to fill their bellies in this harsh winter, which was made even worse by the groups of hungry marauders who plundered their scanty supplies. There were already families in the village who had virtually nothing in their store, and had to send their children round to their neighbours' begging a turnip or a few decaying meat-bones or a heel of bread.

But Zabillet and her family were surviving. Sometimes Jacquemin brought them food from Vouthon, where he farmed his dead grandfather's land, and had more than he needed. But mainly grief had dulled their appetites. None of them fancied the dreary food which was all she could put her mind to. She had no energy or desire to think like she used to of different ways to make a meal tasty. Even in the harshest of times she had sought out different herbs and leaves in the countryside, or baked fragrant pastries. It was a while since she'd bothered to do that.

Zabillet felt a sense of foreboding as Jehanne and Petit-Jean sat down on the benches at the table with their father.

5

'Jehanne, just give me a hand with these bowls, would you?' she said sharply. She didn't need any help; she just wanted to put off for a moment discovering what was making Jacques so on edge. Jehanne got up and did as her mother asked. She didn't seem aware of any tension, for she happily clattered the bowls onto the table, and went outside to get some water, calling a cheerful hello to a passing neighbour as she did so. Zabillet wished Pierre was here; he was always sensible, and never joined in family squabbles, and that helped her to stay calm. But he was at the Baudins', though he was sure to call in later. Zabillet sighed; she knew he was there because he was going to marry and become a member of that family, but maybe also because theirs had been a joyless household since Cathérine died. She'd forgotten how to spend time with her children, how to be amusing or interesting. She was hardly managing to drag herself through one day after the next.

Jacques kept throwing looks at Jehanne, a half-smile on his face, but not a particularly pleasant one. Zabillet watched him closely, trying to guess what might be in his mind. He was harsh with them all now, it seemed, but Jehanne seemed to attract it most. Zabillet watched time and again as Jehanne fought it, fought him, and loved her for her spirit, at the same time as she looked on despairingly. She saw that Petit-Jean was also watching his father, a secretive, unpleasant smile on his dark face. He seemed to be able to sniff out trouble and excitement; he loved it. Her anxiety rose at his expression. Something was going to happen. She had no idea what. The only unusual thing that had happened that day as far as she knew was that Jacques had been made furious by his dreams again. But that had been at dawn.

The dreaming had started soon after Cathérine's death. In one of the rare moments of closeness they had shared since those awful days, he had told her about it.

'I see a long line of troops,' he had said, the memory of the night still heavy on him. 'They are tense and excited, clutching their lances, bent over the horses' necks. The infantry is running alongside, swords and shields held ready to fight. I feel happy because they're French, the livery of France is on their backs and on their standards. "God be praised!" I shout running along with them. "We're going to banish the filthy Goddams and their Burgundian lackeys. France will be free!" A flicker of fear passes through me, and hope. At last we're going to kick out the enemy.'

Zabillet saw the strange exhilaration he had experienced play over his face. 'In the dream, it's a lovely summer day' he continued. 'The army fans out wide as they cross the valley, the sun is glinting on their helmets and the grass, oh it's so green, Zab. Like you never saw, even in spring. It gleams. The men are shouting at each other full of energy and enthusiasm. They're sure to have victory today'.

Zabillet had listened impatiently. It was powerful all right, but what was important about a dream on some fairy-tale battlefield? He should be glad he was dreaming about something interesting, and not seeing the devil come and suck the life out of their daughter all night long, as she did.

'I'm not one of the soldiers', he'd continued. 'It's as if I can see over the whole thing. The commander sits at the head of the army in shining armour on a black horse. Waving a standard high, fluttering white against the deep blue sky, the figure shouts encouragement to the soldiers, the voice sounding clear above the clatter of hooves and all the noise. I feel a jolt of recognition. And do you know what? As the horse wheels round, I see that it's Jehanne. Our Jehanette, heading up the army! Her eyes are afire; she's got that look on her face – you know, so determined and sure. I wake up shocked, shouting "No! No!" trembling all over.'

Zabillet had put her arms around Jacques, pulling his face onto her shoulder.

'It's just a dream,' she had said. 'Who knows what these pictures of the night mean? It doesn't mean it's actually going to happen.'

'How can that be, Jehanette with the army? Not just with the army, but at the head of it? Pff, the only women who ride with soldiers are whores,' he spat. 'She mocks us, Zab.'

'Don't be ridiculous,' she said, gently challenging him to wake up out of his dream-fear and think how unlike a whore their daughter was. 'She may be almost a woman but you know there's nothing whatsoever of the whore about her.'

'But what does it mean? I would rather drown her,' he growled, 'than see her with the army.'

And just this morning she had found him wild with fury again, the dream filling all his mind. He had stormed out of the house before sunrise. When she had hurried after him, worried that perhaps he had heard écorcheurs riding into the village on one of their dawn raids, she had found him outside kicking ferociously at the wood-pile.

'That damn dream again,' he said in answer to her enquiry. 'I'm going to do something about it this time. I've told Pierrelot and Petit-Jean that if I'm not around to drown her, they must, if there's the slightest hint of her leaving with the army. No daughter of mine is going off with soldiers.'

'But Jacques,' Zabillet tried to argue with him again. A dream repeated so many times had to be respected, but he was seeing it wrong. 'Jehanne is not a whore in this dream of yours, any more than she is in real life. She's not going to go anywhere with soldiers; she doesn't like soldiers or their weapons, or anything. Not like Petit-Jean, he would go off to war the minute you gave him your blessing. She doesn't even look at men. You're getting everything mixed up. I can't think of anything she is less likely to do than become a camp-follower.'

Zabillet had looked across the pre-dawn valley. In the grey, shadowless light the landscape looked menacing and unreal, the trees bleached by the moon. She had shivered. Jacques had got it all so wrong, and yet there was somehow a hint of truth in his dream.

'I know Jehanne's not like that,' Jacques conceded finally. 'It makes no sense. But I'm going to put a stop to it, once and for all.'

⚜

Zabillet watched Jacques carefully as they came to the end of their poor meal. He looked smug, self-satisfied, yet she could see that he was anxious too, and kept casting looks at Jehanne. She knew, as he munched his way through a couple of old wrinkled apples, the remnants of last year's harvest, that he was working himself up to tell them something.

'Well, young woman,' he said at last, spitting pips out of the apple core. 'Come mid-summer's day, you'll be married.'

'Don't tell me,' laughed Jehanne. 'You had one of your dreams again foretelling more strange futures for me.' She was busy pouring wine into their mugs.

'No, young madam, more than a dream this time.' Jacques took a large swig. 'I've been talking to Tomas this morning, and everything is agreed.'

Zabillet gasped. So that was where his smug expression came from. He wasn't going to wait for Jehanne to fall for someone and make her own choice of whom to marry, as their other children had done.

Zabillet saw Jehanne look at Jacques, checking out if he was joking or not. She tried once more.

'Don't be silly, Papa.' Fear had nevertheless crept into her voice. 'If I were to marry, which I've told you I shan't, I'd hardly marry a buffoon like Guillaume.'

'Buffoon, is he?' shouted Jacques. He checked himself. 'Guillaume is a perfectly suitable young man. You've known him all your life. And you'll be just down the road at Maxey, what could be better?' He turned to Zabillet. 'That would be good, wouldn't it?'

'It wouldn't be good,' shouted Jehanne. 'But I'll tell you what would be even better. It would be better if you left me alone. I tell you, I'm not going to marry Guillaume or anyone else.'

'Oh yes you are, can't you see it?' chimed in Petit-Jean. 'Jehanne and Guillaume! Guillaume and Jehanette! Very nice!'

'Shut up, idiot.' Jehanne turned on her brother and aimed a blow at his head. He put up his hands in mock horror.

'Ooh, I'm scared.'

'Be quiet, Petit-Jean,' said Zabillet. She turned back to Jehanne. 'At least say you'll think about it.' What was wrong with the girl? Yes, it would have been better if Jacques had gone a bit slower – she didn't even know it was in his mind. But it was quite usual for two families to agree marriage arrangements, after all. They would have been very happy if Jehanne had chosen her own husband, or even talked as all her friends did of marriage in the future, but her stubborn resistance worried her a great deal. What else was there for her to do but marry? Perhaps if she were forced, she would settle down eventually, yes, settle down and be ordinary. Yes, ordinary, that's what she wanted. Much as she wanted to protect what was so unusual in Jehanne, that was the best thing for her. Like Cathérine. She had been only too happy to marry, surely Jehanne would come round. And if she married Guillaume, she would only be in the neighbouring village.

'Maman, please don't say that. You know I don't want to think about it.' Jehanne turned a face full of distress and outrage towards her. 'I am not going to be married. I've always said I wouldn't. I can't.'

'Can't? Can't? Oh yes you can, my girl, and you will,' said Jacques firmly. He wiped his mouth on his sleeve. 'I don't want to hear any more about it. Two cows and a couple of pounds will accompany you. Next week you shall go to church and make your promise.'

'I shall not,' screamed Jehanne, getting up and sending the stool flying across the floor. Her dark eyes flashed. 'You cannot make me, believe me, you cannot.' She ran out of the house, weeping noisily.

'I'm off back to the fields to watch the cattle,' said Petit-Jean jauntily, following her out.

'Don't you go after her,' said Zabillet sharply. 'You'll only make it worse. Let her think about it.' Petit-Jean picked up his stick, saying nothing.

'Two cows and a pound or two!' laughed Jacques. 'To get her settled. That's cheap at the price.'

'Don't, please don't. For God's sake, go easy on her. Why not give her a bit of time to get used to the idea? You know how headstrong she is, especially if she feels forced.'

'Too late, Zab. It's all agreed!' He sloshed some more wine into the bowl.

Zabillet busied herself pouring water from the great pitcher into the pot which always hung over the fire. Then she collected together the bowls and drinking cups off the table and put them by the door to take outside to wash later. She got the broom out and swept every inch of the floor, though she had only done that a couple of hours before. Jacques continued to sit there, pouring wine and more wine into his bowl.

The silence stretched out. Zabillet felt ashamed that she had not tried harder to talk Jacques out of his plan. She wanted him to go, so she could run out after Jehanne. Where would she be, in the woods perhaps, or in the church? She would have liked to sit by her, hold her, weep with her, try to accustom her to what inevitably must happen, whether with this Guillaume or some other man. She had neglected her since Cathérine died. She had no idea what was in her mind.

Irritated, she pushed under the rim of her cap the hair that had worked its way free. She began to fold the clothes which had lain out all morning to dry in the wintry sun. She pulled, straightened, stretched and smoothed each one; the rough work trousers, the strong red skirts Jehanne wore, like all the village girls, and hung them on the pegs around the room to finish drying. She glanced now and then at Jacques, who continued to sit awkwardly at the table, his hand on his cup.

'It's all right, Zab,' he said. His voice pleaded with her to think so. 'She just needs settling down, she's too headstrong by half. Tomas' boy will soon sort her out, you'll see.'

She said nothing. She pulled so strongly on the shirt she was folding that the slight tear in the shoulder ripped into a huge rent.

'It's a wonder he'll take her on,' he laughed, drawing strongly on the drink. 'I thought we might never find a husband for her, with her funny ways. Now she'll have to stop having such fancy notions.'

'You should have waited. It's only this stupid dream of yours that's made you do this. She's young yet.'

'Nonsense,' roared Jacques. 'You talk to her, she'll be all right.' He caught at her as she went past. 'You'll see.' He pushed his face into her breasts, his hand finding its way under her skirt to the soft skin of her thigh. 'Remember what it's like to be getting married, eh, Zab? Eh?'

Zabillet felt a wave of nausea as Jacques got up and tried to tumble her to the floor. 'No, Jacques,' she said. 'Stop it!' She shoved him away hard, furious, and though he was much bigger and stronger than she, he reeled back. 'Don't you dare.'

'It's agreed,' he said sullenly, taking his hat off the shelf. 'There's no changing that.'

'I'll go and find her later,' she said. 'Just don't push her, you know it makes her stubborn.'

2

Zabillet moved around the house and yard, bringing in wood, fetching water, chopping more vegetables into the remnants of the midday meal to make a soup for the evening. If any neighbour spoke to her as she moved from house to lane to river and back and out and in again, she did not hear them. Her stomach churned.

Sometimes anger gripped her, and she would slam a dish down on the table, or roughly push a stool so it went skidding across the hard earth floor. How dare Jacques do such a thing without even mentioning it to her? At other times Jehanne was on her mind. Stubborn girl! Was it not true that Guillaume was a nice boy, taking his turn happily with the sheep in the fields, helping his father with the plough, always careful and thoughtful when they had to flee to the château grounds for fear of the marauders?

Sturdy and steady. Maybe that was the trouble. No, it was more than that. Jehanne did not dislike him, she was happy to talk to him or anyone else if she had to, and was unfailingly kind if anyone was in any kind of trouble. The truth was, she was not interested in any of the village boys, however handsome or exciting.

How she missed Cathérine at times like this. More than a year had gone by since she died, yet every day she still thought of her, longed for her, wept for her. How cruel that her young body should waste away in an agony of pain whilst they all, including her young husband, Jean Colin, looked on in fear. How she would have liked to go out now, walk along the lane to Greux and sit with her talking about their strange Jehanne, mulling over what was the best way of dealing with the stupid, impetuous thing that Jacques had done. The painful image crept into Zabillet's mind of her two daughters lying asleep side by side on Cathérine's death bed, Jehanne's arm carelessly slung over her dying sister; the wasted, old-whilst-young shrunken face of the one against the rude health of the other.

And where was Jehanne after all this time? The spinning-wheel lay idle, where normally on an afternoon like this she would be sitting busy with the spindle, preparing the wool they needed to sell to the people of Neufchâteau, or weave into clothes to keep themselves warm in the winter. She would be in the church perhaps, or one or other of her favourite places, up towards the Fairy Tree where the healing fountains were maybe, or down by the river where it ran away into the woods from the village. Over time Zabillet had learnt it was pointless to look for her in her friends' houses. She was never there.

She sighed. She could stand her confused, grief-ridden thoughts no longer. She would go to the church herself and if Jehanne was not there, she could sit and talk with *curé* Frontey for a while. He seemed to understand Jehanne better than anyone, perhaps he could tell her what to do. She pulled her warm shawl around her shoulders, and was dampening down the fire when she heard shouts from the yard. Through the doorway she could see a horse and cart pulling up outside the house.

'Aveline!' she exclaimed, her mood immediately lifting as she rushed outside. 'And Durand! What are you doing here?'

She laughed as she helped her sister out of the cart and gave her a big hug. 'And you Durand, what a lovely surprise. Are you going to unhitch the horse? Tie her up here.'

'We're not here for long,' said Aveline, linking arms with Zabillet and turning towards the house. 'Durand had some business in Maxey, so I persuaded him to come on here. But we mustn't stay long; it gets dark so soon.'

'You're freezing,' exclaimed Zabillet. 'Come on in. It's not a great day for riding round the countryside in an open cart.'

'That's why Marie's not with me.' Aveline pulled a stool up close to the fire, and held out her hands to capture the warmth. 'She wanted to come, but she's got such a fever Durand said she must stay at home. They're love-birds, Zab, that's what they are. They can hardly bear to be parted, even for a day.'

Zabillet smiled, amused and pleased to see her sister so cheerful. Aveline had despaired of her daughter Marie until a year or so ago; she was far more interested in the soldiers of Vaucouleurs just a step from their little village of Burey, than in spinning or tending the animals. Neither Aveline's tears nor her father's whippings had seemed able to keep her from the inns of the town, flirting, enjoying the company of the soldiers far too much. Whenever Aveline and Zabillet had met, all their talk had been of what they could do to prevent her, fearing pregnancy, disease, neighbours' gossip.

Then she had met Durand Laxart, a young widower who had recently come to Burey from some far village, and taken over a little house and some land from a distant relative who had died. And in a moment, it seemed, Marie had turned from a capricious, rebellious girl into a sturdy housewife.

Zabillet sighed. More recently it had been her turn to be troubled, to seek comfort and re-assurance from her younger sister. She warmed up some wine for them, stirring some spices in, so the house was filled with a cheerful, warming aroma.

'Is Jacques about?' asked Durand, coming into the house after securing the horse. 'I want to tell him what's going on at Vaucouleurs.'

'I hope de Baudricourt is getting rid of those damn Burgundians,' said Zabillet. 'We could certainly do with some of his protection.' The village was paying one warlord a large amount of money they could ill afford to stop other warlords attacking them. It had bought a measure of 'peace' for Domremy, but they feared having to pay more and more if Robert de Baudricourt could not help them.

'It's not going well for him. Virtually everywhere's in the hands of the Burgundians now. His whole land is being attacked, and he's busy trying to make deals – you know what he's like. Truces, treaties, anything to get them off our back for a while. I can't see him being able to help you much. I'll go and see if I can find Jacques.'

'Oh, he's somewhere about. I should try the fields towards Coussey – they were busy digging a new ditch earlier. Pierrelot's probably there with him too.'

'Jacques has arranged for Jehanette to be married,' said Zabillet as she ladled the steaming wine into a cup.

'That's good,' said Aveline, warming her hands on the cup and sipping the hot drink. 'Mm, that's lovely. I can feel it warming all the way to my stomach. It's not good, is it?' she finished, looking at her sister.

'She won't hear of it. She's run off I don't know where since he told her earlier. I'll have to go and look for her soon.'

'She'll be back, don't worry. She's always going off on her own, she won't go far. But what made Jacques do that? She's still young and obviously not interested.'

'He's plagued by dreams. Says he keeps seeing her with the army, and assumes she's going to become a camp-follower.' Aveline's face registered disbelief. 'It infuriates him that she has no interest in the boys of the village, and keeps saying she'll never be married.'

'So he decided to fix it.' Aveline smiled. 'Typical Jacques.'

'Always trying to fix things. It doesn't look good in the village for him to have a daughter who doesn't fit. And she's so stubborn, Avie, so he has to show her who's boss. Oh, he was pleased, I can tell you, even when she stormed off.' Zabillet shifted uncomfortably on the bench, remembering how threatening he had been.

Aveline looked at her curiously. 'What do you think?'

'He needs to leave her be,' said Zabillet indignantly. 'She's still very young. God knows, Jehanne could fall for someone anytime, and then we'd all wonder what the fuss was about. And if not, she's a sensible girl; she'll do what she has to in the end. What other choice is there? As it is, he's just making everyone miserable.'

'Poor Jacques! He thinks he's making it right, and he's just frightening Jehanne. And you.' She clasped Zabillet's hand across the table. 'Look, I tell you what. You tell Jacques he must give her time and not pester her. But if things get bad, why not let Jehanne come to me for a while? You know I can always do with the help, and maybe it'll get you over a bad time.'

'You're an angel,' said Zabillet, beginning to look a little happier. 'I may take you up on that, though God knows I can hardly spare her here. We're such a little household now, you know, with

Pierrelot as good as gone, and so much to do.'

Aveline got up and gave Zabillet a hug. 'That's our fate now,' she said, 'to see our children go off one by one. How's dear old Pierrelot anyway, now he's to be master of his own house, even if it is only three doors away?'

Zabillet laughed. 'Oh, very much preparing to be the lord of the manor. How strangely things work out. He's a mere boy, yet in his mind, his future is all happily mapped out. He'll be married to the Baudin girl. She's sweet and capable; they'll be a good, solid family, I'm sure. He likes to help Jacques with collecting the taxes, and probably sees himself doing more of that as time goes on. He usually calls in this time of day. I do miss him; he's the voice of calm around here, I can tell you – maybe that's him.' There was the sound of someone scraping mud off their boots. 'Pierrelot, is that you?'

'No, it's only me.' Durand stepped into the house, blowing on his hands. 'We'll have to go soon, it's getting colder and colder out there. Have you kept a cup of that hot wine for me, Tante?'

'I have.' Zabillet laughed to be called thus by this self-possessed young man. 'Did you find Jacques?'

'I did, but he was busy with his weights and measures, so I didn't stay long. No, I found young Jehanne down by the river, so I stopped to talk to her.'

Zabillet looked up. 'How was she? We had a bit of a row here earlier.'

'Oh she was fine. She said she would be home soon, and to tell you not to worry.'

Durand shuffled his feet as he swallowed the hot liquid. He didn't want to join in the women's talk; he wanted to think about how he had come across Jehanne in the woods by the river, and watched as she knelt there, ignorant of his presence, her face turned towards the sky. On her face was an intense interplay of happiness, beseeching and radiance. And when she had finally noticed him, he didn't want to forget how that radiance still suffused her face and eyes. And how happily they had chatted and laughed, teased each other. He still felt the warmth of their encounter. He wouldn't have been able to find the words to describe what he felt for her.

'I was just saying to Zabillet, that perhaps Jehanne might come to stay with us for a while, if she wants to. She'd be good company for Marie.'

'That would be good,' said Durand. 'She'd be very welcome, and we could certainly do with the another pair of hands.. But talking of Marie, I think we'd better start back if we're not to worry her to death.'

Zabillet hugged her sister hard as she prepared to climb into the cart. 'I'm so glad you came,' she said. 'I was quite miserable until you arrived to cheer me up. And I might take you up on your offer. You never know.'

'Yes, do.' She touched a finger to Zabillet's cheek. 'And just persuade Jacques to give her time. It'll work out all right, you'll see.'

Zabillet watched as the cart started to move along the lane, and turned back into the house. She glanced at the sky, black clouds heralding early darkness. She must go and find Jehanne.

CONVERSATIONS

Zabillet talks with Our Lady in Domremy

Dear Holy Mother, let me feel near to you in this quiet place. I am confused and fearful. Look kindly on me as I speak with you, and seek ease in your wisdom and compassion.

It seemed so simple when the children were young. Was I foolish to hope for ordinary pleasures like three sturdy peasant sons to help till the land and keep us all safe; for my two daughters to be with me always, living a hard life cheerfully, and eventually to have little ones scurrying around my feet? Apparently so, for one daughter is dead, and the other is so fractious and sure of her own mind, determined somehow to tread a different path, though she does not say what that path is. You must know, Holy Mother, for she spends time in here, perhaps more than I think, talking to you and to the saints here – I've heard her sometimes when I come in – as if they were her friends.

The other young people mock her for being apart, never quite sharing in their preoccupations. It was always like that. I remember when she was little, and we would go to the hermitage at Bermont on a Saturday. Holding my hand tight, she would jump along, full of questions, curiosity, laughter. As we entered the little chapel, she would run up to your statue, an old, wooden thing, as if you were her best friend, and chatter about the baby Jesus you held, and the little dove on your arm, her face alight with love. And when I came out after finishing my prayers, she might be lying in the long grass in front of the chapel, looking up through the branches of the trees as they waved in the wind, radiance streaming from every pore of her face as if she were watching a host of angels. She was such a sweet, loving child, yet in some way never like the others. And that sweetness is still there, though it is often hidden from us as she stubbornly resists her father. Oh, how stubborn she is.

I try to sit quietly, to feel your peace and shake off these worries. Yet, where can my mind rest when trouble is everywhere? Far off wars, far off deals, changes of allegiance. England and France. What are these things that keep changing all the time? Does it matter that I have always lived in places loyal to France, and not given over to Burgundy or the English? I was proud to have been born in Vouthon, belonging to France, and then when I married Jacques to move to Domremy, which also belongs to France. Belonging to Bar as well, of course, or Lorraine, whose Dukes change sides regularly depending on the advantage to be gained from it. Belonging to the de Bourlémonts too, whose castle overlooks the whole valley. Working the land for them, paying dues to them all, one way or another.

Proud to belong to France, and yet in the last few years we've been ruled by a baby English King. How can it be that the Dauphin, son of our old dead King, has been ignored and powerless since the country, our country, was signed over to England, a land over the sea? I have never seen the sea, it is so far from here. Jacques says that we must stand firm with Robert de Baudricourt at Vaucouleurs for France, and wait for the English Goddams to be defeated. Maybe I would not worry so much if it were not for the écorcheurs, from whom we seem to have to flee more and more often to the grounds of the old Château d'Île for safety, and who take away our livelihood.

Something has gone wrong. We are not free, have never been free, yet now we get no return for all that we do, and pay. Protection, that is what we are due. I understand how it is meant to work – we give time, work, goods and money, and they make sure that no-one attacks us. We give to our *seigneurs* de Bourlémont, who even now, though no longer living in the village, own us and look after us who till and harvest their land. And I know that in turn they must pay the Duke, or whoever owns the wider land, and he pays the King. And whilst great wealth is engendered for them and their families, we have not been so discontent with that if they keep us safe. But now we are no longer safe.

Forgive me, Holy Mother, for asking such questions, but what does God think when he looks down and sees our peaceful lives disrupted? The rich and powerful people are scheming to get the best for themselves, regardless of us, to make sure they are on the right side when whatever they see happening comes about. The 'right side' being that of the eventual winner, whoever that might be in this endless war. Does God see his peaceful tapestry's thread drawn tight, broken, blood soaking in to spoil the colours, new borders roughly sewn in daily, and loathsome insects eating up the lovingly stitched-in villages? How much must we suffer before it is mended and cleaned? Is our sinfulness so great?

To my shame, last night I said to Jacques 'Perhaps if the young English King brings peace to France, that would be best, for then we can live free of fear.' 'Never!' he cried. 'Never! The Goddams are not to be in France, we will never accept them.' I dared to tell him some of my fears; what might happen if we fled to the relative safety of the Château grounds, but those raiding the village broke through and murdered us all; and how hard it is to find food for everyone now that so much has to go in taxes, and about Petit-Jean who gets so excited by these stories of the marauders that he would go off and fight too. And surely Robert de Baudricourt's stubborn loyalty to France makes us all targets of the Burgundians. Jacques became angry. He shouted and threatened me, called me ignorant and stupid. I thought he would hit me. I'm not allowed to have an opinion. In this long scale of 'belonging' I am even less, the least maybe, for I belong to him, and so am forced to concede to his views. Even the boys will one day go and have someone else belong to them to do their bidding. Just Jehanne and I will always belong to someone, who belongs to someone else, who belongs to someone else.

Jehanne was sleeping by the fire, and was no doubt woken by our quarrelling. She said in her dreamy voice, 'The English must stay in England. They must not steal our country.' Her father roared with laughter and she got up and put her arms around him. 'That's my girl, my sweet Jehanette!' he said. This was the first loving moment between them since the bother over her marriage, for in truth he more often dismisses her strange ideas, so she never knows if he will hug her or hit her.

Forgive me, Holy Mother, my anger and fear diminish as I kneel here before you. You accept the muddle of my thoughts. After I have told you everything, you eye me kindly as if to remind me that the world was always troubled. The tapestry was never so smooth or ordered and clearly coloured as I like to imagine, though you assure me it could be. Then I cease to worry about it, and feel the strength to carry on.

SUMMER 1428

Refugees

1

How Zabillet missed Domremy. She was glad to have Hauviette and Tante Marguerite with her, and Jehanette of course, for the hustle and bustle of Neufchâteau frightened her. Jacques had done his best to find them lodgings, and certainly their room at the inn, shared though it was, was a great deal better than others had been able to afford. It was strange not to go out of the house in the morning and smell the river and fields, not to push away the chickens pecking around her feet as she fetched water, not to lay out her washing to dry on the stones by the house. Instead there was the breakfast-room full of bodies with their smells. There was nowhere to brew a little hot drink without the incessant chatter of the other refugees, travellers and the tradesmen who regularly lodged there. She would never get used to it.

To make it worse, Jacques, Petit-Jean and Pierrelot, together with most of the other Domremy men, were camped in the fields below the town, keeping close watch on the cattle and sheep they had driven there from the village. Many an evening Zabillet sat with the men down by the river rather than mix with the crowds in the heat of the inn. The little Mouzon was tiny compared with the river that ran past her home, but as the evening mist settled over it, the smell of the water was more familiar to her than the filthy streets of the town.

Six weeks they'd been here, the longest she'd ever been away from home, an eternity it seemed. The endless war had threatened to engulf their village. All she knew was that the Burgundians, no doubt with the backing of the English, had decided they wouldn't put up any more with Vaucouleurs being loyal to France, and would bring it down. For safety the villagers of Greux and Domremy, and others besides, had fled to Neufchâteau whilst Captain Robert de Baudricourt and his troops fought off de Vergy and his soldiers – or more likely did one of his famous deals to buy a few months or even just weeks of peace. Truce, rather, she thought as she sidestepped the rain running down the street; peace was an idea, a fiction, a dream or maybe a childhood fantasy which had somehow slipped away when she entered adulthood.

This time it wasn't enough to flee to the old Château at the far end of the village. It seemed a long time since some of the men, including Jacques, had negotiated with the *demoiselle* de Bourlémont to use the land around the crumbling old house as sanctuary from the marauders. They could survive for a few days there, safe with their animals – had done many times – whenever the unrest in the countryside grew too great. But this time it was more than écorcheurs, unpaid soldiers, looking for food and destroying for their amusement. The Château could not protect them, and they were forced to pack up such possessions as they could carry, and flee to the safety of the town.

But if the stay at Neufchâteau was an anxious and tedious experience for her, it was just the opposite for Jehanne. It was a new world for her, helping out in the inn to pay for their meals. Sometimes she waited at table, sometimes she helped out with the many horses stabled nearby. She loved to be around the innkeeper, a woman called La Rousse because of her shock of red hair which never would stay under her cap, her curls falling onto her shoulders in a way Zabillet found immodest. She was shocked at her no-nonsense way with her lodgers, but Jehanne found it amusing and when waiting at table adopted the same casual banter with the men. But for all her worries, Zabillet had to admit they seemed charmed by her, and were never rough or crude with her as they were with some of the serving-girls.

Jehanne's independence worried her and infuriated Jacques, and in this strange place his dreams started again. Zabillet worried that the brief respite she had gained for Jehanne from marriage might be very short, and she tried to keep a close eye on her. But one day, having coming back late from the market with Marguerite, she found her down the stables riding the horses with Hauviette and some of the stable-hands, her face flushed with excitement. Her eyes were bright as she threw back her dark hair.

'Maman, Maman, look at me! Isn't this wonderful? Just get a sight of this great brown beauty. I could go far on him.'

Zabillet went up to Jehanne on the horse, and wrenched her off. She shook her. 'Get down at once. Look at you, you're showing your legs for all to see.' She tugged at her skirts which she had tucked up. 'Jehanne, you mustn't do this.'

'Do what?' Jehanne was defiant. 'You don't mind if I ride Dizzy at home if there's a need. What's the difference?'

The difference was that these were sleek, fast horses, not slow, fat Dizzy, and they were not in Domremy but in a town which appeared to have many temptations for a young girl.

'Don't let me see you doing that again, do you hear?' shouted Zabillet. 'I don't want to have to tell your father about this.'

Jehanne turned away sharply, and ran back towards the inn.

'Don't be too hard on her,' said Marguerite, sending Hauviette ahead. 'They're good girls, you know. They're just enjoying themselves. You fear that Jehanne is immodest, but when did you ever see her let a man so much as touch her?'

It was true, and yet Zabillet feared these changes; that Domremy and their life there, which she longed to get back to, would seem dull and uneventful to her daughter. She hid from Jacques that Jehanne would sometimes ride along the ramparts on some horse she had groomed and fed in exchange for an hour's ride, or dance in the square with the other young people. And yet she was just as often to be found in the church of St. Christophe in the heart of the town, silent, praying, prostrate before the huge wooden, painted statue of the saint. And if, on searching the town, Zabillet found her there, her face shining and devout, she would kneel with her, and pray to understand this strange daughter of hers.

❧

Had she done right to plead with Jacques to prevent that marriage? She had wearied him with it until he had agreed, to get a bit of peace in the household. And yet when she had told Jehanne that Jacques would no longer make her marry Guillaume, she had just tossed her head and said she would not have married him no matter what her father said.

But that had not been the end of it. Disappointed in these hard times not to be receiving the generous dowry Jacques had promised, Guillaume's father, Tomas, had become angry and abusive. Next thing they knew, they were summonsed to the ecclesiastical court at Toul to answer for it. Their own neighbour had taken out a breach-of-promise suit against them.

What a horrible journey that had been. Jacques was angry and humiliated. It did his standing in the village no good to have such an obstinate daughter, whom it seemed he could not control, and who was prepared to go all the way to Toul, to court of all places, rather than be reasonable and settle down to a marriage with a young man whom she said she had nothing against. She herself was weary of trying to placate Jacques, and understand Jehanne, who seemed to defy everything a young girl should be.

She had never been in such a place before as the bishop's palace; cold stone, immense arches, the clerics in black sitting behind their table making judgements on people of whom they had no knowledge. She had been frightened.

But Jehanne was not frightened. She stood there in her red dress and white cap, and declared that since she had never promised to marry Guillaume, why should she be put on trial for breaking that promise? Were her life and her body not her own, why should her father be able to dispose of it in such a way? The clerics cited from the great books in front of them, and looked uncertain when Guillaume, humiliated, shouted he would not marry Jehanne anyway, no matter what, now.

Zabillet listened, frightened and amazed at their defiance in such an important place. But astonishingly, the court decided to side with Jehanne – that was how she saw it anyway. Of course, her father had the right to arrange her marriage if he wished, they said. She was only a girl, after all. But it seemed no-one was saying that she herself had ever promised to marry Guillaume, and since she still did not wish to marry the young man, and moreover it seemed that the young man really did not want to marry her either, then what was the point? Case dismissed.

Jehanne's face glowed with delight, and Jacques growled, but since he did not have to hand over the dowry as he had feared he might, marriage or no, he was cheerful enough. They enjoyed their day in the town, poking around in the market, astonished at the amount, range and splendour of the goods for sale. Zabillet and Jehanne said a prayer of thanksgiving in the towering cathedral that was so unlike, and yet so oddly like, their little church in Domremy. Jacques was generous enough to buy them a roast dinner at the inn. He even said, 'That's my girl, you stick up for yourself,' in a forgetful moment, and this would be his story, not that he had been humiliated by his daughter, someone he was meant to own and control.

Their walk back home was a lot more pleasant than the journey into Toul, especially when they stayed a couple of days in Burey with Aveline, but Zabillet kept shaking her head. What would Jehanne do next? She feared for them all.

One day, Zabillet decided to walk down the valley to Soulosse to pray to Saint Élophe at his church there She had grown weary of the heat and smells and noises of Neufchâteau and was desperate for the sight of green fields and hills. Jacques told Pierre to go with her, since the journey would take all day and there were still many dangers about, even so near the town. So the two of them, with Jehanne and Jeanne Baudin, set out soon after dawn, Pierre with his stout stick and Zabillet carrying a basket of food.

As they walked along the ridge above the valley, she felt transported into another world. Fresh air, sun, trees, birds and flowers; she had forgotten how beautiful and abundant such pleasures were away from the town. And the young people, chattering away, teasing and chasing each other, gave her an experience of freedom, a placing aside of anxiety, a sense of familiarity with the hills and valleys so similar and so near to home. She had almost forgotten open spaces, home. Mother of God, she prayed, let us get out of that prison of a town soon, before I forget the sweetness of the land.

After a while, they began to dip down into the village of Soulosse. The two girls chased each other down the hillside, running so fast on the steep slopes that they occasionally stumbled over, and Jehanne ended up with a bloody nose where she had gone flying and Jeanne with a grazed elbow. Pierre walked with Zabillet, trying to work out from all the bits of information they had when it might be possible to return to Domremy. She felt happy to be walking with her son, who had virtually left home to live with the Baudins in the sad time after Cathérine's death, and she basked in his gentle kindness.

'What will become of Jehanette?' she dared to voice her fear. 'She is so stubborn and obstinate. And yet so full of life.'

Pierre shook his head, admiring. 'I don't know,' he said. 'Jeanne's mother says she will never make a peasant wife and mother. She isn't going to settle for that.'

Zabillet was silent a moment at the thought that her neighbours were discussing her daughter. 'But what else is there? Go into a convent? Become a stay-at-home that everyone mocks? It worries me to death, Pierrelot.'

The girls ran screeching by, arms out and flapping as if to fly down the hill. Zabillet and Pierre laughed, hurrying along themselves. 'Everything is changing,' he said. 'Maybe there will be opportunities for her, even if not in Domremy. And she is young yet. Don't worry, Maman, I shall always look out for her.'

Down in the village, they stopped by the river and drank, and refreshed their feet in the water, which glistened as it tumbled over the rocks. Pierre and Jeanne were going to call on a distant cousin nearby, and left Zabillet and Jehanne at the entrance to the church.

It was tiny, no larger than the church at Domremy, wood, wattle and candle-wax giving off the same musty smell. The two sank in front of the statue of Our Lady, and began to pray.

'Maman,' said Jehanne after a while. 'Is it true that Saint Élophe walked up the hill after his head had been cut off?'

'That is the story,' replied Zabillet. 'He picked up his head where it had been cut off right here, and carried it to the top of the hill there.' She pointed up behind her, where the hill rose up from the village.

'Tell me, tell me,' demanded Jehanne childishly. Zabillet laughed.

'Perhaps I could tell you that story.' The old *curé* had come into the church unnoticed, and now sat down by them. 'Long, long ago, when people did not yet know about the Holy Mother and Jesus Christ, they worshipped idols and other gods. Élophe came from a family who did know Jesus, as we do, and was a priest in Grand, just over the other side of the valley beyond Bourlémont. One day he became very angry because the townspeople were making sacrifices to their gods, and he went and upturned the altar, and broke the statues of the idols, praying for the people to turn from their devils to God. Nearly all the townspeople became Christians.

'But one, he went and reported the incident to the Roman ruler of the region, Julian the Apostate, who was furious that a mere priest should assume such power. He came to this village, and demanded that Élophe be brought before him. When he arrived, he was taken prisoner and led before the ruler. Julian demanded that Élophe give up his faith in Jesus, and embrace the old gods again. He refused, and at his continued defiance, Julian ordered his head to be cut off.

"Christ will take me into his bosom" said Élophe serenely. "All I ask of you is that you let my dead body lie atop that hill there."

'Julian laughed contemptuously, and at his signal, Élophe's head went rolling to the ground. "Now we shall see if your precious God will help you climb the hill!" he sneered.

'No sooner had he said this, than the murdered Élophe got to his feet, picked up his head between his hands and started towards the hill. He stepped between some rocks, struck one with his staff, and a fountain arose. The Roman soldiers following him shouted with fear, and made as if to slay him once more, but the rocks closed on them, killing them all. Élophe continued, carrying his head up the hill, and lay down on the summit, at peace. A little church was built up there where it is said his tomb is, to remember his great faith and bravery.'

'What a wonderful story,' breathed Jehanne, her eyes gleaming. She turned to the *curé*. 'Do such miracles still happen?'

'We must believe they do, my child, for we are sorely in need of them.'

Zabillet stood up wearily. All these lovely stories, they were so long ago. When had she heard of a miracle in recent times? Who knew what to believe? 'Come on, my sweet,' she said to Jehanne. 'Let's go and find your brother. We must try and have faith, eh, Father?'

The old *curé* blessed them, and they went into the bright sun, where Pierre and Jeanne soon joined them. 'Can we go up the hill?' said Jehanne, still lost in the wonder of the story.

'Why not?' said Zabillet. Soon the four of them were climbing the hill, through the bright green trees in their full summer leaf. Jehanne breathed in the luscious air, tucking her arm into her mother's. 'It is not so different from climbing up to our dear hermitage, is it?'

'What, at Bermont? It's a good deal steeper,' laughed Zabillet, breathing heavily. 'Here, Pierrelot, carry the basket will you, or we shall never get up there.'

Soon they came out on top. 'Look,' said Jehanne, who had jumped on ahead. 'You can see all across the valley.' It was true. Shading her eyes from the hot sun overhead, she could see the Château de Bourlémont straight across the valley, its turrets just visible above the trees in the noon haze.

'Can we see Domremy?' said Pierre. 'It must be just along there.'

It was not possible. The thick trees on the hillside prevented them from seeing any of the villages lying along the river. It was hard to see whether it was haze or smoke that seemed to hang in the distant air.

They sat on the little plateau in front of the church, eating the bread rolls and cheese and fruit which Zabillet had brought from Neufchâteau. Zabillet's eyes feasted on the beauty of the countryside. She tried to follow the course of the little river below flowing in the direction of Domremy.

'We could take an enormous leap and land in Domremy,' said Pierre. 'That would be good.'

'Domremy. Home. What shall we find when we return?'

'Ssh, Maman,' said Pierre. 'We shall not think of that today.'

No, I shall not, thought Zabillet, lying back to enjoy the warm sun throughout the length of her body. 'Don't let me sleep long', she shouted at Pierre, who was brandishing his stick menacingly at the two girls dancing about. 'We must be back at Neufchâteau long before dark. Pray God, it will not be for much longer, and we can go home.'

2

At last the day came when they could return home. The road lay long and reportedly safe before them. Most of the men went ahead with the animals, and the women with just a few of the older boys as guards came on behind, their carts piled high with their few possessions, alarmingly fewer than when they had set out, for they had not managed to prevent other desperate people from stealing some of them.

Glancing at Jehanette, who was walking on the other side of the old horse Dizzy, Zabillet was not surprised that she looked flat, sullen even. She had wondered if she would come home willingly, or if she might put up some sort of tussle to be allowed to stay.

'I'm so glad we're leaving at last,' said Zabillet. 'I don't think I could have stood another day in that town.'

'I liked it,' said Jehanne. 'Domremy's going to seem very quiet now.'

'Will it not be wonderful to be in our house again?'

'We don't know what we'll find.'

'As long as we can get home,' sighed Zabillet, 'then we can sort things out.'

Zabillet wanted to give a more confident ring to her voice, just in case worry at what they might find in Domremy was the reason for Jehanne's silent reluctance to leave Neufchâteau, though she knew it was not. But she felt far from confident. She had a sick, nervous feeling in her stomach, which none of her friend Béatrice d'Estellin's herbal infusions had been able to calm over recent days. Here they were, reduced to the chattels they had in the cart, and the few pots and farm implements which Petit-Jean had hidden deep in the forest above Domremy before they left, if they remained undiscovered. Before, they had been a whole household, poor enough maybe, but with enough of everything to manage – and if not, usually someone in the village could give or loan them whatever was needed. But now, everyone would be poor; just a few animals, less than when they set out, for some had been sold to pay for their food in Neufchâteau, and one bullock that had been sickening before they left had made the journey only to die; and a half cartful of clothes and pots, with the few bags of grain they had purchased before they left.

What would have happened to the chickens and ducks that strutted and waddled around the yard? Would they have been driven away to die of fear, or maybe killed and plucked for some marauder's dinner, and if so, how would they manage for food? And what of the hay, which still lay ungathered in the fields when they fled? If that was burnt, how would they tend the animals during the winter to come? And what about the crops of precious and essential grain? How would they pay their taxes, and find bread throughout the winter? If they had laid waste to everything...

'Maybe we're going to have to live on very little for a few months,' she said to her still-silent daughter, trying to quiet the incessant, worried thoughts which went around in her head. 'But we'll soon get straight, if we all pull together.'

'It's going to be such hard work,' said Jehanne.

'Well, that's what we do, my girl,' snapped Zabillet. 'Work hard! And you'd better get used to the idea.'

Jehanne's face closed in and she dropped back to where Hauviette was chatting to those following the cart, before Zabillet could take back her harsh words.

Marguerite looked at Zabillet. 'You can't really blame them,' she said mildly. 'Such a calamity to fall on them so young. It's no wonder they would prefer the life of Neufchâteau. They've enjoyed it there.'

'They're not helping though, are they? I mean, is this what you or I want? In a short time, we've come to virtually nothing, and who knows how many more times we might have to take to the road? May God forgive me my anger.' She crossed herself and the two women were silent. 'You're right,' she went on. 'I'm thinking only of myself.'

'I don't care about the work,' said Marguerite. 'I just want to be back in Domremy so we can see what we have to do, and get on with it. The girls will settle down soon enough, you'll see. Neufchâteau will soon be forgotten when we are home.'

Zabillet kissed her friend, but said nothing. She knew the

difference between their two girls. For all Hauviette enjoyed the time away, she would soon settle down with a young man from Domremy or a neighbouring village, and make some sort of home for herself. But Jehanne had refused all that. What sign was there of that changing?

❧

Frebécourt.... Coussey.... the morning wore on. As the small procession came towards the brow of the hill from which they would begin to see Domremy, Zabillet's stomach churned so much that she feared she might vomit. She clung to Marguerite. Behind her even the chatter of Jehanne and Hauviette and the other young people had ceased. On either side of the road, fences and the little shelters in the fields where hay was kept were broken, burnt, destroyed. Ahead of them, smoke played through the air, not dense or billowing as of some sudden fire, but as if there had been fire a while ago that had never properly gone out. Despite the heat of the day, Zabillet drew her shawl closer around her head.

'God preserve us, Marguerite, what shall we find?'

Marguerite shivered. 'Someone will pay for this,' she said angrily.

They could see the men and boys now, who had gone on ahead to settle the animals into their accustomed fields. Here and there, little huddles of them stood by a destroyed fence, gesticulating and shouting. Already they were improvising a mend so that the disoriented animals might settle and not wander away. Zabillet creased up her eyes to see if her menfolk were there, but it wasn't possible to distinguish anyone at that distance.

'Come and walk with me, Jehanette,' called Zabillet. She put her arm round her and held her close as they came to the first house.

Michel Lebuin's mother dashed forward from the group around the cart. 'Oh, no! oh, no!' she screamed as she saw the onions, cabbages, potatoes all torn up out of the ground, lying dead or

34

shrivelled on the soil. Many men had ridden through the patch, malevolently upturning all the vegetables in their full summer growth. She began to move slowly towards her house, still hidden behind the trees, holding fast to her baby, whilst her two small children clung howling to her skirts. Her face was anticipating any horror. A sob came from her, and as the other women drew abreast, they could see that what had been the roof was now just a gaping hole, smashed pots and cooking vessels lay littered around the yard, and the once-beautiful laburnum by the side of her door lay parched and uprooted on the path.

The other women stood in a huddle. No-one spoke. They did not know what to do. They wanted to help. How could they leave her? And yet they must look to their own houses. More smoke whispered its way into the blue sky – it could come from any or all of their homes.

Zabillet took a deep breath. 'Come on, Jehanette,' she said quietly. 'Let us go home.' The women separated off into their family groups, each intent on seeing what their own house might be like. Zabillet was no longer dragging her feet, she dropped Dizzy's bridle, and left him there in the road, the cart standing abandoned behind him. She was almost running, pulling Jehanne along behind her. It was as if the pain in her stomach had become insufferable, and could only be satisfied by seeing for sure.

'Come on, Maman,' cried Jehanne, who, catching the same need, ran on ahead.

As they came around the bend in the road, a similar sight met their eyes. How could their village, where they had lived all their lives, look so familiar yet so different? The honey-white of the walls was charred in many places, doors and shutters were broken off and smashed up, vegetable plots looked as though soil and plants had been thrown haphazardly in the air by a giant spade. They could see the blackened remnants of the hay pile in the covered shed. It was the church that was still burning.

They stood undecided on the threshold of their house. Zabillet's hand was on her chest as if she felt a pain, and Jehanne looked at her anxiously. 'Come on, Maman.' She put her arm round her. 'At least none of us or the animals were there. We can put right whatever has been done.'

She stepped inside and Zabillet followed, anxious not to lose sight of her, as if she might be sucked through the gaping black doorway into some chaotic world beyond. The pain in her chest exploded into angry sobs as she saw how the shelves were wrenched off the walls, lids of chests had been used to augment the fire, together with broken pieces of stools and the table, so that now the hole in the roof had been made enormous. Many nights of rain had come into the house creating a thick mud on the floor.

'I must fetch Papa,' said Jehanne in a frightened voice, turning towards the doorway.

'No, don't go!' cried Zabillet. 'We'll go and find him in a minute. We've got to straighten up first.' She staggered as she turned towards Jehanne.

'Come on.' Jehanne turned upright a box which had only been slightly damaged. 'Sit here and calm yourself. It's not so bad. We can soon put this to rights.'

'I hate them, Jehanne,' sobbed Zabillet in a sudden spurt of anger. 'I hate soldiers and I hate this damned war, may God forgive me. This, what has been done, why? There was nothing to steal here. This is just destroying, destroying...'

Jehanne held her whilst she sobbed. Tears fell down her own face. Then she moved about absent-mindedly, beginning to pick up bits and pieces which had been thrown down but not broken.

'Someone's got to do something, it's got to stop,' wailed Zabillet.

There was no sound in the room and Zabillet looked up to see that Jehanne had stopped her restless wandering and was looking through the doorway. Her face was aglow with determination.

'I will, Maman,' she said, nodding her head. 'You'll see, soon I will.'

'You will what?' asked Zabillet, staring in fear at the intense look on her daughter's face.

'I'll make sure it stops. All this. Soon.' She waved her arms around the house.

'Don't be silly, Jehanne,' said her mother sharply. 'What can we do? All that is left to us is to pick up the pieces and carry on. Come on, let's go and find your father and brothers, and see what they've found.'

CONVERSATIONS

Zabillet talks with the Chronicler in Orléans

I can tell that you are becoming impatient. My story is too slow. You say you want me to tell you what it was like to be the mother of a hero, but what you actually want, it seems, is to hear of miracles and divine interventions and portents of future glory and success. But to be the mother of a hero, or a heroine, or however you like to refer to my Jehanette, is to be just a mother – with all the everyday concerns of caring for a child.

I have no other way of telling the story except by recalling our lives in Domremy at that time. You have lived in Orléans all your life perhaps, and have little understanding of life on the land. How it determined all our activity, harsh master and sweet fertile bed. So to tell the story of our family is also to tell the story of the land, the peasants, our *seigneurs*, the dues and levies owed, and the effect on us, people and land alike, of wider events. How the disruptions of that time changed us all irrevocably.

So let me go on. There were several occasions still, even after returning from Neufchâteau, when we found ourselves camped out in the grounds of our old dead *seigneur* Pierre de Bourlémont's Château, as warlords continued to fight over the land, and soldiers descended on our village stealing whatever they could, and vandalising what they could not. We kept such stores as we had well hidden in the out-houses of the deserted château, and the older boys strengthened the fencing so the few animals we had left were safe. We became adept at hiding our possessions in holes in the ground and in the forest, so the damage would be less if they came into our houses, and we kept to hand baskets of necessities we could just pick up and flee with. We lived the lives of those who had been refugees, and might become so again at any moment. It was wearisome.

It was a cruel winter. Snow, rain, cold, fog. Some days we spent in virtual darkness, the low sky denying the sun its power to light and warm us, and chase away our fears. We fed the hungry fire to keep us warm and shed some light, though sometimes the shadows it cast in the corners made me start up with fear. The river was filled with chunks of ice making our hands red and sore. And so little to eat. We had meat just now and then from the poor, thin hungry livestock. But we had to have grain from our *demoiselle*, who sent bread in for us since our crops were destroyed while we were in Neufchâteau. It was bitter indeed, no longer to be able to sustain ourselves.

Despite all our precautions, the écorcheurs often came across the fields, or swooped down out of the forest on the hillsides into the valley where our villages lay. There were losses – cattle, woodpiles, grain, whole houses even. There were brutal rapes and assaults, though none thankfully in our family. The men became tired, demoralised. They had long farmed the land to pay out taxes to so many interested parties, but now they lost confidence in the safety of the crops since it seemed that so much hard work could be torn up in just a few hours. The women grew weary of never feeling safe in their houses, keeping as much out of sight as possible, always counting their children, and being ready to collect up that basket of necessary foodstuffs and run. It was hard to rebuild when everything could be destroyed again in an instant.

Only the children enjoyed it, in ways I did not like. The boys became warlike, practising with sticks and the rough bows and arrows and catapults they carved from wood. Gone were the days when they lay about in the fields keeping a desultory eye on the sheep. Now they had to be like soldiers on guard, alert and watchful, and when they weren't watching the village's livestock, they were rushing around making sure there were no strangers in the village, or chatting with traders and soldiers passing through, eager to learn what was afoot in the countryside. I despaired of Petit-Jean, whose tendency to create excitement where there was none was fed by these events, until our good friend Jean Morel took him in hand and began to help him use his energy in a way more helpful to the village. Pierrelot lived half his life down the lane at the Baudins', and continued to work with his father helping people decide how to prepare their tax-payments, which animals they should give up, and endlessly checking the guard rotas. In the house, we tried to keep everything going, and still occasionally spent happy afternoons when Jehanne would sit and spin, and we would chat of this and that, our neighbours' doings, whilst I kneaded bread. Or we would take the clothes up to the washing-place and beat the dirt of the fields out of the men's jackets and trousers, and lay our skirts and bodices on the stones by the river to dry.

How hard it was. The life of our family and the village was changing through worry, disaster and despair. But despite that, there was continuity in that centuries-old peasant life lived out in the fields and forests that lay alongside the Meuse. It wasn't quite broken yet.

You ask me if I knew Jehanette had been called to save France at that time. How could I? Oh, she'd talked to me once or twice of bright visions, of a warmth coursing through her body when the saints talked to her. And of course I witnessed her utmost devotion in our church, and the private happiness that shone sometimes from her eyes and softened her whole body. I knew of what our neighbours and friends said they saw if they came across her in one of her secret places, and how odd they found her. I don't think that she knew herself at that time exactly what she must do. We didn't talk of it. She knew that I did not like her difference, was frightened at any presumption to be in conversation with the saints; that I wanted to my shame for this oddness to be suppressed, for her to be ordinary. How could I think otherwise? How could a poor peasant girl from the countryside on the remotest border of France have any role to play in larger events? It never occurred to me this could be so. We could not have such aspirations because we were powerless and, it seemed, fit only to suffer much.

No, when she went to stay with Aveline, I had no idea that this was the start of what she called her mission. If only I had. I never even heard that word until much later. But she knew I would have stopped her. From what I saw, this is how it came about. She didn't settle after our return from Neufchâteau. She was often absent in her mind, even when she was with me. Distant, impatient with all of us, restless. Jacques became increasingly furious with her, talking of marrying her to this boy or that, to which she remained quietly unyielding. And he would storm at me for encouraging her, as he said. I was playing for time, hopeful it would all settle down as it must.

At last I remembered that Aveline had said to send her to Burey if things became too difficult. So one day, when Durand Laxart came to bring us some precious flour and vegetables, I asked him if he would take her back with him. Jehanne's face lit up as I spoke, and it broke my heart. Durand was pleased, for he loved Jehanne, and both his Marie and my sister Aveline were to have babies that winter and would need the help.

Jehanne was excited as I got together a few clothes for her to take. She and Durand were laughing and teasing each other. It was the first time I had heard her laugh for many weeks. I put my arms around her. 'Jehanette, are you so glad to be leaving me?'

'Maman, Maman,' she soothed me. 'Don't be sad.' She seemed to want to say more, but just hugged me fiercely.

She knew something of the amazing thing she was about to do. I did not, and I was left with an empty, aching heart.

Sometimes I cannot help but wonder, may God forgive me for it, why such a path was carved out for me and my family, which saw more death, terror and ill-deeds than we could ever have imagined at that time. Why am I old and all but alone, so far from those hills and valleys, when I had expected, if I had ever thought about it, to live a hard but unchanging life in the bosom of my land? I can feel its texture now, smell the spring rain light in the air, see the fresh green fields dotted with munching cattle. Ah, Domremy! Yet I should not grumble, for I chose to come here to Orléans, to be close to those who love and celebrate my Jehanette, and it is not so bad to wander these streets and pray in the vastness of the cathedral, where she prayed. And I can still sit from time to time with Pierrelot, kind and gentle always, and talk of all those things we do not understand, nor ever shall.

FEBRUARY 1429

Departure

Zabillet knew that there was something wrong as soon as she saw Aveline and Durand Laxart draw up outside the house in their little cart. It was a bitter March day, the harsh wind accompanying the blank grey sky, the hostile cold. It was no-one's birthday nor a feast which they might have celebrated together as a family or with the other villagers. Who would gladly travel on such a day? And their faces did not look right.

Surely Aveline could not have come so far on a day like this just to show her new baby, which Zabillet could see only as a bulge held in the arms of her sister under her thick brown cloak. Jehanne was not with them.

'Where is she?' she said as Aveline began to get out of the cart. She gave her sister her arm whilst Durand held the horse's bridle. Zabillet noticed how he fussed with the leather straps in an unnecessary way, keeping his head averted.

'What's happened?' Her words were sharp with fear.

'She's gone, Zab,' said Aveline on the verge of tears. 'She's gone to France.'

'To France? What do you mean, to France? Where in France? Who with?'

Zabillet staggered as she and Aveline went in through the doorway. The fire burned steadily in the middle of the room, and the little light that penetrated the half-closed shutters was dull on this dismal day. The two women stood there, Zabillet searching unsuccessfully for her sister's eyes.

'She's gone with Bertrand de Poulengy and some others,' said Aveline.

'Not with soldiers,' cried Zabillet. 'Please Aveline, you are breaking my heart.'

Aveline put her arms around Zabillet and held her close. 'I had no idea, you must believe me. Though I should have known. She's so headstrong. I thought it would help her to have a few days in Vaucouleurs. She's such a good girl at heart. And now look what's happened.'

Zabillet stared across her sister's shoulder through the door where she could still see Durand loosening the horse from the cart and tying it up to graze.

'Do you know where she's gone?' Zabillet's voice was almost a whisper.

'Durand says they have gone to see the King, at Chinon.'

Zabillet broke free from her sister and started to throw more wood onto the fire. 'To Chinon? Where in God's name is that? She had such stupid notions, but how can this be? How many days journey to Chinon? Presumably it's somewhere on the Loire, wherever that may be, if the King is there. And the English and Burgundians everywhere. Oh, she's lost, surely. She's only a young girl. Please, tell me it's not true.' Her voice became a wail.

Aveline started to take off her cloak, the baby giving little whimpers as she did so. 'There's a lot to tell. Durand knows it all, more than I do. You must fetch Jacques.'

'Jacques? Oh no, he'll kill Durand if he had a part in this. You know he will.'

'He must hear it. You know he must.' She nestled the baby against her and, sitting on a bench by the fire, started to suckle it.

Zabillet moved to the door. Petit-Jean had turned up from somewhere and was laughing with Durand as they stood watching the horse.

'Petit-Jean, go and find your father. He's in the village somewhere. Tell him he must come at once.'

Petit-Jean turned, perhaps to object, but when he saw his mother's white, tearful face, he said nothing, and ran off down the track. 'And if you see Pierrelot, tell him he must come too. Durand, you can get some feed for that horse from the side, then come in.'

For something to do, Zabillet began to put on the table drinking pots and pitchers of beer and wine. She held the tiny baby over her shoulder and winded her whilst Aveline went outside. 'Cathérine,' she muttered. 'Cathérine! Named for my poor dead daughter.' She wept a little, snuffling into the baby's neck, smelling the sweet skin. But she was waiting, waiting for everyone to get here, waiting to hear the whole story, dreading it, longing to know. 'And what about my little Jehanette, is she gone too?' she asked the contented baby. 'I don't want to hear it,' she whispered, weeping. 'I don't.'

Petit-Jean rushed into the house, his brooding face animated by the drama he hoped to see unfold, and Durand followed him slowly, looking uncomfortable. He went to sit beside Aveline who had resumed nursing the baby. Shortly, Jacques' big frame filled the doorway, followed by Pierre.

Jacques went straight up to Durand and dragged him up by his shirt. 'Where is she?' he shouted. 'What have you done with her?'

Zabillet pushed between them. 'Stop it, Jacques. Stop it' Durand fell back onto the bench. 'Sit down and listen.' Jacques looked at her, surprised at the strength she had showed when she separated them, surprised at the command in her voice, surprised at her white, stern face. She was desperate to hear the story.

'Pierre,' she said in the same peremptory voice. 'Pour everyone something to drink. Now, Durand, you must tell everything.'

'She left one day last week,' said Durand quietly. 'Robert de Baudricourt gave her a horse and escort. She was determined to go to Chinon to meet the King, or the Dauphin as she calls him.'

'Robert de Baudricourt? How does he come to be giving her horses?' shouted Jacques.

'Oh, she looked fine,' said Durand. 'You should have seen her, Zabillet, she looked so excited and proud.'

Jacques slammed his drink down on the table. 'I wish I had

bloody well seen her,' he shouted. 'I would have given her something to be proud of.'

'Jacques, please,' said Zabillet. 'Let's hear what Durand has to say.' She was scared he would fight with him and she would never know.

'She was with the King's messenger,' said Durand, perhaps hoping this might make it better.

'She's gone off with soldiers, Zab, like I always told you,' said Jacques.

'There were several of them,' Durand said quickly. 'It wasn't like that, not at all. Bertrand de Poulengy…'

'Dirty dog! If he's had his way with my daughter, I'll…'

'For God's sake, will you listen?' Durand's face was flushed. 'Jehanne was so full of what she felt she had to do, she wasn't going to go off with some rough soldier like Bertrand. No, he went along to protect her, as all the others did. You don't get it, do you?'

'Get what? What do you mean, 'get it'? What is there to 'get'? My daughter's gone off with a bunch of soldiers. That's all I 'get'. And that you were in some way responsible.'

Zabillet knew he was remembering his dream. 'What do you mean, Durand, what was she so full of? What did she say she had to do?'

'Oh, she's been on about it for ages. Last year when you all stayed with us, you know, after you'd been to Toul, she made me go with her to see de Baudricourt. She was on then about going to the Dauphin and saving France.'

'Saving France?' Petit-Jean laughed sarcastically. 'Our Jehanette? She's mad. I always knew it.' He cackled at such an unlooked for turn of events, delighted at the anger and tension in the room.

Pierre cuffed Petit-Jean across the face. 'Cut it out!'

'Avie,' said Zabillet to her sister. 'Did you know about this?'

'I didn't know anything about last year, any more than you did' she said, patting the silent baby on its back. 'But when she was with us after the baby was born, she was so restless and kept talking about having to see de Baudricourt. So I let her go and stay with Cath le Royer in Vaucouleurs for a few days. I sent Durand with her to look after her – I certainly had no idea this would happen. I just thought she liked the excitement of the town.'

'She can save France,' shouted Durand, slamming his mug down on the table. 'Why don't you believe her? If you'd had more trust in her, she'd never have had to go off like this without saying goodbye.'

There was silence around the table. It's true, thought Zabillet. We were so scared about her strangeness, we never dared ask what was in her mind. She looked at Jacques, saw him rubbing his face in confusion.

'You'd better tell us from the beginning,' she said gently.

'Well, when she came to stay with us,' said Durand, 'she kept talking about going to see Robert de Baudricourt. She saw I was going up to Vaucouleurs most evenings, and she would ask me what everyone was saying about the Dauphin, and his chances against the English, now their army had made such advances into the south. Everyday she would ask me if I had seen Robert. What was he doing? How was he managing to hold out against the English when nearly every other bit of the countryside round here belonged to them and the Burgundians? Oh, he must be a hero, she said. Why weren't other captains doing the same? She seemed to understand exactly what was going on. Then she asked if she could come with me.'

'Yes, I knew about that,' chipped in Aveline. 'I assure you I said she couldn't go. I knew you'd be angry if she started mixing with the soldiers up there, Jacques.'

'Go on, Durand,' said Zabillet impatiently before Jacques could speak.

'She went on and on about it. I said, "What do you want to go up there for?"

"I've got to see Robert," she said. "I've got to ask him to help me go and see the Dauphin."

'See the Dauphin?' snorted Jacques. 'The King of France? How ridiculous!'

'You always think the worst of her,' blazed Durand. 'But she had a mission. She still has, you'll see.'

Zabillet put her hand on Jacques' leg. 'Don't you want to hear what has happened to our daughter? Please, let Durand go on.'

'She started to go up there with me,' said Durand. 'She would go straight up to the castle and badger the guards. "I must see Messire de Baudricourt," she would say. "Go and tell him that Jehanne from Domremy wants to see him. It's about the safety of France."'

Durand smiled, admiring, indulgent. He wasn't going to tell them how the soldiers responded to her, or her sharp, insistent answers, their ribaldry she parried. How his heart swelled with love and pride to see her.

'After a few days, her insistence got to them. I said to Jean de Metz, a friend of mine in Robert's guard, "Why don't you do as she asks? You know she'll just keep on coming here every day until you do." Anyway, Jean went off and came back a few minutes later. "Robert's bored to tears," he said. "He's heard about Jehanne and her amusing persistence. He'll see her."

'I don't know what happened between them,' said Durand, 'but when she came out she was furious. She was stiff with rage. Bertrand de Poulengy walked with her to where I was waiting. He was laughing all over his face. "Robert says send her home to her parents and give her ears a good boxing!"'

'Dead right!' sneered Petit-Jean, laughing uproariously and thrashing his fists around in the air.

'Jehanne wouldn't speak to me all the way home,' continued Durand, ignoring Petit-Jean. 'Then as we neared Burey she calmed herself. She turned to me, her face and eyes glowing. "Don't worry, dear Durand," she said. "I'll be back. I will get to go and see the Dauphin, for I must, and it is Robert de Baudricourt who will help me. Now, please don't tell anyone, because there's nothing to be done about it."

The baby cried. Perhaps it was the tension in the room, or the smoke that gathered because the shutters were only half-open on this bitter winter day. Maybe she was overtired from the long journey. She did not want to sleep despite all their petting and feeding of her. Eventually, Pierre made a little crib for her in the corner, and after a few more minutes of wailing and grizzling, she settled down.

Zabillet walked down the lane a little way before taking more wood into the house, trying to calm herself. Pictures flashed through her brain. That autumn, after their return from Neufchâteau, Jehanne had become increasingly withdrawn, rebellious, absent, spending hours in the forest, up at Bermont, at the Fairy Tree. Out, anywhere but in the house where her father might shout at her, her brothers tease her, she herself make some impatient remark about the work that remained still undone because of her dreaminess. She was waiting, thought Zabillet, waiting for an opportunity to get away. No wonder she was so happy to go and stay with Aveline.

She shook her head, tried to blow warmth onto her cold face. Mission, a mission, Durand had said. What was all that about? To see the Dauphin? But why? What did she think she could do?

Baffled, stunned, Zabillet paused a moment looking across the flat land of the valley, grey now in the faded light. The lead-coloured sky with its low cloud threatened rain if not snow. Where was she now? Zabillet turned sharply as all the dangerous possibilities of this dreadful journey she had undertaken began to crowd into her mind. 'Come home, Jehanette,' she wanted to scream, and perhaps would have done were it not for a neighbour calling out a friendly greeting.

Jacques had hardly moved all this time. He looked angry and shamed. Zabillet didn't want to sit by him, and went over to where

Pierre was standing by the fire, stirring the big pot of stew which was to be their evening meal.

'Come on, Pierrelot, we'll eat in a little while.' He was shocked, upset, and she pushed her arm through his as they sat down again. The baby was sleeping.

'Right, Durand,' she said. 'What happened next?'

'Well, as soon as Aveline had little Cathérine,' he nodded towards the crib, 'she was on at me to go to Robert de Baudricourt again. She would sit for ages with me and my friend Jacques Alain. Now all her questions were about what was happening at Orléans, trying to understand exactly where it was, what the soldiers were saying about the English laying siege there. She was very agitated. "I must see the Dauphin. I must get to him before mid-Lent and help him," she kept on saying.

'The soldiers were talking about nothing but Orléans, and how if the English took it, a gateway to the South of France would be opened and the Dauphin would lose everything. This was what Jehanne said she had to prevent. Eventually, I took her up to the castle again.'

'What the hell did she think she could do about it?' growled Jacques.

'Oh, she never said that much to me,' said Durand. 'But Jean de Metz told me that she said to Robert de Baudricourt that she was going to free Orléans from the siege, and have the Dauphin crowned King of France.'

'And you were fool enough to believe her?' thundered Jacques. 'A young peasant girl, make the Dauphin King. That's rich, that is.'

Durand's voice was cool. 'Yes, I did believe it, and I still do,' he said. 'And you should know,' he was suddenly angry, 'that all the people of Vaucouleurs came to believe it too. After she went to stay with Henri le Royer and his family, everyone wanted to help her. I can tell you. They gave her all that was necessary for her journey.' He swallowed hard, calming himself, before continuing.

'But at this point, when Robert sent her packing again without offering her any help, Jehanne seemed to lose her energy and determination. She no longer wept or railed. I was worried about her. She had asked so little of Robert, she said, and that had been refused. One evening, when we were sitting with Jacques Alain, talking things over, he said impatiently, "If these stupid soldiers won't help, why don't we?"

"What can we do?" I said. "Robert isn't going to listen to us, we're just peasants."

"Well, I've got a few pounds, and I expect you have too. Why don't we buy her a horse, and go with her ourselves?"

'I thought he was quite mad. But Jehanne leapt on him and gave him a great hug. "You have just saved France," she said to him.

'Two days later, we set out from the Porte de France. We'd bundled up some clothes and such food as we could get without raising suspicion. Her horse was a poor old thing, the best we could afford, and our own were little more than farm animals. The bitter wind blew straight into our faces as we left. It was one of those winter days when you fear that it may never get light, so low was the dark, grey cloud. The fields lay colourless and as if dead all around. Needles of rain stung our faces, whipped to sharpness by the wind.

'By mid-day, we had travelled just a few miles, and stood huddled under a tree, resting our horses and breaking chunks off the bread that was serving as lunch. Jehanne's clear eyes looked across the horizon, not listening to our brave attempts to keep our spirits up.

"We're going back," she said.

'I thought of my little warm house, where even now my wife would be waiting with food for me, wondering why I hadn't come home. "No, Jehanne," I said. "We're used to the cold and wind. My cousin will give us a warm bed for the night."

"No," she said sadly, her eyes focused on some place far to the south. "The time's not right. I must be patient. Only Robert de Baudricourt can give me the help I need."

'Alain looked at her from out of his cold, red face. He was stricken. "You must decide," was all he said. She put an arm around each of us. Her face was joyous. "My dear, good friends," she said. "Don't look so unhappy. Come on, let us wait for a better day."

'Sitting in the warm bar that night, snow falling outside, Alain and I agreed it would have been hopeless. But we knew that one day soon, she would travel that same road. Perhaps we would not go with her, but we would do what we could to help her get it right.'

No-one spoke. Zabillet felt deep misery. Such folly. Why had they indulged her notions? Anyone could see that she had come to have a fixed idea which warranted no more than a shrug and a smile. Yet it seemed that people had come under its spell. She looked at Jacques. He looked completely bemused too, and was getting through the moment by filling everyone's bowl with some of the rich stew from the pot.

'Next thing, she went off to see the Duke of Lorraine at Nancy,' said Durand. 'Robert de Baudricourt said that he had asked to see her, and I should go with her.'

Zabillet looked sharply at Aveline. Her sister shrugged. 'Don't ask me,' she said. 'It had got completely out of hand. I've never known a girl be so headstrong. She was staying with Cathérine le Royer in Vaucouleurs by then, so there wasn't much I could do to stop her. Believe me, Zab, I was just waiting for her to come to her senses, so I could pack her off home to you. I thought the whole thing would run its course, and she'd settle back in Domremy again. The only thing I could do was let Durand be with her to see she didn't come to any harm, though we could ill spare him from the village.'

Durand stood up angrily. 'I know what you're all thinking,' he said, 'but you don't have to worry. Jehanne had only one thing in mind, to get to see the Dauphin. Even the soldiers, who would sit and boast about what they would do with her if they got her alone, forgot all that the minute they saw her. You don't know what she was like,' he ended, with a slightly contemptuous note in his voice.

Zabillet shook her head. It was true in a way, what Durand said, but the one thing she did recognise as fact in this whole strange story of her daughter, was that she had no interest in men, and utterly despised their sexual approaches. She suddenly felt more cheerful.

'Go on, Durand,' she said, prepared to hear anything. 'What happened in Nancy?'

'Well, the Duke received her in his palace.' There was incredulity in his voice as he remembered the huge magnificence of that place. 'She was most amused, said afterwards the Duke was a revolting old man, and she'd put him straight on a few things. She must have impressed him, though, because she got him to give her a horse.'

For the first time, Jacques lost his sullen, angry expression. 'That girl!' he said. 'Trust her to see what an old goat he is. A horse he gave her, did he? Go on, Durand.'

'When she got back, she'd become a bit of a hero. Nothing was talked of in the town but when she would be leaving for Chinon. Somehow it had become known that Robert had written to the Dauphin, mentioning Jehanne and asking if he would see her. Jacques Alain had been busy and had got clothes for her from people, and a bit of money too. Oh, she was very impatient. But one evening she came back from the church with the most stricken expression on her face. You know, she used to spend ages up there, praying in front of the statue of the Holy Mother. "I have to see Robert de Baudricourt now," she said. "France is in the gravest danger."

'I went with her up to the castle, and somehow we persuaded Bertrand de Poulengy to take her in to see Robert. I don't know what happened, but when she came out her face was calm, and all tension had dropped from her body. "Durand," she said. "I am going to the Dauphin. Robert has had a messenger come today with word that the King will receive me."

'I can't tell you how I felt,' continued Durand, his face loving and excited as it mirrored his feelings of that moment, oblivious to the astounded faces around the table. 'It was all frantic preparation then, I can tell you. But you know, Bertrand later told me how she had wept and cried to Robert that evening, saying that France was in terrible danger, had just lost a battle with the English near Orléans, and she must be in Chinon to help the Dauphin. The amazing thing was, only a few days later, just before she set off, news came of a battle where the French forces got hacked to death as they attempted to stop food reaching the English besiegers. She had known that somehow on that night.'

Zabillet shook her head distractedly. Was this the Jehanne she knew? To be received by the Dauphin, a man as good as King. To know things before they were known. To be so single-minded in her purpose, well yes, she certainly knew about that. But what was she thinking she could do, how could she help the Dauphin, help France get strong again, when it was so obvious that just the opposite was happening? And she was taking so many important people along with her. A peasant girl, and her daughter! It would take a lot of thinking about. 'Go on, Durand,' she said wonderingly. 'Tell us about the day she left.'

'Oh, it was a great day,' he said. 'Nearly everyone in Vaucouleurs was at the Porte de France to see her off. She had quite an escort. There was Jean de Metz and Bertrand de Poulengy, and their squires and the Royal Messenger and his archer. All in their armour, and well-cloaked against the wintry weather. There she sat, our Jehanette, on her black horse in hose and doublet and cloak, all made specially to fit her by the townspeople. And when Robert de Baudricourt came to say farewell, he presented her with a sword. Oh, she looked so proud sitting there. Jacques Alain and I rode with her a way, and all the people cheered and wished her well. She was so calm, knowing that she had started at last on her mission.'

Durand fell silent. It had been the best day. He would have

loved to go with her. How dull everything had seemed since then.

Jacques leapt to his feet so violently that the table rocked and mugs and jars flew everywhere.

'Mission!' he roared. 'What mission? You stupid young fool. My daughter has gone off with soldiers, dressed like a soldier. What were you thinking of? You have brought shame on my house. Do you think anyone except you thinks this is anything but a piece of stupid nonsense? She was in your safe-keeping, yet you encouraged her!'

He had Durand by the throat and pushed him toward the door. 'Get the hell out of here, Laxart, and never return. And you, Aveline, you let this happen, and you never sent any message to us when things began to get out of hand. What were you thinking of? Go! Get out of my house.' And he staggered out into the yard, screaming in rage and pain.

Zabillet sat at the table, sobbing. Pierre came and sat with her, his arm around her shoulder to comfort her, whilst Petit-Jean stood by the doorway waiting to see what would happen next. There was so much more she wanted to know, needed to know. But Jacques had spoken. She did not look up as Durand and then Aveline gathered up their things and the baby, and left.

Jehanne's Mission

1429 – 1431

CONVERSATIONS

Zabillet talks with the Chronicler of Orléans

What can a peasant woman with no resources do when her daughter goes off in the middle of winter on some impossible, deluded mission? I could hardly bear to think of her crossing lands that I had hardly heard of, Burgundian lands. What would defeat her first, the cold, the dreadful floods which burst through the river banks sweeping bridges away, an attack from the soldiers fighting over our land, or some assault from one of the men accompanying her, whom she foolishly thought her friends? Sometimes in the night I fancied I heard wolves howling, and that she was lying scarcely safe in the open, for surely even if any of the party had money, it must be too dangerous to seek shelter.

Where to find comfort? Jacques, his rage never abating, saddled up old Dizzy and went off to Vaucouleurs to find out more of what had happened, and to shout long and hard at Messire de Baudricourt, or at least to claim he had. I wanted to go too. I wanted to talk to Cathérine le Royer, who had lodged my Jehanette, and wander amongst the townspeople trying to discover what it was that had made them support her in setting out on this doomed journey. I wanted their confidence, their reassurance that all would be well; other times I railed against them – why did you not send her home, how could you be so stupid as to be taken in by her foolishness? Why, if one of your daughters had acted so in Domremy, I'd have soon packed her off home, so why didn't you? I wanted to kill Aveline and Durand.

But it was not to be, of course. If Jacques was away, someone had to tend the hearth. And there was the boys – Pierrelot sad and silent; Petit-Jean furious, shamed by the mockery of his silly friends.

Oh yes, it was hard to hold up our heads in Domremy, no wonder Jacques went away for a while. A few friends said don't worry, she's got a good head on her has your Jehanne, she'll soon turn up again (but disgraced of course). Some I knew mocked us all; Jehanne had always been strange, they said, foolish, headstrong, nothing could surprise them about her, especially after that marriage business. Only Béatrice d'Estellin would come round and sit with me for a while, brewing me some strong infusion against despair. Just wait, she would say, keep in good heart, eventually you will hear something. Jehanne is a good girl. And dear Marguerite was there, of course, sad, watchful, not judging.

Yes, they were good friends when such were in short supply. You may look disbelieving and astonished when I speak of these things. It's not easy to think back to that time, given all that we know about Jehanne now and her greatness. But then it was a bitter mystery and shame. I wanted to believe in what Durand Laxart had told us of her mission, but surely God would punish me for assuming so much. After all, we were just a peasant family in a tiny village far from the centre of things.

When I spoke of these thoughts, hesitant and weeping, to *curé* Frontey, he too seemed unsure. We spoke of Jehanette's goodness, her love of God, her strange determination. I spoke of her deceit. He spoke of how a glamour can sometimes lead even the most devout into sinful aspiration. He did not know if that was true of Jehanne, but it was something I needed to consider. I left him, little comforted, fearful for my daughter's body and soul.

Do you want to see the letter she sent? Oh, the joy, the relief, the pain. Here, I carry it yet about me; it's the only letter I ever had from her. It's become quite faded and torn over the years but see, if you piece it together carefully you can just see the writing. Not hers, of course, she had to ask someone to write it for her. Naturally, she knew how worried we would be – she must have had it written as soon as she came to a safe place – Gien she says there, see? A town, they told me, on the Loire, quite a way still from where the Dauphin was at Chinon. A friar passing through Lorraine brought it to us at Domremy. Are you struggling to make it out? Let me tell you what it says, for although I cannot read it, I have asked so many people over the years to remind me of its words, that I know it quite by heart.

Greetings to my father and mother, Jacques Darc and Zabillet in Domremy. I write to ask your forgiveness for leaving without your knowledge or consent. I feared that you would not permit me to come to the Dauphin at Chinon, which I do by the Will of Heaven. I am to relieve the poor besieged people of Orléans and have the good Dauphin crowned King of France at Reims.

All I do is on behalf of God.

My companions are good fellows and we have travelled safely. I will come into the presence of the Dauphin in the next few days.

Think well of me.

That is her cross there, see?

MARCH 1429

Pilgrimage

1

Zabillet would not look at her husband. A great joy swept through her, warming the sad empty spaces of her heart where there had been for so long cold dread. Jehanne was safe! Jehanne was alive! Jehanne had sent them word! Oh, they were strange words she had sent them, they would take much thinking over to extract their meaning. For they were mad words, just as Durand had told them, words that made little sense, of the King, of France, of the English, of Orléans, of a mission. Asking their forgiveness for leaving with no goodbye.

Jacques had not stirred, and that was how Zabillet knew not to look at him. If he had felt like her, happy, relieved, joyous if puzzled, he would be talking, asking questions, ordering her to be hospitable. It was only the fact of the old friar sitting there, sipping the warm, spicy wine she had poured for him, that she knew prevented him from shouting his rage.

He blamed her. That much had become clear over recent weeks. She had been too soft, apparently, had let Jehanne have her own way, been taken in by her goodness and piety. It was her fault, it seemed, because she had sent Jehanne to stay with Aveline, and put her in the way of that no-good dupe Laxart. She had become battered by his anger and accusations, occasionally by his fist, so much so that hearing his unhappiness sometimes during the night, she had not wished to comfort him, and feigned sleep.

The friar stirred, beginning to fold up the paper he held in his hand. 'No!' said Zabillet, her voice sounding harsh in the small, dark house. 'Please, read it once more.' She feared he would go too quickly, too suddenly, leaving behind a letter she could not read. She got up and stood behind him, looking at the page.

'Who would have written this?' she asked softly.

'A priest maybe, or a cleric,' said the friar. 'It was in Gien she had it written, in French lands on the Loire, where she would have been able to move freely and find someone to do this.'

'Would she have had to pay for it?' asked Zabillet. She had never seen a letter like this before, not an official one but between family members.

'Perhaps,' said the friar. He smiled and looked at her. 'I think whoever wrote it would have been honoured to write it for nothing.'

Zabillet digested this. 'Holy brother,' she said at last. 'Did you see my Jehanne?'

'No, I was not in Gien at that time. One of the brothers gave it to me when I passed through, knowing that I was coming this way. But they were talking of little else but Jehanne and her journey and her brave mission, believe me. I would have liked to meet with her.' The friar gathered his cloak around him and made to leave.

'So you don't know if she got to see the Dauphin?' she asked timidly.

'No. She had several days journey before her to reach Chinon. I had to leave before news came of that. But I wish her well, and you, mother of Jehanne.' He blessed her.

He glanced over to where Jacques sat unmoving, his eyes fixed on the floor.

'God be with you both,' he sighed, moving towards the door.

Zabillet stood at the door and watched the friar go. He pulled his hood close around his head, for he had several hours walking in the cold March rain before he would reach the priory near Vaucouleurs, where no doubt he would rest awhile before continuing his wanderings. How Jehanne had loved to run out and greet these holy men, whose vocation it was to travel from one abbey or priory to the other, bringing comfort to the people they met, hearing confessions, encouraging the priests trying to serve God in war-torn villages, carrying news of events throughout the countryside, messages, letters like the one he had brought today. They would accept small gifts of hospitality, nothing more.

I would be like him, thought Zabillet, holy, travelling, not tied. Her heart leapt for a second. Perhaps she might be a little like him for a while – now they had word from Jehanne, might she not be able to go on the pilgrimage? She must think about that later. There was a sound behind her, and Jacques pushed past without saying anything. She pressed the letter to her lips as she watched him stomp down the lane, slipping slightly in the mud as he went. Jehanne, she must have held the letter to make her sign at the bottom. Had she kissed it, a kiss for her mother?

Zabillet sobbed. When would this dreadful time cease? Of course, it was good to have the letter after the agony of recent weeks when they didn't know where she was, or even if she was still alive. But what did it all mean? In her letter, Jehanne showed no regret that she had gone, no sign that others were mocking her and about to send her home as a strangely deluded young woman. No, though the friar had not met her, he talked of her with the greatest respect. There had been no hint of doubt, or that he found her foolish. He had talked of her being fêted, welcome, somehow expected. He had not known whether she had managed to see the Dauphin, but he seemed to expect that she would. He had blessed her as the mother of Jehanne.

If only I had been brave enough to get to know you better, my sweet daughter, wept Zabillet. If I had been able to see that you might do something so different, so courageous, and that you would have the right of it, I might have been able to help. Now there was just the pain of losing her, missing her all the time in the many places where she had been used to seeing her; there was the bitterness of not having understood, of not having tried to understand. She dared for a moment to picture herself at the front of that cheering crowd at Vaucouleurs, sending off her daughter to France with her love and her blessing. But Jacques would never have let her go; he blamed her for not keeping Jehanne at home, not stamping out her foolish notions. Zabillet sighed. Cold rain stung her face. Perhaps he was right too. Just because she was safe and no-one had yet dismissed her did not mean that she was going to do anything significant. How could she? It was foolishness. Certainly the Dauphin would send her straight home. That was most likely after all. Really, she should start to think how she could help Jehanne settle back down again in dull Domremy without feeling totally humiliated.

She folded the piece of paper carefully, and placed it in her bodice near her heart. I must find Pierrelot and Petit-Jean, she thought, how glad they will be to have news of their sister.

2

Petit-Jean clung surprisingly hard to Zabillet as they walked towards the crowd of pilgrims waiting at the end of the village. She held him close to her.

'I want to go with you,' he said in a little boy's whiny voice. Zabillet ran her fingers through his thick curly hair.

'You would hate it,' she said gently. He was taller than her, a big sturdy lad, no, young man. 'I shall be back before the moon is new again, and you must stay and help your father.' Jacques was nowhere to be seen.

'But everyone is going away, Maman. I want to go too.' It made him mad that his sister Jehanne had run off on some crazy pretext whilst he must continue to tend the cattle and milk the cows, cut wood, keep guard through long tedious hours, and do, well, so many very mundane things all day long. His only pleasure was when he could persuade some passing soldier to cross swords with him.

'Pierrelot will come over every day to help,' she continued. 'And you can go over to the Baudins with him for your meal. Tante Marguerite's going to keep the house straight for you and your father. And I'll be home before you know it. That's right, isn't it, Pierrelot?'

As they approached the group, Pierre on her other side leading the donkey that Jacquemin had lent to her, Petit-Jean drew away a little, the familiar sullen expression returning to his face.

'Look,' she said to amuse him. 'Do you honestly want to spend weeks in the company of these people?'

The group was made up of priests and friars, trades people, several peasants like herself walking with their goods done up in a cloth on their back, just a few with a donkey or horse to ride part of the way. Many bore a stick, satchel and hat, trademarks of the pilgrim. A couple of merchants also rode with them, and up ahead were one or two carriages with landowners or nobles off to seek penance for some misdoing.

Petit-Jean laughed. 'No, not the most exciting company, you're right.'

Pierre tucked his hand in her arm. 'It's such a long way to go when you don't know anyone. Why are you going?'

Zabillet stopped. Why was she going? 'They may look a strange lot,' she said, 'but that's just because they're in the middle of a long winter journey. There are friends to be made amongst them. You know I'd planned to make this pilgrimage before ... before Jehanne left. I even thought she might come with me.'

'Yes, but now she's gone, surely ...'

'Now we've had news that she's safe, I want to go for her, for myself too,' she continued. 'Maybe it's a little thing I can do to help and support her, praying before the Black Virgin at Le Puy.'

'You will come back to us, won't you?' said Pierre for the twentieth time.

Zabillet hugged them both. 'Of course, of course. Don't be silly, you two. I'm going to Le Puy and then I'm coming back again. No harm can come to me whilst I have this sturdy staff.' Laughing, she held up the stick which Petit-Jean had cut and crafted for her. 'I shall be the better for it, and then we can all get on with things again. Now you look after each other. Jacquemin and Yvette will call in a few times, you'll be fine. In fact, you'll enjoy not having me at your back all the time.'

As the band of Lorrainers got underway again, Zabillet being the only one to join from Domremy together with *curé* Frontey who would accompany them for a day or two, she felt a little prickle of excitement. She hardly recognised it. For weeks now she had been miserable. The sheer dreariness of not having Jehanne with her, the constant worry about her, had worn her out. And to this was added the burden of Jacques' hostile accusations, and the need to keep a semblance of normality for the boys.

For the first time in all those anxious weeks, Zabillet felt roused from her absorption in her family. Life was going on, after all, and there were other concerns apart from the fate of her daughter. Perhaps through journeying and prayer, she could reach a measure of peace; maybe a little understanding would rub off onto her from some of these wise, humble and far-seeing friars.

The friars set up a chant as they led the group out of the village, holding the cross high at the front. Pierre and Petit-Jean walked alongside Zabillet and the donkey for a while. Familiar sights evoked memories as they passed the Fairy Tree, naked in its winter bleakness, and the Fountains, where today several of the travellers stopped to drink the healing water. At the turn in the road which would hide Domremy behind her, Zabillet stopped a moment. 'Do you remember when we came home from Neufchâteau, how terrible it was to come round this bend and see the smoke above our village?'

'It was horrible. All the crops were destroyed,' said Pierre. 'And we couldn't keep the cattle safe because the fences and hedges were trampled down'.

'It seems ages,' said Petit-Jean.

Zabillet shuddered. How had they survived all that? Well, they had managed somehow. It had been overtaken by other events.

'Now, you must go back home,' said Zabillet as they came down into Frebécourt. The Meuse, wide and slow here, was grey and icy in the cold March wind.

'Maman, it's cold, and you are going so far,' said Pierre, holding her very tight. 'Are you sure I can't come too?'

'Don't be silly, Pierrelot,' said Zabillet, holding on tight to both her boys. 'Now be good, and I will be back before you've had chance to truly miss me.'

She smiled cheerfully, and turned several times to wave at the boys as they stood on the roadside shouting their farewells to her. Only when they could not possibly see, did she allow the tears to flow and she sobbed quietly for a few minutes. How could she leave them, when they too had lost so much?

But as the day wore on, their sad faces began to fade. She enjoyed the journeying, chilly though it was. The rhythm of the donkey, when she occasionally rode him, soothed her. She already felt free of obligation, and anticipation grew in her as she talked to some of her fellow travellers.

It was a great pilgrimage. For weeks, bands of pilgrims had been moving across France to Le Puy, deep to the south in the mountains, to celebrate the Great Jubilee, so called because Good Friday and the Annunciation fell on the same day in this year. 'Oh, you will love Le Puy,' said one of the friars to her. 'Mountains, strange peaks, miracles and the centuries-old church that so many pilgrims have been drawn to. And the Black Virgin, she is so beautiful, Zabillet. And she heals, she heals. That is what we all go for, all of us, to find peace in her smile.'

It was a beautiful picture, and Zabillet longed for it. Yet, it also felt peace enough to be away from home, the endless reproaches of Jacques, and the curious, pitying looks of her neighbours.

Zabillet tossed and turned on the thin pad that was her bed. The cold stone of the convent floor kept striking through into her sleep. Already she had got up to put on every stitch of clothing she had brought with her, and re-wrap herself carefully in her heavy lambswool blanket. And she was tired, so tired that she had expected to sink immediately into the dark unconsciousness she craved. Yet here she was, cold and restless.

It had not been a happy day. The euphoria of the first couple of days had disappeared. She did not feel like a pilgrim, whose thoughts she knew should be focussed on the journey, the destination, on calm reflection of the cruel days before Good Friday, the great sacrifice of Jesus and the pain of his Mother. She could certainly lose herself in the pain of the mother, but it was pain for her own children. It was a blasphemy and she could not help it.

'Father,' she had said to the *curé* Frontey, who had not yet returned to Domremy, and was walking alongside her as she lagged briefly behind the main company, giving her donkey a respite from carrying her. 'I seem to be able to think only of my own troubles, may God forgive me.'

'You have had more than your share of those,' he smiled, encouraging her. 'And you must not reproach yourself. We have all suffered greatly this year, surely without the goodness of our *demoiselle* we would all have starved. God grant that the crops you good people of Domremy and Greux have sowed will prosper. And in addition, you have been worried about Jehanne.'

'It has been the hardest winter,' reflected Zabillet. She could not say more for the anger that rose in her, threatening to burst out of her body in a great cry of rage. Not only have we had no food, she wanted to cry, but I have not had my Jehanne, who for very pity of us all has gone off on some doomed mission. She wiped the furious tears from her face.

'Let the journey do its work,' said *curé* Frontey gently. 'You will come into peace.' She felt his compassion. Some of the words in that angry flare spun in her mind. 'For very pity of us', had been her thought. For the first time, she glimpsed that Jehanne's departure might be something other than stupid, adventure-seeking defiance. She gasped, and wept more gently.

'Come, let me tell you the story of the cathedral at Le Puy, and how it came to be,' said *curé* Frontey, noticing her distress. 'Centuries ago, a young woman was suffering from so severe a fever she thought she might die. One day, she climbed slowly and painfully up Mount Anis by Le Puy. Her chest was aching as her inadequate breath rasped. She must get to that clear, blue air, and when she did, she lay down exhausted to sleep. When she awoke, the Virgin Mother was sitting on a huge rock nearby, and told the young woman that she wanted a church to be built in that very place. Our Lady blessed her, and the fever completely disappeared, and she descended Mount Anis joyfully.

'Hearing of the miracle, the Bishop came to see for himself. It was July, but when he arrived on the mountain, the ground was covered in a thick blanket of snow. He waited a little; no doubt he felt a little of the power of the impossible being made possible, and a stag appeared and traced the outline of a huge church with its hooves in the snow. But the Bishop did not have the money to build a church, and all he could do was lay down a thorn hedge to mark out the plan. The next day, the hedge was covered in the most beautiful blossom.

'After a time, there was another miracle on the spot. You can see how determined the Virgin can be, Zabillet. She was not going to give up showing where her church must be! And finally, the Bishop got permission from Rome to build it and eventually found the money needed. And that was the beginning of the great church of Le Puy.'

But these stories that were so soothing as they walked along, helping the miles pass more quickly, even occasionally making her almost believe that the most unlikely things could happen, were no comfort in the cold night, when the losses of the winter seemed close and acute. Zabillet reproached herself that she had not thought enough about her sons. Jacquemin was all right of course, older than the others, and settled on her dead father's lands at Vouthon. But Petit-Jean and Pierre, thinking soon to be men when they were still boys, had betrayed their youth and dependency as they clung on to her begging her not to go. How could she? As if they had not lost enough, why would she compound their misery by leaving to go on a pilgrimage? Well, she did not know the answer to that. But the pain of them all dissolved into weeping, and Zabillet had to tuck the blanket firmly round her head for fear of waking the other sleeping women. At least she was weeping for her sons, and not suffering the vice of dread upon her heart that clenched painfully each time she thought of Jehanne.

After a few days, roads, convents and hostelries, food and the kindness of people, all rolled into one. Zabillet could hardly remember the names of the places they had passed through; she had never heard of them before, and it was not important. Just the cities she recalled, like the great walls of Langres perched up on the hills, and the safe feeling when the gates clashed shut at sunset. They were in Burgundian territory, but any groups of soldiers who passed them did not bother them much. Pilgrims traditionally had some protection and there was little to gain from a bedraggled group of priests, peasants, women and beggars, though sometimes they found their taunts and contemptuous remarks hard to bear.

No, the countryside had melded into a wet and inhospitable place. Wet and cold, cold and wet, wet and cold, there were no other variations except occasionally a weak wintry sun. When they grumbled, someone would praise God there had been no snow, but it was little consolation. Although the nuns and friars who dedicated themselves to helping pilgrims along the way were invariably kind, food was short everywhere. Zabillet could see that many villages were like Domremy – even worse sometimes, houses half burnt, crops destroyed before they had truly shot through the brown winter earth. And everywhere, people were on the road. Many who joined their group had become landless and moneyless, and hoped to benefit at least from a warm, nourishing if meatless soup at the end of the day. Others, home destroyed and village decimated, travelled alongside them for a day or two just for something to do and somewhere to go.

And yet, as the band formed by people with such disparate intentions moved south, it became stronger too. Pity for the ruined countryside and its people grew, and the priests who led them prayed longer and louder for peace as they walked, and the friars' songs and chants rang out through the rain.

Focussing on her blisters, the cold, her ever-damp clothes, making a piece of bread last all day in case no village could let them have anything as they passed through, occasionally becoming absorbed in a conversation with a fellow-traveller, or responding to the energy of the friars who led them, Zabillet thought less and less of Domremy, of Jacques' hostile anger, even of the lost, sad faces of her boys as she had left them. This was her current world, little larger than the space she and her donkey took up. As long as they could put one foot after another, and her blanket would stay dry on the donkey's back so she could keep warm at night, and she had a little bread and even just a few dried fruits left, that was enough.

Only Jehanne was in her mind, often, like a strong burning light. She refused to agree with Jacques who had insisted she was shamed, they were all shamed by her shame, cavorting around the countryside with strangers, as he put it. No, that was not the Jehanne who shone in her mind. It was the Jehanne that Durand had described – a young woman sitting on a horse, her face radiant; or the girl in her red peasant dress who chatted familiarly to the saints in the village church.

After they passed through Lyon and into the mountains, she learnt they were walking by the Loire.

'Father,' she said timidly to an old monk who walked by her.

'This Loire, is it the same river as where the Dauphin sits at Chinon?'

'Aye, that it is,' he replied. He waved his arm generally over to the right. 'Long way over there, many days away. We shall not see the Dauphin on this journey.'

'Oh no,' replied Zabillet. 'I know we are far from there. It is amazing to me that this is the same river.'

'It is, though who would know? Here it is narrow and tumbles through the stones. There it is broad and deep and slow.'

Now Zabillet could feel a line connecting her to Jehanne. She prayed for her constantly, though she had no idea, could not begin to imagine, what she was doing or why. Just let her be safe, was all her prayer.

It was Maundy Thursday when they eventually came into the little town of Le Puy, just in time for the Great Jubilee, the prayers and celebrations already beginning. It had been a hard push at the end, up and down hills, along paths around the mountain-side, their numbers swelled by other groups of pilgrims as they came nearer to the town, the friars increasing the pace to ensure their arrival before Good Friday. Rain and wind accompanied them most of the way, at best a few hours sun, hard to enjoy for the bitter cold that inevitably followed with the early darkness.

Zabillet felt she had been walking forever, if she felt anything at all. Mostly it was just the necessity of placing one weary foot in front of another, of gentle encouragement to her slowing donkey. Home and destination were forgotten, purpose incorporated into the mechanical movement of the body. But gradually a sense of the journey's end began to take hold of the pilgrims, the friars sang stronger, conversation became more animated. A great cheer arose as those at the front saw Le Puy before them. They were going steeply down and around the mountainside into the valley; on their right the red hillside arose almost vertically in places, on the other side only trees belied the treacherous way the mountain fell away beneath the path.

'Are we there?' asked Zabillet of Marie, a friend made on the journey with whom she was walking. As yet she could see nothing but the backs of those who walked ahead of her.

'It seems so,' said Marie, straining her neck. 'Oh look, Zabillet, we are.'

'Oh, my goodness.'

The little town lay before them in the valley, the cathedral dominant with its surrounding buildings, hospitals and abbeys. Rock formations, peaks of volcanic growth shot up out of the earth. One to the right seemed to have a church growing out of the top, and another stood huge behind the cathedral. It was magical. Zabillet had never seen anything like it before.

'Praise be,' said Zabillet, hugging her friend. The sight of the buildings, immense even at that distance, dark in the late afternoon light, and of the strange rocky growths, lifted from her all weariness, cold and numbness. She and Marie waved their arms, laughed, made a little dance with their companions, and joined in the chant as they picked their way down. And now they could hear the sounds of a town celebrating, its streets full of people. There was a fair, food cooking on open fires, music, dancers, light.

Tears flowed down Zabillet's face. I have arrived, she thought. I am here. I can rest and pray. People are enjoying themselves. Although she had not seen anything like this before, nothing so huge or so vibrant, the normality of celebration resonated throughout her body. She felt connected to the life expressed around her. She found herself clapping and cheering.

Le Puy was overflowing with pilgrims. The Lorrainers had a space set aside for them in a hostelry, and boys took off the horses and donkeys to rest in an enclosed field nearby. Zabillet set out her blanket and few possessions in the dormitory. If I can eat and drink a little, and then sleep, she thought, I will be able to do what I came for – celebrate the Holy Mother's day and maybe speak with her a little, mother to mother.

3

'Zabillet! It is Zabillet, isn't it? From Domremy?'

Zabillet, trying to find her way through the crowds in the cathedral, looked up in surprise as a man in front of her grasped her arm.

'Bertrand de Poulengy? Is that you, Bertrand?' For a moment she felt faint. What could this big, rough soldier whom she'd only ever seen in Vaucouleurs be doing here? Was he not with her Jehanne somewhere far away?

'Jehanne…? She's not…?' Zabillet wasn't sure what the best end to this question was. Is Jehanne here? Or, has something happened to her? Something terrible.

Bertrand smiled at her dismay, and put his arm around her shoulder. 'Your Jehanne's away with the Dauphin,' he said. 'She's doing fine. She's too busy to have any time for us just now, so we thought we'd come and pay our respects to the Black Virgin.' He bowed slightly towards where the figure stood, though obscured from their sight by the hundreds of pilgrims enjoying the festival in the vast cathedral. 'Didn't we, Jean?' He pulled at the arm of his companion and drew him nearer to Zabillet.

'Jean, have you met Zabillet before?' The younger man shook his head. 'This is the mother of our Jehanne.' The younger man bowed extravagantly, and insisted on kissing Zabillet's hand.

'Jean de Metz,' he murmured. 'I am honoured indeed. What an amazing daughter you have.'

Zabillet felt as she had when the friar had brought the letter from Jehanne, puzzled at the respect in which people appeared to hold her. She remembered how Durand Laxart, on that horribly confusing afternoon when he had told them of Jehanne's departure, had said that Jean de Metz was devoted to her. And this respect seemed to extend itself to her, just because she was her mother.

She looked at them, fearful that they might depart as quickly as they had arrived.

'Would you have time to tell me what has happened to her? It sounds as though she got to see the Dauphin. I miss her so much.' Zabillet brushed her eyes with the corner of her shawl, feeling fully the loss of the daughter who had always been at her side until just a few weeks ago.

Jean smiled at her. 'I don't think she would ever forgive us if she knew we had met with you, and not given you all the news of her that we can. She's quite formidable you know when she's cross.'

Bertrand laughed, shaking his head at some memory that phrase evoked. 'Come on,' he said. 'I'm sure we can find a place to sit down for a little while and talk.'

'It was a dreadful journey,' said Bertrand. 'I'm not going to tell you all the details, because it was hard and dangerous, picking our way across a land in the power of the English and their lackeys the Burgundians.' He spat contemptuously. 'No-one could be trusted. It was wet, cold; sometimes we had to make enormous detours because floods had wiped out bridges. We hardly ever dared to go into a town or village until we got into French land. And there were marauders, and small bands of homeless peasants ready to injure and rob to get a little food. It was hard for us soldiers, never mind for a young girl who'd never ridden a horse any distance before.'

Zabillet tried to imagine it. 'Jehanne is used to things being hard,' she said.

Jean broke in. 'Oh, she's tough, all right,' he said, smiling with admiration. 'Made of granite, I'd say; and she kept us all going by never for one moment swerving from her purpose. For her, even the worst hardships were minor obstacles to be overcome in order to get to the Dauphin.'

'She could be a bit reckless, though, couldn't she?' laughed Bertrand. 'We can laugh now we're all safe, but I thought our adventure had come to an end several times – like when she insisted on going into Auxerre to say mass.'

'Yes, it was no joke when we almost bumped into those Burgundian soldiers, I can tell you. Not that she was troubled by it.'

'And what happened when she got to Chinon?' said Zabillet, feeling more cheerful than in many weeks. She found she was grasping the two hands of the men talking to her.

'It was astonishing,' said Jean. 'I must say, for all I had come to admire your daughter and her purpose, I thought this was the end of our journey. The Dauphin is completely unpredictable, you know, and even though he'd written to Robert saying that he'd receive her, I thought he'd send her packing. I dreaded it. She would be so angry and miserable. I wasn't sure what would happen next.'

'He kept her kicking her heels for a day or so, and then he called for her. I'll tell you what happened when she went first into the Dauphin's chamber at Chinon,' continued Bertrand de Poulengy. 'They say the Dauphin was in a merry mood, and he decided to play a trick on her, this country upstart. He put one of his Lords by his throne, and hid himself amongst the courtiers. Jehanne comes in and this Lord, pretending to be King, steps forward to receive her greeting. She just looks at him and says "But you are not the Dauphin!" and starts looking around the room. She makes straight for where Charles is standing in the crowd and kneels in front of him. "My liege," she says in her rough, Lorrainer voice, "I have come to save France and have you crowned King." Apparently some of the knights and ladies started laughing, thinking it just a good joke to pass the cold winter afternoon. But others murmured in amazement because she had made straight for the Dauphin despite his deception. The Dauphin bent over her and raised her up, looking deep into her eyes. "You are welcome,

Jehanne," he said. "Come, warm yourself by the fire here, and take some wine. Then we will go aside and talk." That is what happened, is that not so, Jean?'

Bertrand turned towards the younger man, whose face was alight with laughter, affection, fervour. 'Aye, that's what they say. If only we had been there to see it, but she insisted on going into the castle alone. But Zabillet, she could command anyone, your Jehanne. All through our journey she was so strong, so sure, no matter what happened. Whenever there was any danger, she would say, "Don't worry, be strong, the way is clear. I was born for this." Believe me, she will save France.'

Zabillet stood up and walked a little way from the body of the cathedral where they had been sitting. She was no longer aware of the crowds, the incense, the minstrels, the jostling, the sounds of prayer. She felt dizzy, light-headed. Jehanne was safe. She was more than safe. Not only had she made her treacherous journey to Chinon, but she had been received by the Dauphin. The Dauphin, whom many already called King! The Dauphin had received her daughter. He had not mocked her, ridiculed her, imprisoned her or sent her away. He believed in her as did these two faithful men.

She turned back and sat with them again. 'Bertrand and Jean,' she said. 'I must ask your forgiveness. I have thought ill of you and your other companions since you left Vaucouleurs with my Jehanette. Oh, I've suffered bitter nights, wondering that you could go on such a journey with my daughter, honourable though I know you to be. I cannot think yet what will come of all this, but I thank you for your care of her, your love for her. Shall you return to Vaucouleurs soon?'

'Oh no,' said Jean de Metz. 'I am pledged to follow her to raise the siege of Orléans. You know that is what she is sworn to do when she returns from Poitiers?'

'Raise the siege?' repeated Zabillet. She felt confused. Was it not enough that Jehanne had been well received by the Dauphin and become a part of his company? 'How can you speak of such things? She is but a country girl, how can she ... why, she's never used a sword. She's never even been to a place like Orléans. I don't know where it is.' She shook her head, it was overwhelming.

'The Dauphin loves her,' said Jean, his eyes shining. 'Another day he called for her, and they spoke long in a side room. When they came out, the Dauphin's face was radiant. He was full of resolve to fight for France. She has inspired him where no other could. And those near to her are beginning to hope again, you know, where before they could see only humiliation by the English, and the Dauphin doing nothing.'

Bertrand de Poulengy took Zabillet's hands. 'Dear mother of Jehanne,' he said gently. 'Try to understand your daughter. She is called to save our country, miserable state that it is in. Everything she does is by God's will. She hears voices that tell her what to do and say, and which give her courage. Everything she needs to know, she is learning fast. Even in the few days she was at Chinon, the Duke d'Alençon taught her how to use a sword, how to ride a charger, and it all came to her so easily. She has many friends who believe in her and wish to follow her. You must believe in her too.'

Zabillet felt the tears begin to flow from her eyes. She rubbed them away impatiently. There were things, so many things, she wanted to ask, to say, needed to know, but she did not know where to begin. The great bells began to toll, heralding the Good Friday mass.

'Will you meet me here again tomorrow?' she asked of the two men, her words barely audible within the great stone arches of the cathedral. 'I must think on what you have said.'

The two men bent over her hand, and left her there, her face white, strained and soaked with tears.

The Great Mass continued. Zabillet sat on in the cathedral. The huge space was full, abuzz with pilgrims who had made the long journey for this celebration which happened so seldom; to honour the Holy Mother called by God to bear his son, and on the same day to reflect on his death. Bitter sweet. To have, and then not have. To love and lose. To rejoice and then mourn. To be filled with joy, and face emptiness. Zabillet felt the intense celebration. She sat as the priest incanted and the choir sang, and the holy water and incense sprayed across the cold interior. Sitting, not thinking, lost in the great mysteries, Zabillet felt for a moment the movement of life and destiny.

The next day she was up early. Unable to sleep, her head whirring with sights and sounds she had never experienced before, with unfathomable thoughts about Jehanne, she decided to get out of the crowding around the cathedral and find some air. It was only a matter of a few minutes walk from her hostelry before she stood at the bottom of the tall, thin volcanic peak that rose like a needle into the morning sky. She was not alone; since time immemorial there had been a chapel on the very top, and already, though dawn had only just broken, people were beginning to make their way up, round and round the narrow rock, climbing steeply upwards as if the narrow pathway would take them straight into heaven in the dark blue dawn.

Cold, quiet, peace. Despite the other climbers, Zabillet felt the sharpness of the dawn, saw the stars she could nearly reach out and touch, bathed in the crisp calm. Coming to the top, she entered the little church, full of its frescoes of all living things painted in the sweep of the bays, its elegant arches.

Small beauty, thought Zabillet. Not big, rich, cavernous, like the cathedral, but tiny and perfect. Not so much different, she thought, from Bermont, that small, simple chapel at the end of the little pilgrimage from home and through the woods she had made with Jehanne and Cathérine so many times. Long ago. Very long ago, it seemed.

Zabillet prayed, and slowly made her way down to earth again, as the sun came through.

Later, when she saw Bertrand de Poulengy and Jean de Metz again, a young priest stood with them.

'Zabillet,' said Jean. 'This is Jean Pasquerel. We have been talking of Jehanne.'

Pasquerel inclined his head towards Zabillet. His eyes shone. 'Mother of Jehanne,' he said, 'how honoured I am to meet you. Your daughter is called to do great work. Come, we can go into the cloister, where it is quieter.' Warmth radiated from his smile, gentleness from his gestures.

Zabillet bowed and walked beside him. They entered the cloister and continued to walk in the covered, quiet area. She felt breathless. That a priest, albeit such a young man, should honour her so, was something she had never experienced.

'Bertrand,' she said hurriedly, determined not to become confused again as she had at their previous meeting. 'Why have they taken my Jehanette to Poitiers? I do not even know where such a town is.'

'Oh, it is far from here, nearly as far as you have come from Lorraine, but to the west. The Dauphin has sent her there to be examined by lawyers and advisers.'

'Lawyers and advisers? But I thought you said she was to go to Orléans?'

'Oh, she is so impatient to go there!' smiled Jean de Metz. 'So impatient! She shouts at the Dauphin and d'Alençon and all his people, she cannot stand the delay.'

Zabillet laughed. She understood that Jehanne well enough. 'But you said the Dauphin believes in her?'

'He does,' said Jean. 'But those around him are more cautious. So she has to answer questions and demonstrate that she is truly for the King, and a good woman and a virgin.'

Zabillet shook her head, wondering. She remembered how Jehanne had spoken at the court at Toul when defending her refusal to marry. 'She will not fear them,' she said.

'Fear? No, she fears no-one, only the delay enrages her. It will not be long. They are preparing now for a battle at Orléans, and she will go there with the army. Then we shall all see what she will do.'

Zabillet did not want to talk of battles and armies. She turned to Pasquerel. 'Are you of that region?'

'I am indeed,' he said. 'Though I have not met Jehanne yet. I am lector at a convent at Tours, so I hope to meet her when she returns to Chinon.'

'Ah, you must tell her…. Tell her…….' Zabillet did not know what to say. She felt overwhelmed by the confidence that these three men showed in Jehanne. But was she not just an ordinary peasant girl? How could anyone have confidence in her to achieve these things of which they spoke, as if it were no more than finishing a bobbin of wool, or rescuing a lamb from the river?

'May she not fail?' she burst out.

'Fail?' Bertrand laughed shaking his head. 'Fail! That word does not even enter her mind. That much at least you recognize, do you not, Zabillet?'

Their laughter eased her fear. 'She is so sure,' said Jean de Metz. 'She is so determined, none can turn her from her path. And yet she is so sweet.'

So sweet, ah yes, so sweet. Her open loving face, her smile. Zabillet felt the sheer physical loss of her. She wanted that warm body within her arms.

She turned again to Pasquerel, who sat quietly watching her. 'Father,' she said. 'Please give Jehanne my blessing. I did not… I did not….' I did not give it to her, she wanted to say, because I did not know, I had no idea, I did not try to understand, I was scared. I am scared. She wept.

The young priest bent to kiss her forehead and made the sign of the cross. 'I will,' he said. Zabillet felt he understood all that she had not said.

'Will you give her this ring?' Zabillet eased the rough gold band from her finger. 'Tell her it is from her father and mother. Tell her to think of us now and then, and we wait for her to return home when it is done.'

'She will be so pleased that we have seen you,' said Bertrand gently. 'And we have a gift for you. Here, it is a rosary made especially for this Great Jubilee. Remember us with it. And now we must say goodbye for we leave early tomorrow.'

'Messire,' said Zabillet to Pasquerel. 'Shall you hear my daughter's confession?'

'If she so chooses,' he replied.

'Would you go with her to Orléans, and be with her in this battle and be her confessor?'

The young priest looked startled, and then he said. 'Is that what you wish?'

Zabillet nodded, weeping. Pasquerel's face became calm, bright. 'Then if she does not object, so it will be.'

Zabillet wanted to delay these men, to talk more, much more. But they had to be away. They were going to Jehanne, she was not. It was bitter.

CONVERSATIONS

Zabillet talks with the Black Virgin at Le Puy

Dear Holy Mother, how beautiful you look! And how different it is to see you in this wonderful, enormous place so far from home. It is your very own church which you were so insistent should be built here hundreds of years ago. I like those stories which the good *curé* told me as we walked along, of how the stag marked out the plan for the church in the July snow, and of the thorn hedge which burst into flower overnight.

Although I saw you once before in a cathedral, in Toul, how unused I am to the crowds and smells and sounds of this huge place. And yet I know that you are here, just as surely as in my little church at Domremy, or up at Bermont in the woods. It is of no consequence which town or village I am in; as I kneel here and look at you, I feel a similar peace upon me.

How strange it is to feel the same despite those huge differences. You yourself could hardly be thought to be the same. For there, I am used to your kindly, homely face, and I can sit or kneel just a few feet from you – a few inches if I desire and stretch out my hand to you. But here you are truly in state, on the altar where I cannot touch you, and surrounded with light.

The Black Virgin they call you, holding the little black Jesus on your lap. And dressed! Instead of the wooden, painted robe of your Domremy statue, you are resplendent in rich lace garments, heavy with jewels. Both you and the baby Jesus have heavy crowns upon your heads. You are truly fit to receive the devotion of kings.

I have learnt over these last days how people come to Le Puy for many reasons, healing of body and of mind. Such stories I have heard, of their steadfast belief, and your power. And I have had my miracle, to meet by chance amongst all these thousands of pilgrims the two men who have been with my Jehanne, and could give me word of her. And I thank you.

And now I have come to know you a little, Holy Mother, I must go home tomorrow. Bless me and pray for me. These three days I have been thinking of you, wondering how to celebrate with you both the day you knew you were to bear the Son of God, and the day in which you saw Him die, cruelly hung on a cross in the fierce sun. Experiencing in one memorial day great joy and the greatest loss.

I bought up Jehanne to know you and your great Son, Jesus Christ. You remember how we used to go to Bermont, and Jehanne would light a little candle at the base of your statue, where you held your baby Jesus and the little dove perched on his hand, singing as she did so. And how she was filled with joy when the bells rang across the village, across the river, throughout the fields.

That special light about her – but you know also how I came to fear it. Or fear for her as she grew impatient with our simple way in Domremy, our ordinary peasant life, made harsh as it was by endless war. I feared her radiance because I did not know how she could live life with it in Domremy. And I could not see there might be a life for her elsewhere, a life so very different that even now, when people have told me of it, I can hardly believe it, for I have never heard that a peasant girl could have any part in such a world.

Because I do not know anything about the Dauphin or the court or the army, or a great city under siege such as they say has happened at Orléans, so I still doubt. Maybe she is mistaken; the foolish Dauphin has taken some fancy to her and will spit her out soon enough. Or, God help us, her head will be so swollen that she will rush into some battle and be slain, and none will care enough to protect her.

What can a mother do? Well, I shall try and believe in her, as those good men do whom I have talked with today, despite my doubts and my ignorance, and the utter strangeness of her story so far. If she believes that all she does is by the will of Heaven, then I shall not question it. I am done with sadness and weeping for the past.

I will do what I can to protect her, and pray to you, Holy Mother, that you will watch for her; and that when this is done, or is not done if that is what is meant to be, that she will come home safely. I will look after her, come what may, and be glad to have her by me again. Never again shall I try to make her live a life she does not wish to live.

And in the meantime I will do what I can to love and protect the others in my family.

In your kind and knowing smile may I find the strength and resolve to be patient, calm and loving, no matter what might occur.

APRIL to JULY 1429

Success

1

Zabillet saw Pierre and Petit-Jean before they saw her. They were standing on the top of a little outcrop watching for the band of pilgrims to come into view, and were entirely visible, whereas she was one of many. She walked with her hand on her donkey's head, feeling every one of those hundreds of miles they had walked, wet, ragged, cold on this sunless April day, and hungry. Their hunger had seemed worse on the way home, because the peasants and villagers who had cheered them on their way to Le Puy, happy to give them some bread or a small bowl of soup in exchange for the promise of a prayer before the Holy Mother, now had little interest in them as they made their way back.

It had seemed a long path home to Zabillet. She was impatient. She wanted to tell Pierrelot and Petit-Jean and even Jacques about her meeting with Bertrand de Poulengy and Jean de Metz, tell them what they had said about Jehanne. She knew Jacques might scoff, would certainly scoff, but at least he might be less angry with Jehanne, knowing that she had been well accompanied and come to no harm. And she would go over and see Aveline as soon as she could, and tell her and dear Durand Laxart what she had learnt – surely Jacques could no longer forbid her that.

These had been her thoughts as she made the slow journey home. She still felt too shy to share anything about Jehanne even with Marie, with whom she had shared the hard road, her donkey, last heels of bread and even body warmth when the cold became too much to bear alone. It was hard sometimes not to burst out, for as they passed through the impoverished, wasted villages, saw how few fields were sprouting their winter wheat, talked with women who had little wool to spin and few stores to draw on for food, she wanted to give them hope. 'My extraordinary daughter…' she wanted to begin. 'Soon things will be different…' Other times, that hope seemed stupid, vain, the task much too great, the untended fields and skeletal animals reflecting the bitter reality of years of war and the land's destruction. How foolish to think a girl could do anything about all that.

Pierre and Petit-Jean came leaping down the hill as soon as they spotted her. My boys are men, she thought, admiring their strength and speed as they raced towards her. Then as she heard their cries, she knew they were still boys, her boys.

'Maman, Maman! We've been waiting for you for two days. Hey, there's your old donkey, still standing – just!' She was enfolded, overwhelmed, knocked over almost by their hugs, their thumps on her back, their grins, their gladness.

'It's lovely to see you,' she said, leaning into them, feeling weepy and grateful. 'You look so big and healthy!'

'Well, we haven't been weeks on the road like you. Oh, look at that poor donkey; he's so thin he might tumble over!'

'Don't laugh at him. He's been the best of friends to me. Haven't you darling?' Zabillet gave him a hug and they all laughed, delighted.

'Now, what's been going on at home?' she asked. 'When I've said goodbye to my friends here, I shall want to know every detail.'

Home, what would it be like? At least it was obvious Pierre and Petit-Jean had no especially bad news to tell her, their faces were open and happy. There can have been no further catastrophes. Yet the two boys certainly did exchange a look.

'What?' she said sharply. 'What has happened?'

'Nothing,' said Pierre. 'We have something to tell you, but Papa said we were to wait until we are home.'

'It's good news!' burst out Petit-Jean, unable to restrain himself.

Pierre knocked into him roughly almost causing him to fall into the ditch by the roadside.

'Hey, come on now. No fighting,' said Zabillet, beginning to pull her donkey along. 'We shall be home very soon. We have lots to tell each other.'

Petit-Jean led the weary donkey along whilst Zabillet, holding tight to Pierre's arm, weaved through the group of pilgrims, saying goodbye and hugging the friends she had made. Zabillet had grown fond of these people, they had become her whole world as they covered mile after mile. But now she was ready to leave them, anxious to get back to home and family, however difficult that might be.

Jacques stood at the doorway of the house smiling at Zabillet as she approached, flanked by Pierre and Petit-Jean. She regarded him cautiously. They had been cold with each other for so long, but now he looked welcoming, pleased to see her.

'I've got a pot of soup on the fire,' he said. 'Marguerite sent it over to welcome you home. We guessed you would come today, although the boys have been looking out for you for days.'

'Petit-Jean, would you see to the donkey?' asked Zabillet. 'Make sure you give him a good brush down, and see that he has plenty to eat and drink. Hello Jacques.' She smiled uncertainly at him and followed him into the house. What a heavenly smell! And there on the table was bread, and pastries and wine.

'I say, this is a feast,' she said shakily. She sank down on the bench by the table. 'Thank you, Jacques. It's lovely to be home.'

She could not quite meet his eyes, and anyway he was bustling about, stirring the soup, chopping bread, asking her about the last leg of her journey. Pierre sat close to her, pouring wine and smiling.

'It's been more or less quiet here,' said Jacques in answer to her query. 'No raids, no écorcheurs. But plenty of fighting further north. The truce is just about holding out that Robert de Baudricourt made with de Vergy, but there are still scuffles now and then. Thank heavens the crops are safe so far, and the village has had several new lambs.'

'Yes, Jeanne Baudin and I were out two nights with the sheep lambing,' chipped in Pierre. 'We thought we were going to lose grouchy old Tweezle, but she pulled through. Two babes she had.'

'Excellent,' said Zabillet. 'If only we could have a few months of peace to get ourselves together again.'

Jacques laughed bitterly. 'That's most unlikely. The Goddams and that fiend the Duke of Burgundy will make sure of that. There's no end in sight. We've more or less finished the little wheat our *demoiselle* gave us last autumn. I fear we shall have to go back to her and beg for bread again soon, until the new crops are in.'

Jacques nearly slammed the soup pot down on the table, then laid it gently as he remembered the occasion. 'Now,' he said more cheerfully. 'Where's young Petit-Jean? Food is what we need.'

'You've become quite at home around the stove,' teased Zabillet as Jacques set a little pot of butter on the table. 'Perhaps I'm no longer needed here.'

He laughed. 'You are, believe me, you are. We've slummed it good and proper while you've been away, haven't we Pierre?'

Petit-Jean dashed in through the door. 'Have you told her?' he demanded anxiously.

'Sit down, you young fool,' shouted Jacques. 'I said we would tell her together, and that is what we shall do. Now, you start while I serve us all some of your Tante Marguerite's soup.'

'Maman,' said Petit-Jean excitedly. 'It was a few days ago. Monks came, clerics they were, from the King.'

'Yes, from the King, or Dauphin as they called him, in Chinon,' cut in Pierre.

'Shut up, Pierre,' shouted Petit-Jean. 'Papa said I could tell her.'

Zabillet smiled and shook her head. How could this tall, strong, almost-man of hers be so angry and impetuous.

'Boys, boys,' she said. 'Don't fight or I will never get to know the news. Come on, tell me, these monks, what did they have to say?'

'They came into the village to ask about Jehanette,' said Petit-Jean. He sat back smiling all over his face.

'Jehanette? Our Jehanette?' asked Zabillet. She half-raised herself from the table in excitement. 'Oh my goodness, what were they after?'

'They told us she got safe to Chinon,' said Pierre, 'and was presented to the Dauphin.'

'Yes,' broke in Petit-Jean, 'and he sent the monks to Domremy to check she is who she says she is, and not a witch or something.'

'A witch!' said Zabillet. 'Our Jehanne? How could they think that?'

'They said the Dauphin was taken with her,' continued Pierre. 'She is talking of leading the army to raise the siege of Orléans. If the King is satisfied that she is who she says she is, then that is what she will do.'

'Our Jehanne,' chortled Petit-Jean, 'leading an army!'

'Leading an army!' said Jacques disparagingly as he sat at the table. 'That much is made up by foolish monks. They're exaggerating, as usual. I'm sure they wouldn't think she could do that after they'd heard about her life here, anyway.'

Zabillet looked at him. This was the first time he had spoken since Petit-Jean started to tell the story. He looked puzzled and confused.

'This daughter of ours,' said Zabillet, leaning over and taking his hand, 'is exceptional.' She felt strong, unafraid of him even should he fly into one of his rages. 'Listen to me, Jacques, and you two boys. I've had news of Jehanette too whilst I've been away. It's time to put away worry and anger, for whether we can see it or not, she is going to change things by her power and by her goodness.'

Zabillet started to tell her husband and sons about Bertrand de Poulengy and Jean de Metz, and even about Jean Pasquerel. She told them about the journey from Vaucouleurs to Chinon, about

Jehanne's strength and determination, of how they had tried to fool her at the Dauphin's court, and the long examination at Poitiers, of which perhaps the monks' visit to Domremy was a part. There was hope for the future of France, and it rested on her young woman's shoulders. And somehow, they had to think about this, and not just dismiss it.

The day passed. Sometimes one or the other would come out of the house to fetch water from the well. Jacques at one point paced around the house and up and down the lane, ignoring the greetings of neighbours and their enquiries as to whether Zabillet was safe home. Once Petit-Jean leapt out of the house, made a mad, excited dance in the yard, punching the air with his fist and shouting, sending the hens scuttling in fright. Zabillet herself, still in her worn and dirty travel clothes, fetched wood from the wood-pile. But still she did not go around the village to greet her friends and neighbours and tell them of her long journey.

By evening, when it was time to secure their animals for the night, it had been decided. Pierre and Petit-Jean would go as soldiers to the Dauphin, and fight alongside their sister, if that was how it turned out. For the first time in very many months, Zabillet was happy to snuggle up to her husband in their bed that night.

2

What a feast had been laid on to honour Jehanne! How the townspeople and villagers wanted to celebrate her! Zabillet could hardly believe she was the focus of such attention. It was embarrassing how people kept looking at her and raising their drinks to salute her. She looked across to where Jacques, perhaps conscious of all his doubts and anger, scratched his head and looked uneasy as Robert de Baudricourt spoke.

'Our very own Jehanette!' he said proudly, standing at the head of the tables in the great hall of his castle. 'What did she say when she left Vaucouleurs just a few weeks ago? "I go to bring aid to the

Dauphin, to lift the siege of Orléans and have him crowned King at Reims." Well, she has already raised the siege, and surely she will take the Dauphin to Reims next. Let us all drink to our Jehanne of Domremy!'

All the villagers, the townspeople and the soldiers cheered and clashed their cups. 'Jehanette!' they shouted. 'Jehanette! To our Jehanne of Domremy! She will chase the Goddams out of our country, you see. And we shall have our King crowned ere long!'

Durand Laxart, who was sitting opposite Zabillet with Jacques Alain at the table just beneath Robert's, looked fit to burst with pride. Whilst the cups were refilled, she went round and hugged him for helping her daughter on her journey, and believing in her as no-one else had at that time. Even Jacques went and slapped him on the shoulder, anger forgotten.

'This is what I have heard,' continued Robert. 'The townsfolk of Orléans were in a terrible state. You people of Vaucouleurs have some idea of what it's like to be under siege, but think of them, month after month through the winter with no sign of relief. Everyone is gathered within the city walls for safety. Some supplies can get in, so they aren't quite starving, but hunger is never far away. They have no leader – their Duke Charles d'Orléans is still in prison in England waiting for his ransom to be paid. The English are at the walls, all around, and so far all attempts by Charles' brother to fight them off have failed. No help is coming from anywhere. There's no hope, nothing is left for them but to starve until they have to submit, however much they might declare that will never happen.

'Then they start to hear about our Jehanne. They first hear about her when she comes into safe territory at Gien, on her journey from here with my men Jean de Metz and Bertrand de Poulengy. Here is someone saying she's been sent by God to raise the siege! But they have to wait long weeks whilst she sees the Dauphin, gets examined, then fitted out in armour – yes, our Jehanne in armour – and soldiers gathered together for her. I can see you shaking your heads – you've heard nothing yet! It's an unbelievable story!

'D'you know what? You saw how holy she is, always praying in church and talking of instructions from God. Well, she gets all the Dauphin's soldiers to confess and forbids them to swear. And she sends all the camp-followers away. Mercy me, when they march on Orléans, the army is headed up by priests chanting!'

Robert de Baudricourt burst out laughing, raising his bowl to take a large swig of ale. But Zabillet thought he looked truly astonished. She noticed that *curé* Frontey was nodding, pleased.

'Amazing!' he continued. 'But that's not all. When she arrives at Orléans with her soldiers and all the supplies and several lords and that rogue La Hire with his company, she discovers there's no intention to fight at all! The commanders only intend to get the supplies into the city on the other side of the river, and send the soldiers back to base. Oh, Jehanne's furious, I can tell you. She's all ready for the battle to start, but it looks like she's the only one! Furious, she turns on the Bastard d'Orléans who has come out from the city to meet her, and gives him a right haranguing. "The Counsel of the Lord our God is wiser than yours!" she says. "I bring you better help than has reached you from any soldier or city; it is help from the King of Heaven who has taken pity on the poor people of Orléans." To the Bastard's further embarrassment, the wind's blowing in the wrong direction, so his boats can't even come across the river to pick up the supplies. But suddenly, as Jehanne is telling him about her Counsel from Heaven, the wind changes and the boats can cross and be loaded up with the supplies for the city.

'Next day, Jehanne rides into the city by the side of the Bastard and La Hire and the other commanders. Good townspeople, imagine the delight of the citizens of Orléans! They cheer and fête her – they know something really special is happening.'

Robert de Baudricourt leant over the table and sloshed more ale into his bowl. 'Come on, everyone, top up your cups, for this is the happiest tale we've heard in a long time.

'Over the next few days, our Jehanne is so determined she manages to sweep all those reluctant commanders along and get them to agree to fight off the Goddams. We know how determined she can be, eh, don't we just? The Bastard goes back to Blois to lead the army into Orléans, and Jehanne examines all the English camps and fortifications, sends letters to the English lords telling them to go home, and even stands on the bridge defiantly shouting out what will happen to them if they don't.'

There were cheers and laughter from the people sitting listening. This was as good as a story well told, but it was true, and it was about one of their own, one they had recognised as being special.

'Two big battles are fought before they take out the main fortifications of the English, and regain the bridge into the city. Our Jehanne is always there, at the front with her standard, La Hire and the Bastard at her side. At the end, when it's nearly dark, the French lords want to call it a day. But she won't, not she; she presses on. Night falls as they overrun the English bulwark and take the tower at the end of the bridge. The English commander falls into the river and dies after the crafty Orléannais set a fire-boat under the bridge and burn it. And that's it! Victory! Carpenters lay wood across the destroyed part of the bridge, so Jehanne and the French lords and knights enter the city in victory through the main gate.

'Oh, the celebrations go on all night, I can tell you. And for days afterwards, I've heard, when the English that are left pack up and leave. What an inspiration she is! And now Orléans is free and the Goddams are on the run. Hurrah!'

Robert de Baudricourt turned towards where Zabillet and Jacques were sitting and raised his glass, and all the soldiers and townspeople stood and cheered and shouted Jehanne's name. Zabillet felt so proud, though of course everyone knew how much Robert liked to exaggerate at such times. She saw Jacques shaking his head as if trying to clear it.

After a while, Robert came to sit with them, and Zabillet told him about her pilgrimage to Le Puy and her meeting with Jean de Metz and Bertrand. He laughed uproariously. 'They are completely besotted with her – especially Jean. H'd go anywhere with her, dirty old dog.' Jacques half rose off the bench. 'No, no, good Jacques, don't be alarmed; she's a pure maid, that much has been shown.'

'Messire,' Zabillet put the question she had been awaiting the opportunity to ask. 'One of your men told me that she was injured in the battle. Do you know anything about that?'

'Oh yes, she's blessed indeed, your daughter. In the midst of the battle one of the Goddam's arrows went into her breast. Six inches in.' He slapped the area of flesh above his chest. 'Strong as she is, she fainted with the pain of it as they drew the arrow out. But a good coat of lard and oil saw her right again, and off she went back into the battle. She wasn't going to let that stop her. Don't worry, Zabillet, she is protected, that one.'

'Do you have news of Pierre and Petit-Jean?' Jacques asked. 'Were they with her?'

'They are half-decent soldiers, by all accounts,' he said. 'And now they will go on and get these damned Englishmen off our backs. You can be sure of that. You'll see, once Charles is crowned.'

'I shall never forget this day', murmured Zabillet, hugging herself in the cool evening air. Chickens and ducks pecked and clucked around her feet, peering at her boots and occasionally squawking as they turned on each other. They were only just back from Vaucouleurs. It was late, and they still had many chores to do before settling down for the night. 'Holy Mother,' she whispered to the rising moon. 'Watch over my dear daughter and sons.'

Jacques came out, and Zabillet leaned into him as he stood by her watching the river glisten in the last of the light. 'Is it not a horrible thing,' she said, 'that when we are most at peace here, our children are in the worst danger?'

'Don't think of that now. They've been part of a great victory. It's true those battles are drawing in all the marauders that have been such a plague on the villages for so long. Perhaps this dreadful war has nearly reached its end.'

It was hard without the children. Zabillet and Jacques had to do everything themselves, with a little help in the fields from any lad that a family could spare for a day or two. Yet now, in early summer, there was less work to do. All was planted, and they could use the slack time to mend their house and hedges and see to the animals. The men had even started planning to repair the poor church, its roof still open to the wind and rain since it had been burnt by the écorcheurs the summer before, when they had been at Neufchâteau. It had been a good winter and spring in the village. There had been plenty of new lambs and calves, and it was some time since any raiders had swept down the hills into the village intent on destruction.

'Do you think Messire de Baudricourt told it true?' she asked. 'That our Jehanne was at the head of the army at Orléans?'

Jacques was silent. 'I don't know what to think,' he said at last, shaking his head. Zabillet sighed and shivered. It had been a great day, but memories of Robert's warm hall could not prevent her feeling cold now. The last of the sun's rays were disappearing behind the hills, leaving red streaks in the darkening sky. Where were they now, her three children? Despite their success, and the celebration feast, she could not resist the fierce wish that they were home with her here in Domremy, and that she was shouting at them to finish their evening tasks before night fell.

3

Jargeau, Meung, Beaugency, Patay. Zabillet's head spun with the words. It infuriated her that she did not know where these places were. She would repeat them like a mantra, touching the beads on her rosary. The string, under her fingers, formed a line across the countryside, each precious bead a town, a victory for Jehanne at the head of the army. Three times, four times she had asked a passing monk or soldier to help her see where these places were in that fuzzy world beyond her direct knowledge. They would draw it with the point of a knife on her table, placing apples or drinking bowls to show the towns. Slowly she would think she began to see the path the campaign was taking, until she asked where Domremy was and the arm of her teacher would stretch out to the right, off the table. It was far away, beyond imagining.

And what to believe? Every passer-by seemed to have an amazing story about Jehanne. How to sift and glean, to understand the truth? How to find a touchstone in a story so fantastic that often, after the visitor and the villagers who crowded into their little house to hear the news had gone, she and Jacques would look at each other over the table and shake their heads? They would begin to put together the information they had, to try to understand it, but sometimes, often, it was too unbelievable. Zabillet would look out of the doorway and see the poverty of the village, the chickens pecking in the mud, the shaky woodpile she was learning to build herself, the little church next door with its burnt-out roof, the few wizened apples left in the store. This was their reality, was it not? What had any of the Domremy people ever had to do with the wider world in the past? Yet it was not a fantasy apparently, not some strange affliction of her mind that made her believe her daughter was pulling off victory after victory as if she was a general or a great noble commander. However much rumour and boasting accompanied the tales, it was true that Jehanne was slowly turning it round so that villagers, soldiers travelling up and down the road from Vaucouleurs to Neufchâteau and beyond, and those precious wandering monks and friars who came from afar, began to talk of the suffering of France being over soon, in the near future. Because of her Jehanne.

Zabillet's fingers ran down the line of the rosary, the Loire, to Jargeau, a little town just a few leagues from Orléans, though whether East or West she did not truly know. Here Jehanne had gone with her friend the Duke Jean d'Alençon as commander, son-in-law of the imprisoned Duke d'Orléans. Zabillet rolled the bead in her fingers. They had laid siege to a town full of the remnants of the English army put to rout at Orléans, demoralized but angry. And more miracles, it seemed from what she was told. Looking toward the town Jehanne had seen a great cannon pointing towards them. 'You'd better move,' she'd said to d'Alençon, 'or you'll get killed. I told your wife I'd bring you home safe, so hurry.' And the cannon shot landed just where he had stood. More injuries – Jehanne had been knocked off a ladder by a stone shattering her helmet as she scaled the walls to get into the town, and fell backwards to the ground, momentarily stunned. Zabillet's fingers paused in their caress of the bead, and picked up again as her mind slid from the image of her daughter, a peasant girl of Domremy in full battle armour, leading such an attack, injured. Apparently the town had been taken, the great English Duke of Suffolk had been captured and many of the Goddams imprisoned, killed or driven back. No-one had mentioned Pierre or Petit-Jean; surely they must be safe or she would have heard.

News came thick and fast as the trees grew lush with their green bright leaves, and the sun began to glisten on the Meuse. Occasionally, Robert de Baudricourt spared a soldier, who would come galloping into Domremy, and at the sight of him, cheering and shouting Jehanne's name, villagers would hurry to Zabillet's house to hear the latest events.

Her fingers moved smoothly onto the next bead. Meung and Beaugency. What were these towns like? Little walled towns, she was told, rather like Vaucouleurs with a castle and a bridge across the river. Now the English were frightened, so many men were gathering behind Jehanne, her army was growing every day. And they were determined. Could it be that her own daughter had packed the English lords off, making them promise not to fight for ten days? John Talbot and Fastolf had retired northwards. The Goddams were in retreat.

'What does she look like?' Zabillet asked a soldier, who had reluctantly left the army to come east to see his mother before she died, and called in at Domremy to bring news of its famous daughter.

'She's dressed in full armour, specially made to her size,' he said. 'She is proud and strong on a great horse. Before Orléans, she had a banner made for her which swirls in the wind as she rides before the army, urging them on. On the banner are pictures of Jesus and the angels. Her face, Zabillet, oh, it is full of light and energy, anyone would follow her. And she has pages and heralds and people who go with her everywhere and look after her. It is wonderful to be there.'

'I would go,' thought Zabillet. 'I would care for her.' The thought of the soft, young woman's body so vulnerable beneath her armour, hurt her.

'Is she safe?' She laughed at her own words. How could she possibly be safe when she kept going into battle in this extraordinary and impetuous way? But the soldier understood her.

'She is Jehanne La Pucelle, the Maid. She is admired, worshipped, respected. No soldier would go near her. She is blessed by God.'

The soldier blushed at his words, but Zabillet smiled and thanked him.

One more bead, one more victory. Even Jacques had begun to believe that Jehanette could kick the English out of France. How could that be? Zabillet reflected as she turned the bead within her fingers.

'Is it wrong of me,' she had asked the *curé* Frontey the day before, 'to use the rosary in this way?'

The young priest had smiled. 'I am as bemused as you, my dear, at the great achievements of Jehanne. But I do know, from all the reports I hear, that God is with her and guides her, and even drives her. So if the rosary helps you to reflect on that, so be it.'

Patay. The stories were becoming more and more incredible. They seemed to be taking on the resonance of fairy-stories told round the fireside. The battle lines were all drawn up, they said, each side using the bushes and shrub for concealment and cover. There was to be a long and, it was hoped, decisive battle. But Jehanne's troops had inadvertently started up a stag which had leapt into the ranks of the English infantry, startling them into giving their position away, and creating great disorder. Panicking, they had turned and fled, and the French had hunted them down. Thousands had been killed.

On the night this news reached them, near mid-summer, all the villagers of Domremy and around gathered and lit a great fire. A pig was roasted and there was wine a-plenty. Michel Lebuin played his little flute and everyone danced and celebrated into the night. 'The Goddams have run away,' the children chanted, weaving and diving around the fire and the dancers, 'Jehanette has won the day. Thousands of Goddams are dead. Hurray! The French are victors today, hey!'

How proud Zabillet felt when Jean Morel stood up and toasted Jehanne. 'She has saved France,' he said. 'She has chased the English from the Loire. Their great captains Suffolk and Talbot are imprisoned, and Fastolf has crept back to Paris in fear. Oh Philippe, may you rot in hell for allying Burgundy with the Goddams, you shall pay for that betrayal now. Let all the villages in France explode with joy and thank Jehanne, our Domremy Jehanette, for saving our country. Drink to her! Drink to her!' And everybody, the whole village, shouted 'Jehanette! Our Jehanette!' And Zabillet wept.

The excitement in the village was immense. A messenger had come from Robert de Baudricourt at Vaucouleurs announcing the

King was to be crowned. 'When?' he shouted from his horse. 'Very soon! Where? In Reims, of course.' Had not all Kings been anointed there with the Holy Oil of Clovis since time immemorial? Yes, but how was that to happen when the road from the Loire to Reims went straight through Burgundy territory? 'Jehanne will lead the Dauphin and the army, so all will be well.'

'Shall we go to Reims and see the crowning and our Jehanette?' said Jacques that evening. 'Jean Morel and several others have already decided to go. They say the army is before Troyes, so surely we have time. Shall we go, Zab? The boys will be there too.'

Zabillet's spirits soared. It had never occurred to her they might. It wasn't possible surely, that she might see her children again. 'Can we, Jacques? What about the cattle and fields? Who will tend everything?'

'I'll ask Jacquemin and Yvette to come. And Marguerite and Hauviette will help if we ask; they'll be glad to.'

'You don't think Jehanette will have forgotten us?' breathed Zabillet. 'Or shall we shame her, now she is with the King and the French lords? Oh never mind, let us go. Why don't we ask Durand and Jean Colin to come with us?'

'Get food and warm clothes ready,' said Jacques. 'We shall be several days on the road, and will need to take everything with us.'

Zabillet ran her fingers up and down the string between the beads. The road Jehanne and the Dauphin must take to Reims was full of towns with Burgundian garrisons. Yet now the English army had retreated to Paris, surely Jehanne would be safe. Her fingers paused for a moment on a bead. Auxerre, no surrender apparently, but Jehanne and the King were allowed to pass with the army. And another town, Troyes, where that damnable treaty had been signed so many years ago, that had split France in two. Keep safe, Jehanette, prayed Zabillet. If you can take that city, then surely the road to Reims will be open, and I will see you.

4

Zabillet turned under the rough covers, and turned again, now pulling up the blanket to keep her warm, now pushing it away as the fever bathed her body in sweat. She would sleep lightly, briefly, uneasily, then start awake and sit up with a cry. She knew she was much too ill to go. This fever would leave her weak. Even that day, she had hardly been able to walk outside, and she had taken no food for several days. She had no strength, but not so little that she was not able to beat her head against the bedding beneath her in bitter anger and frustration. I shan't see my Jehanne, she wept, nor my boys. And *they* will go and I shall not be there. And *they* will see them and the crowning of the King and I shall not be there. Jacques, Durand and the others would go, and she would be left behind. Eventually she drifted off and her sleep deepened.

She is standing up in the hills, far above Domremy, in her childhood village of Vouthon, with animals grazing peacefully nearby. Jehanne is with her; a tall, strong young woman. Shoulder to shoulder they look out across the valley of the Meuse below them. The green and golden autumn fields are bathed in afternoon light, the trees on the hillside a great quilt of colour – brown, russet, red, yellow, hundreds of shades of each, bright in the sun. Zabillet notices that her daughter is dressed for a journey, a thick cloak covering her red bodice and skirt, and a rough bag on her shoulder.

An immense, loving sadness comes over her as they share a long and tender embrace. She strokes Jehanne's cheek and looks into her face, her finger clearing strands of hair from her forehead. She can see how full of light and purpose her rich, brown eyes are, and pulls her close so she no longer has to see her intent.

'It's time,' Jehanne says, beginning to draw away. Zabillet lets her go, full of love and pain. She can see that love mirrored on Jehanne's face, together with sadness and pity. They kiss again and Jehanne turns and starts off along the road. Not the road to Domremy, or even to Vaucouleurs, but a long road away, away, she doesn't know where.

Zabillet started up in her bed, shouting. Tears coursed down her face. 'Jehanette!' she screamed, full of pain. Her daughter will not return; her long journey will not lead her back to Domremy.

Jacques had been gone many days before her strength returned, and Zabillet wandered up and down the road between Domremy and Greux, there and back and around again. At Greux she would call in at the home of Bérenice, the young woman who had married Jean Colin a year or so after Cathérine's death. Hearing nothing there, she went on to Jean Morel's farm. She craved news, but there was none. Oh, she knew that the King had been crowned, a proclamation had been sent out, and she knew that Jehanette had stood with her banner by the King's side as he was anointed. But good though this news was, giving rise to celebrations in the villages, and gifts from the *demoiselle*, it was not enough for her. She wanted to know how Jehanette was, what her thoughts were, what she was wearing, where and how she lived. She wanted to know what she would do next. And her boys too, of course. She would kick the woodpile in frustration as she brought in logs for the fire, and if Jacquemin and Yvette had not stayed with her and fed her and urged her to sleep, maybe she would not have regained the strength the fever had taken from her, but have wandered into danger in her restless search.

She kept counting the days on her fingers. It would take six or seven days to get to Reims of course, then she was not exactly sure on which day the coronation had taken place, and it was possible that they would not hurry back immediately. One day she even wandered over to Maxey to see if Isabellette had any news from Gérardin. She had none, of course, how could anyone have news quicker than the men could walk back themselves, unless a special messenger or soldier had something extraordinary to report?

Occasionally Zabillet wept. She wept at the weakness of her

healthy body at such a time. She was haunted by her dream, overwhelmed again by the sadness she had felt at Jehanne going away, far, far away with no return. She had never had so little idea of where her family was. It frightened her. She feared Petit-Jean's recklessness, felt panic at Pierre's lack of soldier-skills. She mourned again the loss of her daughter Cathérine who would have been such a comfort to her. She clung close to Jacquemin and Yvette, though she knew they needed to return to their home in Vouthon. Twice they had to restrain her from packing up supplies and going out to meet the men, wherever they might be on their journey home.

It seemed a long, an endless time before one evening Jean Morel came up the path to her house. Zabillet rushed out.

'Where are they? What's happened?' she cried, full of fear.

'It's all right,' said Jean encompassing her in a big embrace. 'Everyone is fine. There's no need to worry. Jacques and Durand are staying on at Reims a bit longer. The townsfolk have put them up at an inn for a while, in honour of Jehanne.'

'Jean, Jean,' she wept, hugging him and letting herself be held close and comforted. 'It's been such a horrible long wait. Come in, please, you must tell me all about it. Did you speak to Jehanette, and the boys, how are they?'

Jean smiled at her, looking into her eyes. 'Zabillet, calm yourself. Everybody is well and happy and full of success. They send their love to you. I'll tell you all from the start.'

'Thank God you are here. I can't believe Jacques hasn't come back with you. Still he will enjoy being honoured, and if he and Jehanette have made their peace, that's all to the good. Yvette, fetch Jean some beer and bread, so he can eat whilst we talk.'

'Just a drop, thanks. I think a feast is being prepared at home. Yes, we actually met Jehanne at Châlons,' Jean began, sitting on the bench. 'When we put up at an inn there for the night, they told us that the army would very likely arrive the next day, or the next, so we knew we were in good time and could wait for them. Well, along they came, Jehanette riding there at the front alongside the Dauphin, as he was then, and all the knights. Oh, it was splendid. Our little Jehanne in her armour, Zabillet, she sat so proud and happy on that great horse. And when she saw her father and Durand and the rest of us, her whole face lit up, and she had her own page help her off her horse so she could come and talk to us.'

'Her own page?' Zabillet wondered at such a thing. No-one in her own family, or anyone else's family she knew, had ever had their own page.

'She asked after you, of course,' continued Jean, 'and was much saddened that you were too ill to come. Then she was called to go and receive the surrender from Châlons. It was so exciting, Zabillet! Our own Domremy girl, so important. I didn't get chance to speak to her again, but next day saw her enter the great cathedral of Reims at the King's side.'

'Was she in her armour?' asked Zabillet, trying to get some idea of how her daughter might have looked.

'She looked wonderful. She wore a beautiful cloak of red and green and gold over her armour, and her face was so proud, holding that wonderful standard.'

'And what about Pierrelot and Petit-Jean?' asked Zabillet. 'Were they with her? How goes it with them?'

'Very good!' Jean nodded his head proudly. Had he not had a hand in those two boys learning to fight? 'They are in Jehanne's own company, all kitted out in armour too, and doing well. Pierrelot in particular sticks close to Jehanne and goes wherever she does. And Petit-Jean is turning out to be a good, responsible soldier.' Jean drained his bowl and stood up. 'But now, I must get on home, for I've done nothing but say hello to my wife before coming on here, glad though I was to do that.'

He began to move towards the door. 'Jean,' said Zabillet in little more than a whisper. 'Does she speak of coming home?'

'I don't think she will do that just yet,' he replied, watching her face. 'They need to press on to Paris to take advantage of their victories over the English. And of course, she must lead them, for the French army is swollen by men who will follow her, and only her. That's how important she has become. So we must be patient for a while yet, and praise God for her successes. But she did give me this.' Jean reached into his cloak and took out a rolled-up bundle. 'Jehanne gave it to me. And now I must away home.'

He bent and kissed her, and left, promising to return soon to tell her everything in more detail.

But Zabillet did not hear him. She was fingering the bundle that Jean had given to her. It was Jehanne's red skirt and bodice, the clothes she had been wearing when she left just a few months ago.

Zabillet shook the clothes out and pressed them to her face. She could smell Jehanne in the fibres of the cloth, and she breathed in deeply. She moaned and sat crushing the clothes to her chest. Jehanne was not coming back home; she had discarded her peasant clothes because she had no further use for them.

CONVERSATIONS

Zabillet talks with the Chronicler of Orléans

How much does anyone know of Jehanne's story after the coronation, after the Dauphin was made King? Over time I have come to have my thoughts about politics and betrayal and sheer stupidity, but then I was living in the enclosed world of Domremy and Greux. I had got a glimpse of a wider world from trying to understand what my impetuous daughter was up to, from my talks with her friends at Le Puy and from our occasional meetings with Robert de Baudricourt. But I had a simple world view – Charles was King, and especially now that he had been anointed at Reims, that was not much different to being God, and his decisions must be good ones. Events were to chip away at that belief until it was quite destroyed.

We sat through that summer and waited. We got news of towns surrendering to King Charles between Reims and Paris, most of them without a fight, glad to return to the rule of France; lots of towns – Provins, Soissons, Compiègne, and others too, and we knew that Jehanne was close by him. We waited for the attack on Paris, and waited. We thought Charles must be delaying whilst he gathered together more troops, because they said that Paris was a huge city mightily fortified, and almost totally in the grip of that Goddam Bedford and the traitorous Duke Philippe of Burgundy.

But it was only when Jacques finally came home from Reims that I realized we had cause for worry. He had stayed there for nearly two months, holidaying on the money King Charles had given him, and eventually riding home on a horse that was a present from the people of Reims. Oh, he was so full of himself. How bitter it was for me who craved to hold my daughter in my arms, to have to listen to him boast of Charles this and d'Alençon that, and to hear his endless recital of Jehanne's rich clothes, her squire, her pages and her heralds. Of course, he had actually spent very little time with her, for she had ridden off at the King's side soon after the coronation, whereas he had stayed behind in Reims enjoying himself.

On the night of his return, there was a feast in the village. People wanted to hear once again about the coronation, and how Jehanne had stood there by the King, and what the lords and knights had been up to. They wanted to hear about her household and her standard, shouting their celebration of her as they raised their tankards. And of course, Jacques had wonderful news for us all as well, for it was from him that we first learnt of a great gift from the King for all of us in Domremy and Greux – we no longer had to pay taxes. Not just this year, or next year, but for all time. King Charles we felt, as we hugged and kissed each other, truly appreciated Jehanne and the villages that had nurtured her. Our lives could only be easier after that.

But a couple of evenings later, whilst keeping the tankards filled of Jacques and Jean Morel and other village men who had gathered in our house, I realized that perhaps it was not so simple, after all.

'I just don't understand it,' Jean Morel kept saying. 'Why didn't they just swoop on Paris after the coronation? After all, the army was huge, and it was obvious they would follow Jehanne anywhere.'

'Surely after all the towns fell around Reims, the English must have been dreading that was exactly what was going to happen,' said Jean Colin.

Jacques said that whilst in Reims he had heard people talking with dismay of King Charles' caution, and of his attempts to make truces with Philippe of Burgundy. I remember Jean Morel shaking his head anxiously.

'Oh no!' he said. 'Philippe is going to give us nothing. He made up his mind long ago that he had most to gain by sticking with England. If he made a truce, it was only to gain time to strengthen his position. Oh Charles! What are you doing?'

A cold chill swept over me. This was a world I did not understand, and however surprising and clever my daughter had turned out to be, not one that she would understand either. And certainly not one she would want to be part of. Come home, Jehanne, I cried, as I busied myself within the house. Come home! Leave them to their endless manipulations.

Jean Colin said, 'You know, when we were at Châlons, Jehanette was so pleased to see Gérardin. They'd always been close. He told me that when they were saying goodbye and he was telling her to be careful and so on, Jehanne said to him, "I fear nothing but treachery". I'm sure she already knew it was going to be difficult to keep Charles focused on ridding the land of the Goddams.'

Treachery! Treachery? What did he mean? I didn't dare ask.

It was only a few days afterwards that Robert de Baudricourt sent a soldier to Domremy to tell us that Jehanne had been injured outside Paris and the whole attack had been called off by the King. She was absolutely furious, he said, because King Charles seemed not to want to fight, had not supported them, despite the plans she and the Duke d'Alençon had made, and the fact that many people within Paris were rallying to their cause. Of course, I cared nothing for that. I couldn't bear the thought of the arrow piercing her thigh – did she not wear armour to prevent that happening? The villagers began to mutter, discontented with the King and his advisers, especially when we heard later that the army had returned to the Loire and been stood down. My heart was heavy – that army which had won all those battles with Jehanne at its head, and forced the road to Reims, was disbanded. How could that be, when it had seemed so likely that the English would be sent packing back to their island home?

Thanksgiving and celebration turned to entreaty in my prayers. Surely she had done enough? Surely the rest was up to the King himself, and if he missed his chances, that wasn't her business any more. Tell her to come home, I pleaded with the Holy Mother and the saints. I wanted their will to be at one with mine. But their faces were turned from me. She did not come.

MAY 1430

Capture

1

It was not a good spring. The only news Zabillet and Jacques had
of Jehanne was from an occasional passing monk, who told them
that nothing much was happening at the King's court. The army
had been sent home, and King Charles was enjoying himself here
and there in his châteaux on the Loire. Only Bertrand de Poulengy,
who came to see them whilst acting as message-bearer between
King Charles and Robert de Baudricourt at Vaucouleurs, had any
real news of Jehanne. She was angry, he said, bored, frustrated like
a tiger prevented by some incomprehensible force from pouncing
on the prey it can clearly see before it. The King, he said in a
contemptuous way that Zabillet had not heard before, and which
scared her, had not allowed her to go with d'Alençon to strengthen
the campaign in Normandy against the Goddams. He had become
irritated by her entreaties and sent her off on a fool's mission to
retake some small towns which were being held by some irrelevant
warlord.

Bertrand's own frustration had broken through. 'The King
didn't even support her with equipment and supplies for the men
who are faithful to her. After taking Saint Pierre-le-Moutier, she
was holed up outside the gates of La Charité in the bitter winter.
Some of the towns that love her, like Orléans, sent her food and
armaments, but it wasn't enough. In the end she had to give up
and return to court unsuccessful.'

Zabillet had felt a terrible confusion at this account. So much
so, that she had not known what to ask. She heard Jacques say

'That damned King! What do you think, Bertrand? Has he missed his chance?'

'They say La Trémoïlle and that vile Bishop of Chartres advise him to make truces all the time. But there is no truce to make. We must rid the country of the damn Goddams for all time. Only the spring will tell.' Bertrand flung the huge cloak he wore as protection against the wind over his shoulders. 'Then we shall see, we shall indeed.'

Zabillet pondered all these things as she spent the dark, dull days of winter at the spinning-wheel, feeling the soft wool form beneath her fingers. It was bad enough to think of Jehanne victorious, proud and confident in battle, with all the risks she kept taking. But sitting in the December cold and rain and ice, unsupported, laying siege to a town because the King asked her to, yet which had, from what Bertrand said, no real significance even if won, that was hard to understand. And to have failed too. The English, it must be assumed, were strengthening their position in the north, when they had been so weakened just a few months before.

'Why doesn't she just come home?' she asked the statue of Mary in the church at Greux. She did not like to ask this question of anyone else. Once when she had tentatively put it to Tante Marguerite, she had not really liked the look on her face. 'Maybe Jehanette has got used to the finery of the court,' she had said gently, and as she thought kindly. It had stung Zabillet into a sharp retort, but she had forced herself to think about it. Jehanne always said that what she did was by God's will. Was this not still true? Could Jehanne be enticed by lovely clothes and food and entertainment, so she would stay at court even if there was no action to rid the country of the English, no attempt to bring the Burgundians back to the rule of France?

In that quiet place, under the calm eye of the Virgin, who appeared to demand rigorous examination and honesty, Zabillet reflected. Jehanne is not perfect; she is impetuous and likes the company of interesting people. She had done unheard of things for a young woman, great military feats, and stood beside the King at his coronation. She has become used to the man's world of armour, strategy and weaponry. She has her own household, and people to look after her.

Zabillet could see how difficult it would be for her to come home.

That was a bitter, bitter thought. She wept and berated herself for her selfish longing to hold her daughter in her arms, to look at her face with all its funny, changeable expressions, just to have her here.

She sat some more, gazing on the face of Mary, a face which was almost more familiar to her now than Jehanne's. 'She still believes,' she said out loud. 'She knows there is more to do. She has to persuade the King. She is waiting for the next phase.'

Zabillet was making a final check to ensure that all the animals were fed and secure for the night, when she heard the slow trot of a horse approaching the village, and then saw the mounted figure begin to emerge from the dusk. It was a beautiful evening, almost dark now, carrying the scent of blossom and the early summer flowers. Jacques was already asleep.

Zabillet peered up the lane as the slow but steady trot of the horse came closer. She could just see the rider almost slumped over the horse's neck, and she waited to see if he needed some help, water perhaps or even shelter for the night. She shivered in the night air as horse and rider approached.

'Maman! Maman!' she heard the figure cry. It was a weak, weary cry and she ran towards the horse. When the rider saw her, he dropped to the ground and put out his arms to her.

'Petit-Jean? Is that you?' Zabillet enfolded her son in her arms. 'Are you all right? Are you injured? Come on, let me help you inside.'

But Petit-Jean resisted her attempt to guide him towards the doorway of the house. 'Is Papa there?' he asked.

'Yes, he's asleep, but we'll wake him immediately. He'll be so happy to see you. Come, let me look at you.'

Despite the fading light, Zabillet tried to look into his face, but he kept it turned from her, looking at the ground. A terrible sick feeling came into her stomach. She put both her arms around Petit-Jean and held him to her. She feared to look into his face now.

'What's happened?' she said.

'Captured. Oh Maman, they are both captured.' As if a stone had been dislodged from a dam, tears and sobs started to shake his body, and Zabillet held him, stroking his hair and wiping his face. Although he stood head and shoulders above her, it was little different from when he was a young boy, on the few occasions he would let her comfort him when upset. She crooned and made soothing noises and rocked him as he stood there. She wept herself.

Despite the lateness of the hour, Zabillet brought the fire up to a roar, and started to prepare some food and drink for Petit-Jean. She went into the other room and knelt down beside Jacques where he lay asleep and snoring.

'Jacques, Jacques!' she said quietly. 'Wake up!' She took his hand and rubbed it and patted his face.

He came to slowly. 'What is it?' he mumbled.

'Jacques, it's Petit-Jean, he's come home'. He started up, beginning to smile, until he saw Zabillet's face. 'He's very tired and exhausted. He's got bad news for us. Pierre and Jehanne have been captured.'

Jacques started up, pulling on his trousers. 'Captured? Who by? Where are they?'

'I don't know anything yet,' said Zabillet, turning back to the room.

Jacques went through to where Petit-Jean sat hunched at the table and put his arm on his shoulder.

'It's good to see you,' he said. 'Come, take off your cloak and sword. You must be hungry. Eat first and then tell us.'

Petit-Jean lifted his head and looked at his father. Jacques flinched at the misery he saw there, and started to help with the fastenings on his cloak.

'Eat,' said Zabillet, placing a bowl of soup in front of him, and cutting a hunk of bread from the loaf. 'Come on, son,' she said as she saw him hesitating, confused by something as mundane as food when his mind was so full of loss. 'You must be very hungry. Then you can tell us what has happened. Jacques, why don't you go and give Petit-Jean's poor horse something to eat and drink.'

She wanted to give Petit-Jean a little time to emerge from his exhaustion. She could hardly remember seeing him so quiet and withdrawn. He had always been angry, demanding, and sullen if thwarted. But now, he needed drawing back before he could tell his story.

Zabillet did not want to hear what he had to say, although she knew she had to. Part of her wanted him to be too weak and exhausted to tell it tonight – perhaps after he had eaten he would just keel over and sleep. No, that would be agony. She must hear it now, however painful it was. She needed to know what she had to deal with, although she was dreading it. Where were her Pierrelot and Jehanette now, right now?

Petit-Jean had started to eat tentatively, more out of some habitual obedience to his mother than anything else. But now, as the fragrant lamb and vegetables teased his taste buds and sense of smell, he began to eat properly, greedily, mopping up the rich sauce with his bread and drinking deeply of the ale his father brought for him. Zabillet filled his bowl once more, watching carefully as the colour began to return to his cheeks.

'When did you last eat?' she said gently, stroking his hair, hoping he might smile up at her.

'I don't know,' he said. 'I just came here.'

'Where did you come from?' asked Jacques.

'Compiègne. It's near to Paris.' He looked puzzled. 'I must have stopped, it's so far. I think someone must have given me a new horse.' He shook his head.

'It doesn't matter,' said Zabillet. 'You're home now, and it's wonderful to see you, no matter what has happened.'

'I wasn't with them, Maman, when they were captured. I should have been there. Pierre and me always rode with Jehanette, just like you said. But I wasn't that day. I should have been captured too.'

'Don't, please don't,' said Zabillet. 'Is it not enough for two to be captured? How would we ever know exactly what'd happened if you hadn't been able to come and tell us?'

'It was all such a mess,' he continued. 'Our army was split up into several sections, and there were only a few of us in Compiègne with Jehanne. They loved her there, you know. They were right in the middle of the Goddams, but they were one town that never thought to go over to them, no matter what. The enemy were all around determined to have a go at taking it. They'd captured the bridges around the town, and were going to lay siege. Anyway, you know Jehanne, she would never sit back and wait for the attack.' Petit-Jean smiled admiringly, but Zabillet shook her head. This was a Jehanette she did not really know. Oh yes, of course she recognized all the characteristics – her impetuosity, bravery, confidence. But how these were applied on the battlefield, she only knew from friends and passers-by. The battlefield! What was her daughter doing on a battlefield anyway?

'A company of us went out to see what was out there and have a little skirmish. Jehanne always liked to do that wherever she was; she said it gave us a taste for the battle ahead, and scared the enemy. I don't know what happened really, there were far more of them than we expected. They seemed to be coming from all sides, more and more of them. We weren't prepared for a full battle. Captain Barretta gave the signal for us to retreat, and we turned back into Compiègne.

'We were all racing across the bridge. I didn't realize that Jehanne and Pierre and a few others had slowed so they could help those at the back, and I kept riding straight into the town with Barretta. Just as we came in through the gate, there was a terrible noise from behind us, shouting and the clash of arms. I turned round, and at that moment the captain of Compiègne shouted to raise the draw-bridge. Jehanne was still out there beyond the bridge, and there was a whole group of English soldiers between her and the gate.

'It was horrible.' Petit-Jean's eyes slid from Zabillet to Jacques and down at the table again. Tears were running down his cheeks. Zabillet could see the tension in every line of his body.

'Go on,' Jacques said. 'What happened next?'

'I screamed at Guillaume de Flavy to wait until they were in. But he just signalled at the soldiers to keep pulling up the bridge. I could see that the English soldiers who were between Jehanne and the city might get in if the bridge didn't come up. But we could have fought them and given time for the others to get back. But de Flavy would have none of it. He wasn't going to risk a single Goddam getting into his city.'

Petit-Jean stopped. In his face was written the agony of that moment, seeing the drawbridge go up, and his sister and brother and dear friends fighting beyond the bridge with no possible help from anywhere.

'They were completely outnumbered,' he whispered. 'Oh they fought, how they fought. We tried to get to the drawbridge ropes, but de Flavy stood his soldiers all around. There was nothing we could do. That group out there, they were so brave, Maman… In the end, one of the Burgundian soldiers,' there was such contempt in Petit-Jean's voice, 'one of them reached up and grabbed Jehanette's cloak. You could always see exactly where she was, by her rich scarlet and gold cloak – you know, Papa, like the one she wore at Reims – and her standard. This pig pulled on her cloak and down she came off her horse. She fell and that was that. They surrendered; there was nothing else they could do except be killed. Oh, it was horrible, horrible. They were cheering as they led her away, and Pierre and the others, while we looked on.'

There was silence in the house. It had grown completely dark and only the glow of the fire illuminated the table where they sat. A great restlessness took hold of Zabillet, so that she had to get up and go outside. She found herself walking around the yard, weeping and praying to whoever might listen to protect her son and daughter. Behind her, she could hear Jacques getting more wood from the woodpile, and stoking up the fire whilst Petit-Jean talked gently to the horse and led him into the shed for the night.

Eventually they all sat at the table again.

'What happened next?' said Zabillet.

'Oh it was hopeless. There was nothing to do. There were only a few hundred of us, and without Jehanne we didn't have a leader. Captain Barretta and everyone just began to drift away. I begged de Flavy to help, to mount some sort of rescue attempt, but all he was concerned about was keeping Compiègne fortified against more attacks. Everyone was bitter, blaming each other, and the company just wanted to get out of there. I hung around for a couple of days to see if I could find out what had happened to them. I couldn't do anything.' Petit-Jean slammed his fist into the table. 'And then all I could think of was to come and tell you.'

Jacques put his hand over Petit-Jean's fist to quiet it. There was silence round the table.

'It was a terrible couple of days. Everyone in Compiègne was distraught, they couldn't believe what had happened. Jehanne's name had been on everyone's lips for over a year; she had made us all believe that if we held firm, the Goddams would be chased out and the Burgundians would be forced to make peace. And lots of people still believed this, even after a winter of the King doing nothing. The army was gathering again behind her. But now she was captured. The people of Compiègne were very determined not to be taken over by the English, but you could see they were frightened. There was no sign of the King or any other lords or captains coming with the French army proper.

'Those vile bands of soldiers kept coming into the fields below the city and mocking us, shouting about how they had got 'La Pucelle' now.' Petit-Jean stopped and his face flushed. 'I can't really tell you what they said, terrible things, horrible words they used.'

For the first time whilst telling the story, Petit-Jean sobbed. Zabillet wept with pity for him, and his ordeal, and in fear for her daughter and son.

'The bastards!' shouted Jacques, standing up in his anger.

'Petit-Jean,' said Zabillet eventually. 'Did you manage to find out where they have taken them?'

'Not really. Someone said that the knight she surrendered to was in the service of Jean de Luxembourg, and he had castles in the area. She would be taken there perhaps.'

'Did you talk to this Captain Barretta about her?' asked Jacques.

'No, I didn't get the chance. He left the next day.'

'Did anyone mention whether they might be ransomed? Isn't that what would normally happen?'

'It was mentioned,' said Petit-Jean. 'Some said she would be ransomed for a fortune, and that Jean de Luxembourg had suddenly become a very rich man. Some said the English would never let her go.'

Zabillet felt a deep weight of anxiety within her. 'But we have no money for a ransom, and there's Pierrelot too.'

Jacques stood up. 'Don't worry, Zabillet. The King will surely ransom her.'

'The King?'

'Of course. If you had seen how he admired and depended on her at the coronation, you would know that. Maybe he'll ransom Pierre as well. He's been generous to us all.'

Petit-Jean shrugged. 'I don't know,' he said. He looked pale and exhausted.

'Let's get some sleep,' said Zabillet. 'Look, it's light already, and soon we shall have to see to the animals.' The thought of the day ahead was utterly dreadful to her.

'We shall go to Vaucouleurs and see Robert de Baudricourt,' said Jacques. 'He'll know what to do.'

2

Petit-Jean was sick the next day. He would sleep a little then get up and vomit violently. He had no strength. He cried a lot. He berated himself for not saving Jehanne and Pierre. He hated himself for not being captured too. Zabillet sat with him, soothing him. She did not want him to blame himself for what had happened. Sometimes he was like the tempestuous boy who had left home little more than a year ago. Other times she could see the man he was becoming. Not just big and strong in his body, immensely strong it seemed to her when he uncurled from the hunched up position he mainly kept in his bed. But his whole language had changed. He used words she did not always know the meaning of, and they were not always to do with fighting. When he talked about the King or some of the most important men at court, there were tones in his voice that she did not understand.

'But the King must be right, surely,' she ventured once. 'That is just how it is. He is of God, and he knows things we do not.'

'Oh, that's what I used to think,' said Petit-Jean. 'And so did Jehanette and Pierrelot. Right up till after he was crowned, we all adored him. Of course, Pierre and I never spoke to him, but Jehanne spent a lot of time with him. Everyone said that if he had gone on to Paris after the coronation, the whole country would have been won. But he wouldn't support Jehanne and D'Alençon and the others. Instead, back to court he went, standing down the army, with all of us including Jehanne at a loss to understand why.'

'I'm sure the King had good reason for it,' said Zabillet. 'They say he has no money to keep the army, and he wanted to make peace with Burgundy. Perhaps he was ill-advised.'

'Oh, he was that,' said Petit-Jean bitterly. 'He certainly was that.'

Zabillet sighed. She did not like this talk. Such complications made her worry that it would not be a simple matter to see Jehanne and Pierre freed.

Another day, when Petit-Jean was well enough to sit outside, Zabillet heard more about Jehanne and the life that she and the two boys had led over the past year. She was beginning to piece it together.

'How they love Jehanette in Orléans,' Petit-Jean said. 'I had only just joined her when they began to break the siege, if you remember, and I didn't really know what was going on. I just stuck close to Pierrelot in the group with Jehanne, and tried to remember what Jean Morel and the soldiers passing through Domremy had taught me. I must have been a pitiful sight.' Petit-Jean paused and laughed. 'A real country bumpkin! But now, I think I'm quite a good soldier. A knight even!'

Zabillet laughed too. A knight! Another incredible thing. The King had made both Pierre and Petit-Jean knights, and ennobled their whole family. It was of no benefit to her and Jacques, did not bring them a single penny or help with the fields; but she was happy for the children, of course. 'I'm sure you're a very good soldier,' she teased. 'You always enjoyed fighting, even when you were very little. Now, you were telling me about Jehanne and Orléans.'

'Yes, I don't remember it that clearly. As I say, it was all confusion for me. All I can recall is that afterwards all the people came into the streets and cheered her, and she led this huge procession round and round the town.'

'What did Jehanne look like at such times?'

'Not like my little sister, I can assure you. In her armour with that amazing standard, she looked so... so ... not exactly happy, though she was, but more glowing. Yes, glowing. She looked completely... complete.' Petit-Jean laughed, embarrassed.

But Zabillet could understand that. She had difficulty imagining the young woman whom she had only ever seen in her simple peasant clothes on a beautiful horse with full armour, with people around who were only there to help and serve and follow her, and hold her banner. But she knew that face. Yes, glowing, that was a good word, her eyes lit, confident, knowing things inside herself that were not from the solid world around. She had seen that. She hadn't really recognised it, certainly hadn't liked it, but she had seen it.

'Anyway,' continued Petit-Jean. 'We went back to Orléans several times before the coronation, when we were fighting for the Loire towns. We all felt quite at home there. In this winter just gone, they gave an enormous feast for her, with presents for her and Pierre and me. They love her, they really do. They consider her solely responsible for liberating their city.'

They were both quiet for a while, Zabillet shaking her head at the thought.

'I can't bear to think of her captured. She hated to be penned in. Imprisoned! It'll be hard for her. You know, whatever she wanted to do, she wanted it now. She had no patience.'

After a while, Petit-Jean continued. 'It was like this when we left the court. After we got back from the disaster at La Charité, nothing seemed to be happening. I don't know what was being said when she spoke to the King, of course. Lots of captains had gone off either to spend the winter at home, or conduct their own campaigns. She hated the inactivity. She said to me one day that she'd been writing to the people of Reims because they were worried for their safety, and there was little protection for them, or the other towns up there loyal to the King. And Burgundy and his filthy English allies were on the move again. She loved the people in those towns, because they had come over to France at the time of the coronation, and she felt that King Charles was letting them down, and she worried about it. A few days later, she came to find me and Pierrelot and said we were off again the next day, going north with Captain Barretta and a few hundred men. We were happy to be on the road again, I can tell you.

'We stopped at Lagny-sur-Marne, just east of Paris, to find out what was happening, and decide exactly where we were most needed. And do you know, the strangest thing happened? Wherever we went, Jehanne always went into the church to pray. Anyway, in the cathedral at Lagny, this woman came up to Jehanne, very upset and carrying a bundle. This bundle was a baby – a dead baby, Maman. It was a grey wizened little thing. Jehanette said "Why have you brought this baby to me?" People were always coming up to her, wherever she went. They wanted to touch her and get some sort of blessing from her. She used to laugh at them, not nastily you know. Just completely amazed that anyone should expect such things from her.

'Anyway, this woman was distraught. "Jehanne, Jehanne La Pucelle!" That's what people had started calling her, the Maid. "Please help me. My baby died before she could be baptized. Now she will never become one of God's children." I don't know why, but Jehanne seemed really upset, and she took this tiny dead baby from the woman. She looked into its face and just touched its forehead, and suddenly the baby came to life, its skin became pink and its eyelids fluttered. "Baptize her!" she said to Pasquerel who was standing nearby. As soon as the baby was baptized it died. It was incredible. Jehanne was crying, the women were crying, but you know in a happy way because the baby was baptized.'

Petit-Jean fell quiet and Zabillet leant back to feel the warm sun of this lovely summer day on her face. There was nothing to say.

3

Petit-Jean insisted that he must go with Jacques to see Robert de Baudricourt at Vaucouleurs, so Zabillet made them wait for a few days until he felt stronger, and the nervous, exhausted sickness he kept experiencing had passed. Zabillet was determined to go too. Jacques had asked Michel Lebuin to go to Robert and tell him about Jehanne's capture, and say that they would come as soon as possible.

It's not easy to get rid of this sickness, it is affecting us all, thought Zabillet as they walked along. Her own stomach had been weak and queasy since she'd heard her two children had been captured. The sun hadn't appeared yet, if it ever would that day, and a dreary drizzle dampened their clothes from the low cloud that obscured the hills across the valley. Jehanne, Pierre, Pierrelot, Jehanette – their names were continuously in her mind. Sometimes she felt she might conjure their release just by saying their names over and over, and willing it. Other times the sick feeling in her stomach threatened to overcome her. None of them said very much.

It was a pleasant diversion when they came to Burey-le-Petit to stop for a while with Aveline, who immediately sent to the fields for Durand Laxart. They already knew of Jehanne's capture, of course, everyone did, but there were many things they wanted to know from Petit-Jean. Sharing some of her pain, and talking of how brave and strong Jehanne must be after a year away, banished some of her fears, and she was able to eat the food Aveline set out before them.

Durand accompanied them when they went on to Vaucouleurs. As they walked up the steep streets to the castle, several people stopped them. 'Do you have news of Jehanette?' they asked expectantly, their faces saddening as Zabillet shook her head. Then remembering the determined, impetuous young girl who had left from their town to go to Chinon not much more than a year ago, they added, 'I'm sure she'll be all right. You'll see, the King won't forget her.' Zabillet wept when she learned that on the Sunday before, the townspeople had processed around the town behind the priest, praying for her release, and she took comfort from their supportive words.

They continued the climb up to the castle. Zabillet could hear

Petit-Jean telling Durand about the winter months, about how the King had sometimes been irritated with Jehanne because she kept trying to persuade him to continue the fight with the Goddams. They talked about his advisors, Regnault de Chartres and La Trémoïlle, how they had the ear of the King and seemed to counsel only treaties and truces. She did not like what she could hear of Durand's responses, his thoughts formed by the time he spent in the inns of Vaucouleurs talking with the garrison soldiers. All she could hear was missed chances, lost opportunities and even treachery, indignation and contempt in his tone. She thought that if Jehanne had become such a nuisance to the King, might he not be glad to have her off his hands?

She turned to Jacques, the question beginning to form on her lips. 'Come on, Zabillet,' he said, taking her arm and urging her on. 'There's always this sort of talk amongst soldiers. Nothing is ever right for them. Let's wait till we hear what Robert has to say.'

Zabillet found herself enfolded in an enormous hug as Robert greeted them in his hall. 'Come in, come in,' he said, drawing them all towards the fire, necessary even on this June day in the cold stone castle. 'Good to see you, Petit-Jean.' He thumped him on the back. 'And you, Jacques, and Durand. Sit down, there's some wine here somewhere. Let's have something to drink.'

'Now,' he said, not wasting any time. 'I've been trying to find out what has happened to our Jehanne and Pierre. It looks as though she was captured by Jean de Luxembourg and is being held by him. It's not easy to find out where – she's probably at Beaurevoir at the moment, to the north of Compiègne.'

'What sort of a place is that?' asked Zabillet.

'I've never seen it, but I think it's a fortified castle. Probably much like this, I should say, though it's out in the countryside.' He gestured around the castle where they sat.

'Will they treat her well?'

'Oh, I think so,' replied Robert. 'Someone said they've allowed her squire Jean d'Aulon to stay with her. She's a big prize, you know, so they'll definitely look after her. She is bound to be fought over; she's worth a lot of money. I haven't found out yet where Pierre's being held.'

'What can we do?' asked Jacques, his face closed. 'We haven't got anything. How can we pay for her release?'

Robert started to laugh, and then saw the distress in Zabillet's face. 'No,' he said more gently. 'It will be up to the King. It'll be beyond what you or I could pay for.'

'What about Pierrelot?' asked Zabillet. 'He mustn't be forgotten in all this. Oh, it's terrible. Their freedom, reduced to what someone can pay. When we have nothing.'

She started to weep, and Petit-Jean came and put his arm around her. 'Maman,' he said, 'don't, please.'

'Pierre's situation should be a lot simpler,' said Robert. 'Like any other soldier, he'll be ransomed. The sum is bound to be more reasonable, though it will not be easy to find.'

'What is this Jean de Luxembourg like?' asked Jacques.

'Oh, he's a complete bastard,' responded Robert, nodding apologetically to Zabillet. 'He's been in the pocket of Burgundy and England for decades. Plus his brothers Pierre and Bishop Louis.' He spat contemptuously into the fire. 'But he is also the youngest of the brothers, and not rich, so he's bound to want a good price for Jehanne. One good thing is that his aunt Jeanne, who apparently lives at this castle at Beaurevoir, is godmother to our King Charles, and her husband died fighting for France at Agincourt. She'll be good to Jehanne, I'm sure, and let's hope she has some influence with the King. The worst is that Jehanne's going to be imprisoned for a while.'

'Is there not something we can do?' asked Zabillet. She got up and started pacing the floor. 'A lot has happened to our Jehanette since she left home, I know that, and when Petit-Jean talks about her in her armour at the front of the army doing amazing things, I can hardly believe it is her. But you know how impatient and impetuous she is. She won't tolerate being locked up.'

'Oh, I do remember indeed,' said Robert. 'How could I ever forget that little peasant girl in her red dress ordering me to send her to Chinon? Outrageous! I'm going to write to the King telling him how upset we all are here, and urge him to get on with it. In fact, people are very upset everywhere. Bertrand told me that at Orléans they wouldn't even believe she was captured at first, and all those Loire towns have had processions to show their grief. At Tours, the monks even walked barefoot around the town chanting the 'Miserere'. Oh, there'll be a lot of people urging the King to get on with it and ransom her.'

'That is what we must do too,' said Jacques. 'We must write to the King and tell him that we cannot pay Jehanne's ransom, and beg him to do so for all that she has done for him. And you shall take the letter to him, Petit-Jean.'

'Shall I?' asked Petit-Jean excitedly. 'Am I to go back?'

Zabillet bowed her head. He was going back. He wanted to go back, rather than take up his life here again. 'Yes,' she said. 'You must go. You must not let the King or the other Lords forget her.'

'Now then Zabillet,' said Robert. 'Can I ask you to lend me Petit-Jean for a couple of days? I want to hear all about life at court, and find out what everyone is up to. Meanwhile, I'll try and find out more about Jehanne. When you have had your letter written, I'll send a couple of my men with Petit-Jean back to wherever the King is.' He stood up to usher them out. 'And try not to worry. I'll send someone down the road to tell you if I hear anything.'

CONVERSATIONS

Zabillet talks with Our Lord in Domremy

I kneel low before you, the crucified Christ. How I miss the dear face of Our Lady whose statue remains in the church at Greux, and whilst I often walk over there, I have started to come here sometimes because I know I'll be alone and uninterrupted. No-one comes here. The roof is open to the sun and rain, just as we found it two years ago on our return from Neufchâteau, the charred wooden beams forming a strange skeleton when I raise my eyes. What a terrible time that was, yet at least I had my children with me, and no idea of this horror to come.

I like to hold their picture in my mind. Jehanette, intense, serious, joyous, even if at times a worry and a puzzle. How could I have ever guessed that she would become loved by the whole of France, not just by her family and friends in Domremy, and come into such grave danger? But I must thrust those thoughts from my mind, that way lies despair. I must try to see her as she was, playful, loving, bright. And gentle Pierrelot, always there to help, sure to have been a leader in the village if events had not taken him away. Far away now, in some castle, I don't know where, whilst we all try to raise his ransom money. A hopeless task, it seems, for we have no money or any way to get what is needed, but I must have faith he will be home eventually. And Petit-Jean, angry, sullen, always just on the outside of things. Excluded again, for which I thank you every day, Lord, from the dramatic capture of his sister and brother. He has been forced by it to grow up, become responsible, and become a link between Domremy and that frightening world of the King.

Help me not to feel such bitter anger towards the King! I had never thought to have such feelings, they go against everything I ever thought or learnt. But my Jehanette has done such amazing things for him, for France, guided she believes by the Will of Heaven, of you Lord, in a way that I can only glimpse; yet still she remains imprisoned. She has fought and won battles which France's best captains previously despaired of winning. She has freed swathes of the country from Burgundy and the Goddams, numerous towns and villages, and inspired people, us, trodden down and impoverished by long, long years of conflict. It was she who by her single-minded determination got the Dauphin, as he was then, to Reims for his coronation. And Charles knew her importance, or he would not have placed her, a mere peasant, by him in the great cathedral. My Jehanette.

But there are bitter, poisonous drops to swallow. I must not let my mind wander from this pain and take refuge in previous happy family times or in Jehanne's great achievements. Because no matter how great these are, the plain truth is that the King has not ransomed her. He has let her be sold to the English so that now she must face trial. And she is no longer imprisoned in some nice château with friendly ladies and her squire to care for her. They tell me that she tried to escape even from there by leaping from the tower, risking her young limbs in a fall, so terrible is it to her to be imprisoned. And now it seems she is in a hideous castle in Rouen, another town whose name I had never heard before, way over, beyond Paris, as good as in England itself. Her suffering must be great. Please Lord, keep her safe there.

Help me try and get this straight. Your face is sad, impassive as I try to work out things that are so far beyond my knowledge, realities that I had never expected to have to understand. Normally, they say, a soldier taken in battle would be ransomed. This is what is going to happen to Pierrelot. When we eventually raise the money, which I must believe one day we will, we hand it over and he is freed. But what Robert de Baudricourt said is that because Jehanette is such a prize, the ransom would be set very high, though of course the King would pay because of all that she has done. And sometimes, Petit-Jean said, if the ransom is set very high, it can take ages, years even to raise, and during that time the person just stays in prison. That is what has happened to Charles, Duke d'Orléans, who has been in prison in England for years, waiting for his huge ransom to be raised.

Forgive me, Lord, I must stand awhile to relieve my aching knees. I keep repeating what people tell me, I know, because this world is so strange and unknown that I have difficulty making sense of it. It has different rules and considerations to anything I've known before. Ooh, it's grown cold in here, let me pull my wrap around me. The winter sun's never truly warmed up the little church today, and now it's dropped behind the open roof. It's shadowy and dark in here now, and there is no candle. But what do I care? It is not a prison cell.

Poor Petit-Jean, he's become bringer of bad tidings. How angry he was that the King would not receive him to accept the letters he brought. We still don't know if the King read them, those letters from Domremy, carefully written by a passing friar only too happy to help. We must trust he did. All that Petit-Jean was able to learn was that yes, the King was concerned, and did care; he was sending a messenger to Philippe at the Burgundian court immediately … then nothing.

What a bitter night that was, hearing that. You have given us strength somehow, to talk about these things, and bear them. There we sat, Jacques, Petit-Jean and me at the table – it's become almost a dread routine – talking through the night, trying to understand a world so far away, so different from Domremy life. A world where words mean different things in different situations, and games of deceit and webspinning are played, and there is no trust or simple truth. And it is hard having to hear the frustration of Petit-Jean who has somehow become the bridge between these two worlds, without as yet having any foundations in that one, and not being able to help him. We guess at what the King might have meant when he said …are we to believe he has not the money to … what can he do anyway if La Trémoïlle and the Bishop of Chartres are saying … but think of how the people of France love her, all the prayers and processions … backwards and forwards, round and round. Yet it does not matter how much we talk, or understand, or fail to understand – Jehanne remains in prison.

There is such restlessness in me, such desire to understand, as if by understanding I could change things. I pace up and down beneath your compassionate eyes. Despite the darkness, I can see the sadness in your face, and it makes me weep. So the King, for whatever reason, hasn't offered a ransom. Even so, they say that the worst should be that Jehanne remains in prison. That would be bad enough. So how has it happened that she has been sold to the English by Jean de Luxembourg, and the King does nothing to stop it? Where is that in their so-called code which is meant to control all these things? What does that mean for her?

Forgive me Lord, but I could scream with the frustration of my helplessness. The thoughts go round and round in my mind; surely if I keep thinking, trying to understand, an answer will be there. Right. Robert de Baudricourt told me the English hate Jehanne. They hate her because prior to Orléans, they had been overcoming France bit by bit, and not only had Jehanne humiliatingly chased them out of Orléans and all those other towns up and down the Loire and to Reims, but she had turned the tide. Captains, Lords and the people rallied to her. And although the few months before her capture had been quiet, who knows what she might have achieved at Compiègne and elsewhere, given the chance? I can certainly see how much they would want to keep her prisoner.

But however hard I think, there is no answer to the King's neglect of her. It has had a devastating effect. How did we get mixed up in all of this? It seems that in some terrible, upside-down way, it has become more important to the English to stop Jehanne, than it is to our King to have her by his side. Let me kneel again in front of you. I try to understand, I am weary with it, but where does that get us all? In the end, all I can do is pray. Lord, help me to have the faith which you demand of me, that all will be well, whether I understand it or not.

I hear a voice behind me say 'Zabillet', and feel a touch on my shoulder. I turn, startled to see the tall figure behind me, wondering what my mad thoughts have delivered to me. But it is only *curé* Frontey, cloaked against the cold, and in the light of his candle I can see his kind and gentle face smiling, but deeply sad and concerned. 'There are men here from Rouen asking about Jehanne,' he says. 'I think you should come.'

SPRING 1431

Trial

1

'She's not …?' Zabillet spluttered. Dead. The word screeched in her head, unspoken. Why else would men come from Rouen?

'No, no,' said the *curé* quickly. 'Let's go to Greux and see what they have to say. We've been looking for you for a while. It is Nicolas Bailli and the Provost of Andelot, a man called Gérard Petit. They've been commissioned by her captors at Rouen to ask about Jehanette. That is all I can tell you.'

'Nicolas Bailli?' said Zabillet as they hurried along the lane to Greux. 'We know Nicolas, don't we?'

'Apparently so. I'm told it is the same who came to write out the agreement when the men of Greux and Domremy leased the old Château from the de Bourlémonts. We've seen him now and then in the villages when there's been legal work to be done.'

It was bitterly cold and nearly dark. Zabillet looked across the floor of the valley to where the hills ranged, great black mounds across the grey, cloudy sky.

'Then why is he doing the bidding of the English?' she asked.

'Zabillet!' reproved *curé* Frontey gently, smiling at her childish, sullen tone. 'People are having to earn a living and obey their masters even in these chaotic times.'

'Of course, of course, forgive me father,' murmured Zabillet. She was surprised at her own petulance sometimes.

As they were approaching the house where Nicolas Bailli and Gérard Petit had set themselves up, Zabillet saw a man coming out. 'There's Jacques,' she said, then louder: 'Jacques! Jacques!'

Jacques stopped and waited for them to approach. Zabillet hurried up to him, stopping short as she saw his face in the light of the smouldering torch he carried.

'Don't go in there,' he said, taking hold of her arm.

'Why not, what is it? Do they not have news of Jehanne?' She felt panic rising up in her. 'What's happened?' The priest stood a little to the side. 'What are these men doing here?'

'They are collecting information on our Jehanette,' said Jacques. 'What she was like as a young girl, you know. It is information for her trial.'

'Yes, yes,' said Zabillet impatiently. She understood that these things happen. What she could not understand was what it could be that was causing Jacques' agony and *curé* Frontey's grave concern. After all, they weren't going to learn anything bad about Jehanne here in her village. 'Tell me,' she demanded, her voice rising to a high pitch.

'She is to be tried as a heretic and a sorceress.'

'Heretic? Sorceress? Why on earth....? But that's nonsense. They won't get anywhere with that, will they?' Zabillet turned to the *curé*, expecting him to smile reassuringly at her. But his face remained sad.

She looked around wildly. 'They can't do that!' she screamed. And as she began to take in the significance of the vile, untrue allegations, nausea attacked her whole innards and blackness overcame her. She fell against the priest who stepped forward to break her fall, and lowered her gently to the ground.

When she came to, she was lying in the home of Jean Colin at Greux, being cared for by Bérenice. Zabillet still looked on Jean as a son of sorts, though many years had passed since they had shared the agony of Cathérine's death, and he had done many kindnesses for them in these months when she and Jacques had struggled to manage without Pierre and Petit-Jean. She was glad to see him sitting there, love and concern in his eyes, whilst Bérenice cooled her face with a wet cloth and gently stroked the wisps of hair from her forehead. How strange that she had neither son nor daughter at home to care for her, she thought, smiling gratefully at them, the tears starting to her eyes.

'Ssh,' said Jean Colin taking her hand, even before she had chance to speak. 'There's no need to say anything. Jacques has gone to see to the animals, and you are to stay here tonight with us, if you wish.'

'Did you go and see them?' she asked after a while.

'I certainly did,' said Jean Colin. 'All of us have been who know and love Jehanette, and those few who haven't been able to go today will go tomorrow. It's outrageous…'

'Here Zabillet, let me help you sit up, so you can drink some water,' broke in Bérenice. 'You need to keep calm until you feel a bit stronger.'

There was silence in the room again, except for the crackling of the fire.

'Am I to lose another daughter, Jean?' murmured Zabillet. 'Heretic and sorceress! How could they? My Jehanette.' And now the tears flowed, angry sobs and despairing wails. The two supported her in the bed so she should not choke, and so they could hold and soothe her.

'Nicolas Bailli is embarrassed,' said Jean eventually, when the storm had subsided a little. 'And so is the other man, though he never knew Jehanne. They are having to ask such stupid questions about the Fairy Tree, and the Fountains, and whether there was anything improper about Jehanne and if she went to church and confession.'

'The Fairy Tree?' repeated Zabillet, puzzled. 'What has that got to do with it?'

'Nicolas said to Jean Morel that they were trying to make out that Jehanne did some ancient magic ritual there.'

'Magic ritual? But it is the priest who always leads the procession up to the Tree every year.'

'It's completely ludicrous,' said Bérenice fiercely. 'The whole thing is. They're not going to learn anything bad about Jehanne here. That's for sure. And Nicolas is writing down everything the villagers say about how good and holy she was, and people are signing it.'

Zabillet lay down under the covers, drawing them closely over her head, and Bérenice threw another one over her to keep away the bitter winter cold.

'I'll leave the lamp burning,' she said. 'You just call us if there's anything you want. Anything at all.'

'Thank you,' said Zabillet. She wanted to think, to try and understand what all this meant. But she was exhausted, and all she could focus on was the Fairy Tree, and how they had always had their late winter festival there.

The Fairy Tree. The Fairy Tree. Zabillet could see it so clearly in her mind. Perhaps it was being in the home that Cathérine had shared with Jean Colin that made her remember the celebration in the year after they had been married, how Jehanne waited impatiently for them to come by so they could all go up to the Fairy Tree together, equipped with wreaths of winter flowers, ferns and berries to place on its bare branches. How, once they had checked that the boys were happy tending the cattle, she and Jacques had gone up later with baskets of food to share with all the other villagers who had done the same. It was a festival they held every year, heralding the coming spring.

In sleepy memory. the warm sun strokes her face. It will be brief, so early in the year, and as soon as it begins to fall down the sky the bitterness of the season will return. But it speaks of the summer to come. How hard this winter has been, so much grain and money going out in taxes, so little left to see to their own needs. And day after day, the cold grey sky has given no sparkle to the cold grey river as it moves through the bare landscape. But on this festive day the water is bright. Zabillet can smell the spring; the buds on those trees which more easily catch the sun have already popped into small green clusters of leaves, and tiny flowers are beginning to show their faces in places sheltered from the wind, so often harsh up here.

The young people are tasting this renewal. A crowd of them dance near the old beech tree, which is virtually unrecognisable. Its bare branches are festooned with garlands and bouquets and ribbons, and a fiddler stands nearby bowing out a tune so vibrant that even before Zabillet can get her breath back from her climb up the hill, she wants to join in. But as befits her age, she begins instead to move toward the other women who are still taking bread, nuts, slivers of meat, pastries and hard-boiled eggs from their baskets.

She looks around for her family. Cathérine and Jean Colin are dancing, celebrating their first outing together as man and wife. Zabillet smiles. Her daughter, usually so quiet and demure, is thrusting her body towards Jean in a provocative way, then archly turning from him, head held high, as the dance demands. Jacquemin and Yvette wander around the great tree, their arms intertwined, admiring the posies and readjusting any that threaten to fall off. Zabillet feels a surge of happiness that her two eldest children have made love-matches, and so close to home.

But where is Jehanne? She hardly expects her to be with Hauviette and the other village children, though she hopes she might be, who are dancing, turning somersaults and cartwheels between refilling their mouths with food. Jehanne's joining in such activities is always temporary, as if she is keen to be seen to do what her mother expects before wandering off alone.

Zabillet knows where to find her. She walks towards the tree and, parting the branches carefully so that none of the flowers tied and balanced there will fall off, steps inside.

The way in which the spreading branches of the ancient tree

bend over to the ground give a sense of stepping into a different place. The noise from outside is immediately muffled though glimpses can still be seen of the colourful twirling skirts of the dancers. Because little light ever comes to this 'inside', there is no grass except at the very fringes, and the dark ground is soft with years of compressed autumn leaves. It smells musty, mysterious and damp. It is brown and dark, just a glimmer of sunlight showing through the gaps between the wreaths and flowers.

Right in the centre of this quiet, shaded space is the huge trunk of the tree. Zabillet can feel the long, long length of its years. As her eyes grow accustomed to the dimness, she can see the small figure of Jehanne sitting cross-legged at the base of the tree.

'Hello, little one,' she says quietly. 'I thought I might find you here when I couldn't see you with the others.'

'Come and sit with me. I'm waiting to see if there are any fairies here.'

'And are there?' Zabillet laughs.

'I've never seen any. Do you think they really come here?'

'Who can say? Your godmother Tante Béatrice talks of fairy ladies being here often when she was a young girl. Who knows what to think? People have always come here to celebrate the spring, even the Lord and Ladies de Bourlémont used to join in when they lived in the big house.'

'How I would love to see them! Are they tiny, do you think? Green like the leaves, or brown like the branches. I wonder. What would they say to me?' Jehanne's voice has taken on a dreamy quality which Zabillet finds disconcerting.

'Listen!' she says sharply. 'The fiddler's stopped playing. Let's go and see what's happening out there. And we haven't eaten any of that lovely food yet.'

Zabillet sat up straight, the covers falling away from her in the cold night air. She struggled to get up, but within seconds Bérenice was there.

'Do you want to go outside?' she asked. 'Let me help you.'

'I must go and see Nicolas Bailli,' she said. 'I must go now, and tell him about the Fairy Tree, what we did there. I must go now. Then he will know that Jehanne is no sorceress.'

'Ssh,' said Bérenice. 'Look, it's still dark. Come, let me cover you over again. We are going to see him in the morning.'

Over the next few days, Zabillet was hardly ever alone. She did not spend any more nights with Jean Colin, wanting to return home. Jacques decided to go to Vaucouleurs to talk over events with Robert de Baudricourt, and try to find out what was happening, so villager after villager called in on her. Many brought something with them, some eggs or a chunk of cheese or a few slices of salted pork and some apples taken from their sparse winter stores.

They all wanted to talk about Jehanne, tell Zabillet what they had said to Nicolas Bailli and Gérard Petit; to express outrage, amazement, support. Some laughed, saying how stupid the English would look, trying to make Jehanne out to be a heretic. Had they not seen her hundreds of times praying, hurrying to church, leaving her work to make confession to a travelling friar, listening eyes-shining to the bells ringing out across the fields? Why, they said to Zabillet, she was more religious than the whole of the rest of the village put together. Do you remember how she'd drag your poor Cathérine and young Michel Lebuin off to the hermitage at Bermont? Nearly every Saturday they went until it wasn't safe to go anymore because of the écorcheurs, damn them. Heretic indeed!

Others thought the sorcery idea even funnier. Oh the Goddams would soon realize they were on a wild goose chase, they said. The very thought! Our Jehanette, she was as pure as could be. She never had a bad or evil thought. Saints was what was in her mind, not some old Lorrainian devilry. You could tell Nicolas knew there wasn't an iota of truth in it – he'll tell 'em all right when he gets back to Rouen. You know what Gérard Petit said before he left – I've learnt nothing about her I wouldn't be happy to hear about my own sister!

Although Zabillet, full of foreboding, could not laugh with them, she liked to have them near, and accepted gratefully their bread and fruit and pastries. She could not focus on tasks like cooking, but she could eat a little of what they brought. Friends came and sat the afternoon or evening with her. Marguerite, of course, Jean Morel on his way back from the fields, or Béatrice d'Estellin who made her infusions of some sharp herb, its scent filling the air as they sat in the dark wintry house.

She was glad of their company; she needed the quiet loving support they offered her. They didn't talk much, if they did it was about trivial things, the number of lambs and calves they might expect that year, the old priest at Maxey who had not lasted the winter as they had all foreseen. And she was glad they did not talk of what was on her mind, for sometimes as she hugged them goodbye, she might look into their faces and see their eyes clouded with tears of pity. That she could not stand, for it spoke to her fears and brought back the nausea that most nights had her retching into a bowl.

There was no word from Petit-Jean, and from that she assumed that the King was doing nothing.

2

'Old Robert thinks the Goddams are determined to get her one way or the other, Zab,' said Jacques as they took up their customary places at the table on the night of his return from Vaucouleurs.

'What does he mean by that?' asked Zabillet after a pause. She began with her finger to gather into a little pile the crumbs that had fallen onto the table from the savoury pie that Jacques had brought back with him, a present from Cathérine Le Royer.

'Everyone knows this witchcraft and heresy stuff is complete nonsense,' said Jacques. 'Robert wished he'd known Nicolas Bailli and his mate were here, he would have soon chased them off.'

'They heard nothing ill of Jehanne,' said Zabillet. 'Can we not trust an old friend like Nicolas to report the truth of what he heard? Surely, if they send people here for stories about her, they have to heed what they actually hear.'

'Robert's point was, why would they charge her with something so completely stupid, if they haven't already decided she's guilty and they're sure they can show she is?'

'Don't say that. It's as if you've given up hope. Nicolas said the Church would try her. Bishops and priests. They will see her for what she is, pure and innocent.'

Jacques was silent for a few minutes. 'I don't know how to say it,' he said at last. 'When Robert talked, I could see it. It's not about justice and truth; it's just the Goddams finding whatever way to dishonour her.'

Zabillet relinquished the little pile of crumbs on the table and got up. She was trembling all over. She poured water into the pot over the fire, but with such inaccuracy that the flames hissed and fizzed as the water hit them. She kicked at the pile of wood by the hearth, sending some logs scudding across the floor.

Jacques got up and took hold of Zabillet's hands. 'Stop it,' he said. 'Come on, sit down.'

'I don't believe it,' she shouted, struggling free. 'You men, you just sit there and think the very worst. Well, I shall never give up on Jehanne, no matter what you say.'

Jacques pushed her hands away from him, causing her to stumble backwards. 'Don't you accuse me of giving up on her,' he shouted, threatening her. 'I'm just trying to understand what's going on out there, where perhaps truth and justice don't matter that much. If Jehanne hadn't been so brilliant and successful, no-one would give a damn. But she was. She roused that pathetic King for a short while, and the whole of France against the English, and they're not going to forget that or risk it happening again.'

'What is going to happen to her?' asked Zabillet after they had sat down again. She studied the pile of crumbs.

'You mustn't expect her home for a long time,' said Jacques gently. 'No matter what happens, they're not going to let her go. Despite all that our Jehanne achieved last year, the Goddams still hope to rule in France. She's much too dangerous to let go, in case she leads more campaigns against them. No, I think she's going to be in prison for a long time. Let's hope eventually it will be in a church prison or convent with women to guard her.'

'That's what *curé* Frontey said would happen if she was found to be a heretic. Or should I say, if they decided she was a heretic. So Robert really thinks that is what will happen?'

'Yes,' said Jacques. 'That is how they are going to keep her quiet.'

'My poor Jehanette,' said Zabillet. 'How she must hate her prison. She has spent all her life outside, in the valley, by the river, in the forest, with the animals, under the sun and rain. Petit-Jean told me that even when she was with the army, she would always prefer to sleep outside with the soldiers, rather than find shelter. What must she be feeling now, right now, this minute?' She sighed deeply, rubbing her face with her hands.

'I don't think anyone would prefer to be out on a night like this,' said Jacques, smiling. He threw some more wood on the fire, and used his foot to gather in the logs that Zabillet had kicked about.

'Why doesn't anyone help her?' she broke out. 'After all that she has done. I can't understand it. You say how much the King loved her at Reims. Petit-Jean talks about La Hire and the Bastard and d'Alençon, all so happy to be fighting alongside her. What are they doing? Everyone seems to have abandoned her. Everyone!'

'Robert reckons the King is completely in the clutches of La Trémoïlle and that Bishop of Chartres. They hated Jehanne for her unusual ways, and for having the King's ear for so long. And you know Jehanne is held deep, deep inside the land the Goddams hold.'

'No!' shouted Zabillet. 'Those are just excuses. I don't know why no-one has helped her. Shame on them! Shame on them! They're meant to be proud fighting men. They felt her power when she was with them. I'll never accept that they can't free her; they haven't even tried, so we shall never know if it might have been possible. And that's why Petit-Jean doesn't come home, because he doesn't want to have to tell us about this, that everyone, not just the King, has abandoned her.'

'Zabillet!' exclaimed Jacques, deeply shocked. 'What are you saying?'

'You heard me,' she replied, gathering up the pots and tamping down the fire for morning.

3

Zabillet was folding and smoothing the clean washing which had been lying out to dry in the warm spring sun when she saw Robert de Baudricourt leading his horse towards her house. Jacques was walking at the other side of the horse's head, and behind hurried Jean Morel and Tante Marguerite.

When she saw their faces, the winter cover she had been stretching and checking for holes or tears slipped from her hands, and she stood waiting, unable to move.

'Come inside, my dear,' said Robert gently as he came up to her.

'Tell me, tell me,' she demanded looking deep into his face. He put his arms around her, and held her tight. She started to shake throughout her body.

'She is dead,' he said. 'Our Jehanette, they've killed her.' Zabillet was aware of a great wail rising from the pit of her stomach, and breaking out through her mouth, quite outside her control. It was a great, cavernous despair.

'Come on, darling, come into the house,' said Marguerite, now weeping noisily. 'We can sit down there,' she added as Zabillet swayed in her arms.

The man with Robert took his horse as he went into the house with them. Jacques was already sitting at the table, his face white and his eyes staring, whilst Jean Morel stood anxiously waiting for them to come in.

Zabillet went to sit on a stool by the hearth, the wail dying in her throat, emerging now and then as she rocked herself, occasionally grabbing Marguerite as she hovered around anxiously. She was aware of Jacques demanding to know of Robert what had happened, and of his occasional outbursts of shouting or angry weeping.

Robert was telling the little he knew, but she could only grasp odd words, incomprehensible words that seemed to float around in the air as he spoke them, hovering as if defying anyone to believe them. Heretic, he said. A relapsed heretic. The market place in Rouen. Burnt at the stake. Fire, flames. Burnt, burnt, burnt, until she was dead. The stake. Her body, burnt, dead.

They were horrible words, a terrible travesty, for they did not describe her Jehanette at all. They must not describe her thus.

And why did Jacques keep leaping up and shouting, slamming his fist into the table, swearing and threatening? How pointless, thought Zabillet, carefully smoothing the creases out of the shawl Marguerite had pressed round her shoulders. How completely pointless.

And as her heart broke, another wail, a terrified agonized screaming that might never end, broke out of her body.

Years of Bitterness

1431 – 1440

CONVERSATIONS

Zabillet talks with the Chronicler at Orléans

She was dead. However much I might rage or faint or cry, it was done. However much Jacques might threaten and curse and shout, she would not return. It took days, weeks even to realize that. We wanted to believe it was a foul English trick – cruel rumours put about to deter the King and dispirit his captains as they planned future attacks. It was impossible to believe that any enemy, however heartless, could kill such a young woman, scarcely more than a girl, in cold blood. No court that had any regard for the law could be responsible for such injustice and put that young life, that young body to death by fire. My daughter, tied to the stake, burnt, dead, impossible.

Many believed – or wanted to believe – it was impossible. They couldn't face the cruelty of what had been done. I had to make myself disregard such ideas; there was hope and comfort in them, and that had to be denied. Little stories drifted around to tempt me. No-one knows where these stories come from or how they move around the countryside; they are as light as gossamer and swirl in the currents of air that gently blow across our fields and villages. They touch down and become known as a fact.

A dove flew, it was said, from my Jehanne's mouth, and turned southwards towards the court of the King at the moment of her death. Or, as her body burnt and the fire sprang up, the name of Jesus could clearly be seen in the flames. Or, her heart would not burn, no matter how the executioner raked the cinders and re-stoked the fire. It still pulsated when all else was ashes.

It was these silly things, these impossible mutterings that filled my heart with stone. Maybe I couldn't understand a world where eminent judges, all men of France though traitorously in the pay or under the influence of the enemy English, could send a young woman to a pitiless public death by burning. But I could understand those gossamer-light tales. It was by them, by their improbability, that I knew she was dead.

For a while, Jacques was with those who believed she had escaped, or been allowed to escape, or was to be kept in prison until the right moment came to release her. They had proclaimed her death, he said, as a show of strength. No-one could be so cruel; some common criminal woman had been burnt at the stake instead. Our Jehanette was still alive, somewhere. We just had to wait and we would have her with us again.

I don't know why, but I could not believe this. Maybe I knew by now how brutal men can be in war. Why should they spare someone who had been so successful against them? It made no sense and I turned my back on Jacques when he talked of it, for fear my heart would find solace in such an idea, and be betrayed again.

Although I was ill with grief, there was much that had to be thought about – about why this death was so different from others I had known, even from my poor Cathérine, long dead from some dreadful disease. We may rail against God in our despair at allowing a young person to die before her time, as we think of it. But we do understand that many of us don't live through to old age, and will waste and die of this or that. Even death in battle seemed quite acceptable compared to this.

No, this was something cold, intentional, very different from the natural though dreadful hazards of life, even of war. Men sat there at tables and desks, and decided she must die. Men, French men, who should have cared just as much as she did that France should not fall to the English, condemned her for her loyalty to her country. Clever, learned men.

I did not know the half of it then, of course. I don't know that I could have borne it if I had. I didn't know that small groups of men went to interrogate her daily, twice daily, in her cell, rather than in an open court, so frightened were they that people might judge them harsh. I didn't know that she had only rough common English soldiers to guard her, no women. I didn't know that she had no advocate to speak for her, no friend, not even anyone appointed to advise her. I didn't know that at the end she was tricked to renounce all that she held dear. All we knew was that she had been accused of witchcraft and heresy. And that crazed me with anger, because it showed me beyond all possible doubt that they did not care for the truth, and had not looked for it.

It was all the harder to understand because the acts of which they found her guilty were so very far from the reality of her. So very, very far that you wondered if there were not other worlds out there with different truths. So very, very far that it could send you mad thinking about it. It was Robert de Baudricourt who helped keep that madness at bay, holding me close as I wept on his shoulder.

'Don't think about truth,' he said, 'because it doesn't apply here. It is entirely political, Zabillet. They decided our Jehanne was highly dangerous, so they used whatever they could get away with to find a way to disgrace her, and ultimately to kill her. We know what she actually was; don't let that knowledge ever be shaken. We will never forget the truth of her.'

That was it then, murder dressed up. But you know what? However I felt about those French judges, lackeys of the English, it was never a patch on my anger against our King. Jehanne had sacrificed home and family to secure his throne, and he did not lift one finger to prevent her having to sacrifice her life too.

AUTUMN 1431

Flames

1

Zabillet had no body to mourn, to bury, to say goodbye to. It was hard to understand the fact of death. Jehanne had not been at home for so long, what was there to make it clear that she no longer existed anywhere in the world at all, rather than just being absent from Domremy? Not only had they extinguished her beautiful young life and had her healthy body consumed by fire, but it was said they had flung her last ashen remains contemptuously into the river.

Flames licked across Zabillet's dreams. Leaping fire pricked her awake, the stench of burning flesh in her nostrils. Blistering flesh clung to her eyelids. The smoke of burning wood blinded her and wrenched her out of sleep, coughing. Men in ecclesiastical robes cackled and gloated and clapped as the young burnt body fell from the stake, the bonds melted away into the fire. Time after time, night after night, Zabillet woke screaming to God for mercy. My daughter, my flesh, my body.

She had not realized how much she had been waiting for her to return home. A hundred times a day she would store some thought or event in her mind to tell Jehanne 'when she comes home.' And every time she suffered again the body blow, the sick jerk of the stomach – she is not coming home, she will never be here again. She is dead; she has been robbed of her life, and I have been robbed of my daughter. At such thoughts, cold anger would sweep through her.

2

It was a bright, hot day, a last remnant of the summer before the leaves would begin to turn, and Zabillet sat in the relative cool of the little chapel at Bermont. There were few days when she did not come here, away from the kind eyes of her neighbours. The act of climbing the hill away from Domremy and tramping through the woods along the hillside to emerge into the clearing where the hermitage stood, made more bearable the heavy burden of getting through another day. It was harvest time; she should be outside in the fields with Jacques, but her restlessness made her useless to him.

Sometimes, especially on holy days, there were pilgrims here, their children playing in the trees. They did not know about Jehanne, or, if they did, not that she was her mother, and she could sit and pray with them, or listen to the laughter of the children, and find a measure of forgetfulness.

But today there was no-one here. The chapel held the intense stillness of a quiet place on a hot day. Just the old priest pottered about brushing the floor with his twig broom and, as always, he knelt for a short while besides Zabillet to pray at the foot of the old Virgin Mary, whose brown kindly face gazed out above the body of Jesus on her lap. Its familiarity over years was a comfort to her.

After a while, she heard a different, more purposeful footstep coming down to where she knelt; it stopped behind her. She felt a hand on her shoulder and looked up and around. It was Jacques.

'Jacques?' she said, wondering. As far as she knew, he never came to Bermont, she never even thought he knew for sure that she came here. And seeing him unexpectedly in this unusual place, for him, she could see how thin his face had become. The weathered skin of a man who spends most of his life outdoors had sunk into leathery grooves. There were deep lines around and between his eyes which had not been there before. Before what? Zabillet did not know. They had not suffered the loss of Jehanne together. They rarely spoke or looked at each other.

Once or twice she knew he had been to Vaucouleurs to see Robert de Baudricourt. He said he needed to find out exactly what had happened to Jehanne. At first she had been hungry for any snippet he could tell her, until she realized that no amount of information could change what Jehanne had suffered. She had lost interest, but it was all fuel to his anger, which sometimes seemed to fill the house until there was no room for her.

But she did know that he was always trying to get news of Pierre, who was still held prisoner by Jean de Vergy. De Vergy, how Jacques would spit that name. That whole family had long been Burgundians in the pay of the English, wreaking havoc throughout the countryside. It was due to his endless fighting they had become refugees and had to flee to Neufchâteau. No mercy could be expected from him. He had set the ransom even higher than was decent for a peasant-soldier, reflecting Pierre's ennoblement by the King, and no doubt he hoped to cash in on his close relationship to Jehanne.

Impossible, impossible, how could this ransom be found? They had no money; they knew nobody who had any money. Yet although she could not join in, could not look ahead or hope for anything, she knew that Jacques was trying to see what could be done. One evening he and Jacquemin had gone to see Robert Baudin, father of young Jeanne whom Pierre loved so much, and had married on one of his brief trips home from the campaign with Jehanne. And Yvette had told her later that even if it took years, they had all pledged to work their land and try to raise the money. Or at least, to raise enough money to get some sort of loan and free him.

Zabillet had hardly been able to respond to Yvette. She was locked into a view of her life in which there was no hope and only long weary days ahead, far ahead, unbearably long. None of her children who had been lost had ever come back to her. Would it not be easier to accept that truth about Pierre now, rather than hope for something that could never be? And this daughter-in-law, who had always been there but who had strangely never become close, had held her.

'Come, Zabillet,' she had said. 'We must not give up on Pierre. Think of him a little. He must know that we care, and that we are all working for his freedom.'

And Zabillet remembered that she must be responsible for all her children, always, even though she could not feel it just now. She laughed shakily.

'Don't think I don't care, Yvette,' she said. 'But all I seem to know is the absence of so many of my children. We haven't seen Petit-Jean for so long, I know he must be blaming himself for Jehanne's death. I don't even know where he is. I can't see how life will ever raise itself out of this despair. I hardly dare to hope that one day we shall raise the money and I shall see Pierre again, for I can only see hope being trodden underfoot whenever its shoots rise.'

'We all need you fighting for us,' said Yvette, stroking her forehead. Zabillet shook her head; she had no spirit for any fight.

Now she looked up at this husband of hers who stood in the dark quiet of the chapel.

'What is it?' she said dully, drawn reluctantly from the solace of her prayers.

'Zabillet,' he said, and stopped as if unused to talking to her in any real or intimate way. 'I thought I should come for you.' His voice seemed to come from afar as he stood twisting his cap, his eyes now on the dark face of the Virgin Mary, now scanning the arches of the little chapel.

Zabillet stood up, shaking her legs a little to ease the stiffness which had crept into them during her lengthy prayers. Her eyes searched his face. 'Not bad news, surely?'

'No.' His voice was hesitant as if not sure. 'There is a man come into the village, and he has walked with me up here. He is one of our countrymen, and he has come from Rouen.'

155

'From Rouen?'

'Yes. He has business in Neufchâteau, but he has come out of his way to see us.'

Zabillet darted glances around the chapel. 'He has come to see us because he was there, is that it?'

She swayed slightly, and Jacques stepped nearer to her and held her, looking anxiously into her face. 'Where is he?'

'The old priest has sat him down outside with a glass of ale. He thought we might want to know a little of what happened.'

Zabillet pulled at a loose thread on her shawl.

'I can send him away, Zab. You don't have to see him if you don't want to.'

'I must. We must,' she whispered.

'Come,' he said, putting his arm around her and holding her close as they walked out of the chapel. The priest was hovering near the door.

'Come and sit on the bench under the trees here,' he said anxiously. 'You won't be disturbed. Look, I've put out some bowls and drink for you. Sit as long as you want. I shall be here in the chapel or my house if you need anything. Just call.'

'Thank you, Father,' she said, clasping the hand the old man stretched out to her. He blessed her.

A large young man in the clothes of a tradesman came towards her. He bent low over her hand.

'Zabillet,' he said gently. 'I'm honoured to meet the mother of Jehanne. I am Richard Moreau of Urville, not far from here, and a bell founder. I'm travelling from Rouen to Neufchâteau to collect a new bell that has been made there.'

'You are welcome,' said Zabillet looking into his sad, compassionate eyes. 'Thank you for coming this extra way. We must make do with the priest's hospitality, I'm afraid. Forgive me.'

'It's beautiful here,' he said, looking at the trees in the bright autumn sun. Jacques poured wine into the bowls.

There was silence except for the many birds making their song.

'Tell us everything,' said Zabillet suddenly. 'We have not heard from anyone who was in Rouen at that time. Did you know my Jehanne?'

'No, I did not know her,' said Richard Moreau sadly, shaking his head. 'How I would have loved to. I don't think she could even have known a countryman was near her when she … at the end. But I was there by chance on business, and I can tell you Zabillet, that many wept for the cruelty done to her. I hope she knew that, despite the devilish jeers of the soldiers. The Goddams.' He spat onto the grass.

'I first saw her,' continued Richard, 'at the Cemetery of St-Ouen. That is by the city of Rouen, and they brought her there one day to read the verdict and the sentence. It was at the end of the trial. They built raised platforms, you know, and your Jehanne was led up onto one of them, and Bishop Cauchon and his cronies were on the other.'

'Was she alone?' said Jacques.

'More or less. There was a man standing by. Jean Massieu he was called. Someone said he was the usher, and he'd been sort of looking after her. He was kindly, but of course he wasn't a friend or advocate.

'The Bishop read this sermon. I don't think any of us understood it or listened to it. There was much evil said about our King. Even in those dreadful circumstances Jehanne leapt in to defend him. We may not have been paying any attention, but she was. It ended up with this priest saying she was a heretic because she refused to obey the church. He said that if she didn't turn her back on her beliefs, she would burn. He pointed to the executioner who stood nearby with his cart full of stacks of wood, ready to take her to the stake.'

'Richard,' interrupted Zabillet. 'Did you understand why they made her out to be a heretic? Oh, I understand that once they had got her, they were never going to let her go Both England and those damned Burgundians weren't going to risk her getting the

King and the French army more victories. I know that now. But heretic! You ask the villagers or anyone that knew her! Why, her love of God and obedience to him was deeper than that of all of the rest of us together.'

'I have heard that,' said Richard. 'Do you know, you could see it? Even on that day. She was dirty and tired and in great danger. Someone told me that she had been questioned day after day in her prison cell by those Paris clerics, with no-one there to help her. But you could still see how pure and trusting she was. They chose that lie to hurt her most. And you know a lot of the English soldiers said she must be a witch and a sorceress to have won those great victories over them. They couldn't understand how a young girl could have done so otherwise. They were determined she shouldn't get another chance.'

'That's what they kept asking the villagers when they came here before the trial,' said Jacques. 'Trying to get them to say she had been a witch. None of them did, you can be sure of that.'

'I know that,' said Richard. 'A few weeks before, I had met my countryman Nicolas Bailli in Rouen. He'd just come from Domremy with the evidence he and Gérard Petit had gathered here. It was what they told me that made me interested in Jehanne. But he also said that when Bishop Cauchon, you know he was the judge, found that no-one had anything but good to say of Jehanne, he would not listen to it. He wouldn't even pay Nicolas for his trouble.'

'Oh no' said Zabillet. 'So all those things which the villagers said about Jehanne were never reported at the trial?' She started to weep.

'That is what I heard,' said Richard gently.

'Go on, lad' said Jacques. 'Tell us what happened. What was it they said made her a heretic?'

'All we could make out was that she insisted on listening to what she called her Counsel rather than the advice of the priests, and wearing men's clothes. It seemed to enrage them. It was very intense. Suddenly,' he continued, 'she shouted that she agreed she was a heretic. She would sign their bit of paper. A silence fell over the crowd when she said that. They knew it wasn't right. But we were so happy. There was a great sigh of relief from those who were with me. The Goddams and their French supporters were furious, of course, and those who dared jeered at them. We thought it was over, she would be kept in prison of course, but she would live. We cheered and cheered. Some people mocked the executioner with his great pile of wood.

'One of the judges – priests they were, all of them, bishops and scholars – gave Jehanne this piece of paper to sign. The crowd went silent. Although we were so pleased, you could see that she was struggling. She had to deny what she believed in. It was horrible, Zabillet. She had gone through that great long trial, and you know the people of Rouen – those that had never accepted the English occupation anyway – said she had withstood all their arguments, and never lost heart. But how could a young girl choose death? Oh, she looked sad and alone alright as she signed that paper. She wasn't sure; but as for us, we were glad. We didn't care much about the rights and wrongs of it. As far as we were concerned our Jehanne, our Maid, was going to live and who knew, she might fight another day sometime. And just as good, those priests and the English had their nose put right out of joint.'

Richard fell silent and drank hugely from his bowl. Zabillet could see the look of delight on his face begin to fade. The old priest brought out water and fruits and knelt nearby, praying silently. The autumn sun was just beginning to fall in the sky, and the light breeze caused a whirring sound amongst the leaves.

Zabillet felt for an instant the terrible conflict of that moment and wept. My poor Jehanne, she thought, little more than a child and asked to choose between life and death; a life based on forswearing her faith in what she heard, her saints, her revelations. When all the people around her were telling her they meant nothing anyway, were illusions, misinterpretations, glamours. Had she come to believe that herself, or had she said whatever was needed to avoid the burning?

'We shall never know what was really in her mind,' she said, shaking her head. 'It must have been a bitter moment.'

She got up and started pacing around the clearing. She noticed that the young man was shaking and pale, and went to put her hand on his shoulder.

'Thank you so much for coming to tell us,' she said. 'I can see that the burden of telling lies hard on you.'

Richard turned towards her and she held his head against her. He was choking on his tears, tears she knew for what he still had to say.

'They played a filthy trick on her, didn't they?' Jacques' voice broke harshly into their tears. He slammed his bowl onto the table and the priest looked up in alarm.

'What do you mean, Jacques?' said Zabillet, looking across at him. 'I didn't know you had heard anything about this. You haven't said anything.'

'Oh, I hear bits and pieces when I'm in Vaucouleurs,' he said. 'I don't always tell you because for all I know it's rumour and lies. But we were told several times that even if the worst came to the worst, she would be looked after in a church prison with women to care for her. She probably believed that too. But it didn't happen, did it? Oh, they tricked her alright, somehow.'

Richard shook his head. 'I don't know about those things. They said the English were furious that she had gone back on her beliefs because they wanted her dead. That's all they cared about. Anyway, she was taken back to the prison in Rouen castle. I went about my business – we thought it was all finished. Then I don't know, three or four days later the word went round she was to be burnt next morning in the market place.'

Zabillet sat down close to Richard on the bench and clasped his hand. 'Do you know what had happened?' she asked.

He shook his head. 'The whole town was talking,' he said.

'There were stories of this and that. One of the things that was said was she'd had to agree to wear women's clothes, but after a couple of days she'd put hose and doublet on again. Others said that they had interrogated her again, and she had said she was wrong to deny her beliefs. And then there were those that said she would rather die than live in an English prison with those rough soldiers to guard her.' He shook his head sadly. 'I just don't know.'

Zabillet could hardly bear the picture of misery he portrayed even in those few words. That her daughter might prefer the cruellest death in preference to the life she was offered was a thought of the utmost bleakness.

'We should never have let her go,' she said. She knew it was a foolish thing to say; they had never let her go in the first place, yet she had gone.

'Those Goddams,' said Jacques. 'They would stop at nothing to make sure she was going to die. It wouldn't have mattered what she said or did, Zabillet, nothing could have saved her life. There wasn't a right step she could take. They were scared of her. She was much too powerful and honest and true for them to deal with. They weren't going to let her live. So if it wasn't one trick, it would have been another.'

'But she was just a girl!' cried Zabillet. How could a child of hers have grown into someone so mighty that her destruction had become so important?

'She did look like a girl that morning,' said Richard, 'as they brought her out. Everyone knew that this was no ordinary witch-burning, no everyday execution. Something terrible was going to happen, and it did.'

Zabillet looked around the clearing. It was so far from the scene this young man was painting; the trees, the long grass rustled by the wind, the big round sun beginning to sink, the little chapel and the old priest clinging to his cross as he knelt praying. How often Jehanne had run about here, chasing the rabbits, spinning, dancing about the trees. A great sigh escaped from her. She knew the time had come to hear the rest, and she sat forward in her seat and nodded at Richard.

'It was a fine May day,' he said. 'It was early when they brought her down from the castle, but even so the streets and the Old Market Place were full of people. Ordinary people, tradesmen and washerwomen, shopkeepers and those come in from the countryside to sell their goods at the market. And hundreds of soldiers of course. Because even though the Goddams have ruled in Rouen and all the countryside around for years, they knew not everyone was going to be happy about this. And more platforms and canopies for those priests who were her judges, and the English Lords, you know. And the sheriff of Rouen, oh they were all there.

'Jehanne was pale and weeping. The usher Jean Massieu stood close to her, and some of the judges looked troubled as though they did not approve of this at all. There was another long sermon, and amazingly Jehanne listened to it. Her face was alive, Zabillet, listening to what was said. But towards the end, as they started to call her a relapse and a heretic, she fell to her knees sobbing. And then she started to pray. We were all weeping with her as she called on the saints to help her. She asked forgiveness of everyone she had wronged and forgave those who were doing this evil to her. And though she often broke down in terror at what was to come, she gathered herself again and again. The whole crowd was silent except for our sobs and tears.

'But the English soldiers were getting restless. They didn't care, and they felt this was all going on far too long. They were worried the crowd might turn, and it would all get more difficult. They kept urging that pig Cauchon to be done with it, and suddenly one of them shouted across the silence of the square 'What, priest, will you make us dine here?' All the soldiers and some of the crowd laughed and jeered. The executioner set fire to the wood that was already prepared at the base of the stake. Cauchon rushed through the sentence and before anything more could be said, Jehanne was seized and the executioner started to tie her to the stake. Whilst he was doing so, Jehanne cried out for a cross, and an Englishman broke through the crowd and gave her a little cross made out of two sticks. She pushed it into her clothes next to her heart.'

Richard fell silent, and Jacques came to sit by Zabillet who could no longer control the wailing that rose out of the excruciating pain she felt. Eventually she quietened, and leaning against him, the three sat and looked towards the setting sun. The old priest came and stood behind them, his face streaked with tears as he held out his cross in both hands before him.

'Oh that executioner knew his job,' continued Richard at last. 'I suppose we can be thankful for that, for as soon as the fire was lit, huge flames started to rise up towards her body. Two of the priests, who I later learned had befriended her as much as they could, and tried to avoid this end, went into the neighbouring church of St Sauveur and brought the great gold cross from the altar. They held it up before her so she could see it even as the flames started to burn her. And she continued to pray and call on the name of Jesus and the saints.'

Richard leant forward on the table and lowered his head onto his arms. 'I didn't see any more. I couldn't stay any longer. I'm sorry, it was too much. I heard it was over very quickly.'

Zabillet stared into the dusk as the priest continued his prayers, tears streaking down his face. Out of her great confusion she said 'What happens now?'

Jacques eased his arm from where it had clasped her tightly and swayed gently on the seat.

'Nothing,' he said. 'It's over. Our Jehanette's life and the sweet promise of peace for France. Over.'

CONVERSATIONS

Zabillet talks with Our Lady in Domremy

Dear Holy Mother, here you are back in our church at Domremy at last. I hope you are content. You have been so long in Greux that I thought perhaps you might have forgotten our little church here. But of course, you are happy wherever you are, for you are everywhere, and it is only weak mortals like me who care where it might be that I sit or kneel before you.

Bringing you back here today has filled me with sadness as well as making me glad to have you nearby again. For as our good *curé* Frontey carried you at the head of the long procession from Greux, we were all remembering our Jehanette and her life, so wonderful yet so short, as well as her suffering.

Look, can you see? The roof has been mended and restored, and everything inside made clean and beautiful again, fit for your return. I don't know how many summers have gone by since that time we were at Neufchâteau when the marauders burned this holy place, and laid the roof open to the wind and the rain. It is not so many years, perhaps, though they've all been long and hard for me. For a long time, there was neither the time nor the money for the men to repair it. Every year it seems to get harder just to see to the necessities – to sow the grain and see it through to the harvest, to tend the animals and protect their young, to keep our houses and yards and tools in order; and for us women to spin the wool, and eke out the poor grain, tend a few vegetables and keep the wood-pile high. Harder because of war and sickness and the never-ending raids.

Last year during the late spring, masses were said for Jehanne's soul in all the towns and villages that had loved her, all over France

I'm told, a year on from her death. And after we had done so before you in your church at Greux, all the villagers sat on the meadow by the river eating the food we had prepared, and enjoying the warm sun that already promised a long summer.

I don't know who it was, Jean Morel perhaps, said he wished we could do something in the villages so that Jehanne would never be forgotten. And others spoke too, wondering how to remember her in a way that would show anyone who passes through that both villages love Jehanne and want to show the world that love.

It was a beautiful afternoon. One by one they stood up, so many of them, and said that Domremy and Greux would always be proud that Jehanne had been born and brought up on their soil. The Goddams had done an evil thing to her and extinguished her bright light, but that didn't change the fact of how pure and true that light had been. And despite the fact that the war showed no sign of ending, and the country was still being split apart, we would always remain loyal to the French King, despite everything, whom Jehanne had put on his throne.

Oh there was such cheering, and tears too. Like today, as people have sat here in this church, they had so many memories of Jehanne that they wanted to speak about. It was wonderful to hear her friends speak of her and of her funny little ways. They had experiences of her and with her that I had never known about. They began to penetrate my blanket of sadness. Their memories and warmth pierced holes in that grey numbness and I became able to smile and celebrate with them the astonishing life of my daughter. I think it was the first time that I had laughed since we heard about her death. And though Jacques and I couldn't bring ourselves to join in the dancing, for the first time we were able to go round and talk to these good people whom we have known all of our lives, and hear their good wishes for us.

By the end of the afternoon it had been decided that the villagers would remember Jehanne by repairing this church so near to our home, which she loved so much and where she spent so much time, and making it beautiful again. And you can see that they have, though it has taken a whole year, everyone working on it when time allowed. See the sweep of the wooden arches, and the strongest roof that we could make.

There are so many things here that she was part of. I like to touch them all, the font where we christened her, her godparents standing proudly around. And the dish of holy water she dipped her fingers in so often. And do you remember how she would wander around and talk to Saint Cathérine there, and the other saints, as if they were her friends? It was those saints who she said spoke to her. My poor Jehanne, she is with her friends now, bless her.

And now the roof is mended, the bell has been mounted again, and today it rang out and rang out. It is this bell she loved so much. How she would scold the old churchwarden if he was late ringing it. I have a stupid fancy, for which you must forgive me, Holy Mother. And that is that when the bell rings, she might yet hear it. This sound, which she heard every day throughout her childhood, pealing across the valley, and which she loved, might it not penetrate to wherever she is, so that she remembers us here in Domremy, and knows that we think of her, and that not a day goes by but I weep for her absence?

AUTUMN 1436

An Imposter

1

Zabillet looked anxiously from Jacques to Petit-Jean, and from Petit-Jean back to Jacques again. Something was wrong. All day the two had seemed to be avoiding each other, and now they were sitting awkwardly at the table, pouring drinks, popping up continuously to fetch some forgotten item. She watched them as she busied herself with the last preparations for their meal, a meal which she had tried to make special to welcome Petit-Jean home despite the continued shortage of food. She hardly cooked for herself and Jacques nowadays; there was little change from the daily potage which was all they could afford, its quality depending on the freshness and type of meat she could find. But today she had killed one of the scrawny old chickens which had stopped laying eggs a while ago, and used some of the precious fine flour she had left to make some pastry. The house was unusually fragrant with baking smells.

She had been so excited to see Petit-Jean. One or even two seasons had gone round since he had been at Domremy. He was always away fighting with one of the captains who had been close to Jehanne, the Bastard of Orléans or La Hire, in this senseless war which surely must come to some conclusion eventually. It had been stupid of her to think that he might come back to live in Domremy. The fact that he had been ennobled by the King, in what seemed to her now to have been a last dismissive gesture before he washed his hands of them, meant that he would no longer contemplate the life of a peasant. But ennoblement meant

167

nothing to her and Jacques; it had brought no funds, no safety or security of any kind. Nor did they have any way of making their living except to continue to farm the land and tend the animals. All the villages had gained was the exemption from tax.

But for Petit-Jean it was different. He had made his life as a soldier, though she did not like to think of it. Occasionally they felt proud of him when he was in one of the King's rare campaigns, making some spasmodic effort to relieve a town from the Goddams. But when the army was stood down, which happened frequently, he did not return home, and she suspected that then he was little better than the écorcheurs who still swooped at times into Domremy and no doubt all the other villages dotted over France, to steal and pillage to meet their needs.

She didn't like to think of that. She loved Petit-Jean, that was not in question, but she did not like his love of war and fighting. He had never been a loveable child, often sneering and sullen, delighting in others' discomfort, stirring up needless conflict. Seeing his sister and brother captured had undoubtedly deepened scars which she knew he tried to assuage through action. He had grown harder since Jehanne's death and the continued imprisonment of Pierrelot. Oh yes, she could see that he would be a good, even fearless soldier, though he might also be merciless. And in truth, she could see no other life for him.

On the occasions when he did appear at their door, he was affectionate and concerned for them, often leaving small gifts of money and occasionally bringing her a bolt of good cloth or a strong jacket for Jacques. And if sometimes she doubted their provenance, and felt that the stories of his exploits were carefully edited, well, that was the way it was. Any money he gave was carefully stored towards Pierre's ransom. She could only love him and pray for him as she did for all her children, alive or dead.

And today, surely, there should have been things to talk about, not this strange silence between him and Jacques. They had not seen each other since they'd heard about the treaty which had been signed at Arras the autumn before, ending the split between the King and the Duke of Burgundy. France was united again, against the English, and if it had not yet seemed to make much difference, this was something that she knew Jacques talked about endlessly with the other men in the village, and she would have expected him to quiz Petit-Jean for any bits of information he might have. Was the circle turning? La Trémoïlle, Jehanne's great enemy at court, though she may never have known it, always advising the King to caution and treat, was disgraced. The Duke of Bedford who had tried everything to make France belong to the English, including snuffing out the precious life of Jehanne, was dead. A treaty was signed bringing peace with Burgundy. Paris had been retaken, and surely other towns would soon fall back to France. But on all of these things, which had dominated Jacques' mind and conversation over the past year, he was now silent.

Zabillet sighed as she served out the food and sat down to eat. The two men, she could see, were making an effort to appear normal, helping each other to bread and wine, complimenting her on the tasty food. Petit-Jean asked about this and that of the villagers, and Jacques gave responses. But it did not feel right. Zabillet wanted everything to be normal, and she returned to the subject they always discussed when they were together.

'Petit-Jean,' she said. 'Jacques thinks that now there is peace between the King and Burgundy, we might have a better chance of ransoming Pierrelot. What do you think?'

Petit-Jean shook his head as he bit deeply into a pear, wiping away the juice that dripped down his chin. His face was sour, angry.

'I wish that were so,' he said. 'Lots of men have been freed since the treaty was signed, even before. But Pierre is held by that bastard Jean de Vergy, and he's in the pay of the Goddams. He's not obliged to give him up and I'm damned sure he won't. Not without the full ransom.' As always, he made a spitting gesture of contempt. 'When I saw the King a while ago, I asked if he would help...'

Suddenly Petit-Jean stopped and flushed bright red. He continued in a rush. 'As usual, he said he hadn't two pennies to rub together, and though he would love to, how could he afford to pay the ransoms of all his loyal soldiers? Blah blah!'

Zabillet noticed that when Petit-Jean mentioned the King, Jacques' head had come up sharply, and he had shot his son a harsh, menacing glance. Now Petit-Jean sat with his head in his hands, worrying at the pear stalk in his mouth.

Jacques was rushing in. 'I've been talking with Robert Baudin,' he said. 'He's worried about his Jeanne; she's a faithful girl but she's fed up of waiting for this husband that she feels she's forgetting. He's been seeing someone about getting a loan on all his land. Maybe if he can, and with all the money we have got, we might be able to raise the ransom this year, or next at the most. I didn't want to tell you before in case it didn't come off. What do you think, Zab?'

Zabillet was silent. All at once, Pierre's face was clear before her, his gentle brown eyes, his kind smile. What did he look like now? In those long years, he would have changed from a boy to a man. She longed for his presence. She took the hands of Petit-Jean and Jacques where they lay opposite her on the table.

'That would be wonderful,' she said slowly, forcing them both to look at her. 'It would be a great thing. We must hope and pray for it.'

'I shall go up to Vouthon tomorrow,' said Petit-Jean, 'and see what Jacquemin might be able to give. Oh Maman.' He came round the table and gave her a big hug.

2

The two men disappeared into the village, Jacques to ensure that the animals were being safely tended, Petit-Jean to exchange news with his childhood friends. Zabillet gathered up the pitchers and walked down to the river for water. Although she felt happy about what Jacques had said about the ransom, she had learnt not to hope for too much. Anything could still go wrong before Pierrelot strode up the path towards her door. It was so long since anything good had happened, it was hard to believe anything might. Besides, she knew when good news was covering bad, and she wanted to think what this awkwardness between the two men could be.

Tante Marguerite was just rinsing off the last of her washing in the river, and starting to gather her things together as Zabillet came towards her. She thought Marguerite looked searchingly at her as she folded her wet clothes.

'Hello, Zabillet, how are things with you?'

'All right,' said Zabillet puzzled. 'It's lovely to have Petit-Jean home again. It's ages since we saw him.' Again she felt her friend's eyes on her.

'Marguerite,' said Zabillet slowly. 'Something is wrong.'

Marguerite was silent as she gathered up her soap and wash board.

'Oh, he's quite the grown-up soldier now, your Jean,' she said airily.

'You know what it is, don't you?' said Zabillet flatly.

Marguerite stood up, leaving her stuff on the ground, and took hold of Zabillet's arms. 'If he hasn't told you, you must ask him,' she said gently.

Zabillet put a hand to her mouth. 'There is something then. Oh, Marguerite, can you not tell me?'

'It's not for me to say,' she said. She gently pushed a wisp of hair back that had escaped from Zabillet's cap. 'But you must ask him.' She leant forward to give Zabillet a kiss, held her close for a minute, and bent to pick up her things again.

When Zabillet got back to the house, Petit-Jean was tending his horse, brushing her whilst she ate from the special trough they kept for her.

'Petit-Jean, you have something to tell me.'

'Me? No, Maman, I've given you all the news.' He teased the last tangles from the horse's tail, keeping his face turned from her.

'You have something to tell me,' she repeated. 'Now come into the house.' Her voice was little different from how it might have been ten years earlier, and sullenly he followed her indoors.

'I've got nothing to tell you,' he said with a slight tremor of bravado in his voice.

'Look,' said Zabillet. 'There's something wrong between you and your father. I don't want to pry into your secrets – you're a grown man now, but maybe there's something I should know about.'

'It's nothing you need to know about, honestly. Just some silly disagreement we had.'

So there was something. Zabillet stood at the hearth pouring the water she had collected into the big pot over the fire.

'I can see you don't want to tell me,' she said. 'It's something serious enough to worry your father, but if it's just something you have done that he's not happy about, then I'm content to leave the two of you to sort it out. Even though you know these things are best out in the open, and I would prefer you to tell me. Things happen, I know that, especially in the world you live in.' Petit-Jean looked flushed and sullen. 'But if it's something that affects this family, then I swear I'll never forgive you if I hear it from someone else.'

Zabillet took the fire-irons, and started furiously to poke and re-arrange the fire, piling on fresh wood as if it were the middle of winter. She had frightened herself now.

Petit-Jean gave a great groan and sat down on the bench, covering his face with his hand. 'You will never forgive me anyway,' he mumbled. 'I have done a terrible thing.'

Zabillet found her hands shaking as she sat down beside him. She could not imagine what she was about to hear. 'Tell me,' she said, feeling panic rise in her throat.

'I thought I saw our Jehanette,' he said slowly, keeping his face turned away. There was silence in the house. The clucking of the hens outside and the birds singing in the soft autumn air seemed far away.

'Jehanette?' repeated Zabillet, stunned.

'Yes,' said Petit-Jean, his tone flat. 'There were rumours she had escaped the fire, and now there was peace between the King and Burgundy, she could come out of hiding.'

'There were always rumours she escaped the fire,' said Zabillet. 'I thought we had agreed long ago that they were foolish, especially after Richard Moreau came and told us about her death in Rouen. He had witnessed it, Petit-Jean.'

'Well, I was not here when he came.' Petit-Jean shook his head. 'Anyway, when I heard this, I thought I should check it out. She was living in Metz and I went to see her.'

'Did you believe these rumours?'

'I didn't know. I wanted to believe she was still alive. Oh, it would have been wonderful.'

Zabillet took his hands. 'Petit-Jean,' she said, weeping. 'If there had been any chance … but there wasn't, you know. You knew that, didn't you?'

'The rumours were so persistent,' said Petit-Jean. 'They had even heard about them in Orléans and sent messengers to find out. I thought I should go too.'

'Go on,' said Zabillet. She knew there was a lot more to hear.

'A knight in Metz was looking after her. He laid on a dinner, and this woman was there. She could have been Jehanne, Maman. She looked so similar to her and talked of Orléans and the Kings' coronation. She knew a lot.'

'And?'

'I thought maybe it could be her. At the end of the dinner I went to talk to her, but she was always surrounded by so many people, and then it was time for her to go.'

'You did not speak to her alone? Did she not ask after Pierre, or about us here in Domremy?'

'No, I wasn't able to get close to her.'

Zabillet sighed. She could not see where the story was heading. All that had happened was that Petit-Jean had allowed himself to be taken in momentarily by this imposter. She could understand the wild hope that must have risen in him that Jehanne might still be alive, which he had not been wise enough to stamp on immediately. It did not reflect much credit on him, that he had allowed himself to be seduced into believing for a moment that it might be her, but it certainly did not explain Jacques' anger or that sad look on Marguerite's face. She braced herself.

'I have betrayed us all.' Petit-Jean burst into a noisy fit of weeping. 'And I have betrayed Jehanne. Twice. First by allowing her to be captured. And now this.' He got up and began to walk out of the door.

'Sit down,' said Zabillet sharply. She rushed to the door and stood blocking his way. 'You are not going to walk out on this now.' She looked at him defiantly.

'Papa told me that I must never say anything to you,' he said miserably.

'Well, it's too late for that now,' said Zabillet angrily. 'I will know what has happened. And you will tell me.'

'I came back here,' he said quietly. 'You had gone to Vouthon for a few days to see if Jacquemin could spare anyone to help with the harvesting. I told Papa I was going to Orléans and then on to see the King to tell them about this.' Petit-Jean paused. 'We had a fight out there on the road.'

So that must be how Tante Marguerite knew about it.

'What was the row about?'

'Oh, you know how Papa can be,' he said. 'He thought I was going to say I had really seen Jehanne.'

'And were you?'

'I thought I could get some money, Maman,' said Petit-Jean desperately. 'You know, if they believed that Jehanne was still alive, they would want to reward her with some money, or at least make sure she had enough money to live comfortably.'

Zabillet felt as though she had been punched in the stomach. She felt the heat rush to her face and she sat down to steady herself.

'Let's get this straight,' she said to Petit-Jean, who stood sunk in misery, stabbing at the fire with the poker. 'You were going to lie to the people of Orléans, who have shown nothing but love for Jehanne and honour to her memory, and pretend to the King that she was still alive and needed money. Presumably you weren't going to take any money they gave you to this woman in Metz?'

'Oh my goodness, no. I knew she wasn't our Jehanne,' said Petit-Jean surprised.

'Oh well, that's something, I suppose,' retorted Zabillet angrily. 'At least you weren't completely in the power of the people who are supporting this imposter. You were going to keep the money for yourself, is that it?'

Petit-Jean shook his head. 'You don't know what it's like,' he burst out. 'Being a soldier is almost as miserable as being a peasant. At least when you're a peasant you know you're going to have some food as long as the land is tended. But to be in one of those companies, Maman, we hardly ever get paid except those few times when the King mounts a campaign. Oh sometimes a town or a village will be grateful to us for something we've done and feed us for a few days, but the rest of the time we have to take what we can ourselves. To have a bit of money makes all the difference. And then you know, we are trying to find the money for Pierre…'

'Don't you dare mention Pierrelot,' shouted Zabillet. 'Don't bring him into this sordid story. Don't start making pathetic excuses or tell me how hard life can be. The fact is you were willing to pretend Jehanne was alive to get money for yourself. You were right when you said you had betrayed us all. As if the suffering of Jehanette was not enough without having her own brother…' She stopped, choking. She couldn't believe it, what he had done was dreadful beyond measure.

'What is this? Petit-Jean? Zabillet?' The loud, concerned voice of Jacques cut across the tension in the room as he stood in the doorway. He removed his cap and stared into the house, blinking into the dark after the bright afternoon sun outside.

'You've told her, haven't you, you young fool?' He strode towards Petit-Jean where he stood miserably by the fire. 'Exactly what I told you not to do.' He hit him in the face.

'That will do, Papa!' shouted Petit-Jean, anger tightening his face. 'That's it! That's the last time you are going to hit me as if I was a little boy. It was a stupid idea anyway, not to tell her. She was always going to get to know, somehow.' He squared up to Jacques, his hands lightly on his hips, his body tense.

'But she hadn't got to know, had she? Not even those who heard us fighting that day said a word to her. And do you know why? Because she's had enough, that's why, and the last thing she needs is trouble from a money-grabber like you.' Jacques poked a jabbing finger near to Petit-Jean's face.

Petit-Jean grabbed his wrist and forced it down.

'Stop it!' screamed Zabillet. She rushed towards the two men and tried to separate them, pushing against their arms. 'Stop it!'

The two men dropped their arms and stood glaring at each other. Zabillet breathed deeply. 'How dare you keep things from me? How dare you?' She stared at Jacques. 'You may have persuaded people in the village not to tell me, even Tante Marguerite who is my friend, but you're stupid if you didn't realize I would know something was wrong as soon as I saw Petit-Jean again. Anyway, who are you to decide what I should know and what I shouldn't know? As for you…' She turned on Petit-Jean, but he put his hand up.

'Don't tell me,' he said angrily, wiping tears from his eyes. 'I'm despicable. I don't deserve to share the same soil with the rest of my family. The very worst you could think of me would not be a fraction of how I think about myself. I'm going. It was a mistake to come, or ever think I could do anything to please you.'

Petit-Jean took his sword and cloak from their place in the

house and strode out. Zabillet sank down by the fire, weeping and listening as he freed his horse and rode away.

It was well after nightfall when Jacques came into the house again. Zabillet served his supper silently. Her anger had drained away and she felt empty. What was the point of reproaching Jacques? It wasn't his fault that Petit-Jean had … done what he had. For all the faults she knew her son had, she was nevertheless profoundly shocked. His laugh as he strode out of the house kept ringing in her ears. It was full of hatred for himself, for them, for the whole world.

'Where will he go now, I wonder.' It was not really a question.

'Back to his company, I expect,' said Jacques. 'It's not that far away.' He sighed deeply. Zabillet thought that he looked old, tired, sad.

'Do you know what happened when he went to Orléans and to the King with this crazy story?'

'I tried to stop him, believe me, Zab, I did. That's why we fought out there in the road. He knew it wasn't our Jehanette, though he desperately wanted it to be. All he told me was that the people of Orléans had also heard about this woman claiming to be Jehanne, and sent a messenger to find out more. I don't know if the King had heard about her before Petit-Jean went to the court to tell him.'

'What did they say?'

Jacques laughed shortly. 'At Orléans? Who knows? You can never quite tell when you only have his word for it. I got the impression from what he said that they didn't believe him, but gave him a good supper for love of Jehanne, and sent him on his way.'

'What about the King?'

'Well, I suppose the King must have been interested because he allowed Petit-Jean to come and speak with him about it. One good thing was that he was able to remind the King about Pierre. In the end, the King paid for his journey, that was all.'

'Would the King care whether Jehanne was alive or dead?' said Zabillet bitterly. 'I doubt it.'

CONVERSATIONS

Zabillet talks with the Chronicler in Orléans

Do you remember that shameless imposter, who became known as Claude des Armoises? You are probably too young, but maybe your parents might remember her if they are Orléannais.

I didn't hear any more about her until I came to live here in Orléans myself, and some of the townspeople told me how cruelly they had been deceived. They love Jehanette here, and although they knew, like we did, that she had suffered a horrible death by burning, they didn't feel they could just ignore this young woman, in case it was indeed her. There were so many stories of how Jehanne had escaped the fire, or even how she had been substituted on the morning of the execution, and another woman burned in her place. Oh, how all of us would have like to believe them, and these good people here didn't want to ever be in the position of having turned her away, if it turned out to be true. So they sent messages to her when they first heard about her appearing in Metz, and of course Petit-Jean arrived here in Orléans with his false stories about her, may God forgive him.

Pardon me if I weep a little. I was angry and disgusted with Petit-Jean, of course, but isn't it natural to wish so much that our dead loved ones might be alive? Don't our hearts leap with joy when we see someone who might, just might, be them? Of course, we curse our own stupidity a moment later; it has caused us pain again. But I could forgive Petit-Jean his desire for that young woman to be his sister. What I could not forgive was his desire to use that brief moment of deception to try and profit from those who loved her and honoured her memory.

I had to think over what he had told me of how hard and

impoverished the life of a soldier was. I hadn't really understood that. How unbelievably glamorous such a life would have seemed to us a few years previously, and especially to Petit-Jean, when we were just a family of simple peasants living a traditional hand to mouth existence. Yet when I reflected on what Petit-Jean had told me of his life, I could see how very uncertain it was. I did come to some understanding of what he had done, though he had shamed us all and Jehanette's memory, and that I could not forgive.

When eventually, by making a huge effort, and borrowing money from any who would lend it, Pierre was ransomed and came home, he was frightened and amazed by the change in the countryside. You don't always notice it when you live through it, do you? And maybe my mind had been troubled too long to bother to try to track it. But Pierre could see immediately how poor we'd all become. Of course Jacques and I had long been unable to tend our lands. We'd managed to let out a bit here and there, though few had labour to spare to work it, but most remained fallow, for we could only manage to work just enough to feed ourselves. We were a very small household.

But Pierre, as he made his journey home eventually, and walked around the villages, kept exclaiming how different it was. I had hardly noticed how many of our young men had drifted off to join the fighting, how many families had gone to live with relatives in other villages to pool their resources and their luck to survive. It wasn't just us who no longer cultivated all our land. Acres lay abandoned. Ditches remained uncleared, and weeds and brambles grew over the banks of the Meuse in places where we had always kept them clear. Écorcheurs had wrecked houses and outhouses and animal shelters, and they had not been rebuilt. The village life of his childhood was gone. It seemed now to have been prosperous, sunny, orderly. How cruelly this ceaseless war had treated us all.

Oh, it was joy indeed to have Pierre back in Domremy, though it was a difficult time for him. He had thought that now Burgundy was reconciled to the King, the English would rapidly be chased out of France, and the dream which Jehanne had inspired in him and all of France, would soon be fulfilled. But although it was true that the English were retreating further and further into Normandy, France was still far from being united under the one French King. So after a brief period of recovery, he all too soon went off to place himself in the service of the King again, as he must.

But I have strayed far from what I was telling you, about this abominable imposter. As far as I know, no-one heard any more about her for a few years after she first proclaimed herself in Metz. Now we know that she travelled around the border country for a while in my land of Lorraine, and settled down in marriage to Robert des Armoises. She had a couple of children, and when her husband died she found herself in poor circumstances once more. Unbelievably, she began again the imposture of Jehanne.

She must have learnt my Jehanette's past well, for I'm told that when she eventually turned up in Orléans, just a short while before I came to live here myself, the city treasurer and others thought it might well be her, and honoured her with supper and presents of money. They said she talked about so many things concerning the siege of Orléans, and of the Bastard and La Hire that they did not know what to think. But she soon disappeared when people who had known Jehanne better got to see her a bit closer, and knew it was not her. They say she was later captured in Paris and put in prison.

I couldn't help but find out all I could about her story. That someone should pretend to be my Jehanne filled me with the greatest anger and revulsion. It was an outrage to her memory, a theft of her achievements, and an incessant pain in the hearts of all that loved her. She caused me to lose for many years a son that I loved, at a time when I had already lost so much. And in addition, there was the deception of the loving generosity of the people of Orléans, although that never stopped them for a moment from remembering and celebrating her.

WINTER 1439

Farewell to Domremy

1

It was the first time that Zabillet had wept. Sitting there in the dark house with Pierre, lit only by the flickering flames of the fire bright in the early evening darkness, the full weight of her grief overcame her. Pierre sat by her, holding her and talking gently to her, though occasionally his own sobs could no longer be contained.

'There is no comfort, is there, Pierre?' she said. 'It seems that our suffering will never be over.'

'Sshh. Don't say such things. These are such harsh times we are in. Everyone is suffering.'

'I know that,' she said. 'I try not to be vain and believe that our suffering is greater than others. Misery is everywhere. But it is hard.'

'Poor Papa,' said Pierre. 'How he fought that illness. Despite everything, he didn't want to leave us. Even when his body was covered in sores.'

Zabillet sighed deeply and they sat quietly for a while, dull with sorrow. Eventually she stood up, stretching herself and yawning deeply. She began to get down bowls and pour some ale.

'The village has done Jacques proud today,' she said. 'They all have so much of their own to grieve about, and yet they came to bury him and say kind words about him. You could see their fear; this horrible illness has cut short so many lives in the villages around.'

'People are starving,' said Pierre, 'and so poor. I don't know how Tante Marguerite and the others made such food for everyone today when there is so little.'

'We were honoured. They are still proud of the family that produced Jehanne, and glad to have been part of her life, despite everything. There has been kindness upon kindness for us. And Jacques was an important man in the village of course.'

'They're so loyal,' said Pierre. 'When they look around, they must wonder sometimes if it was worth it, what she did. We could never have foreseen it would take so long. But like the people of Orléans, they have perfect faith that things will get better. Which they will, Maman, they must.'

Zabillet looked deep into the flames of the fire. It was true that things must get better, for they could scarcely get worse. When she thought about it, there were only half the people living in Domremy and Greux that there had been when the children were young. Long gone were the days, which now seemed so orderly, when at the threat of écorcheurs or any other danger approaching, they would hide their possessions and drive the cattle into the Château d'Île for safety. Soldiers would pass through, and their guard at the end of the villages or on the church tower would shout out warnings, or just whatever news there was. They felt unsafe then, but that seemed to have been a secure existence compared with now. When Zabillet remembered how the *demoiselle* had helped them get their cattle back when they had been stolen by one of the warlords, or how she brought them bread and wheat after their crops were destroyed the year they fled to Neufchâteau, she could see that these were crises which were managed within their traditional existence.

But now those times were gone. It was not a matter now of holding firm with Robert de Baudricourt against the Burgundians. They were meant to be at peace. But what a peace it had turned out to be. The King seemed to have forgotten his people. The local lords fought each other, and the soldiers took their living from the land where they could. Not just soldiers either, for groups of landless peasants wandered the countryside, begging and stealing to remain alive. In Domremy and Greux, as elsewhere, it was about the survival of each individual family, who could hardly tend their own lands and contribute to what was perhaps the last communal activity, keeping the cattle safe, never mind find people to post as guards, or lend the neighbourly help they had been used to giving.

'It was so lovely to see Béatrice d'Estellin and young Michel Lebuin and the others today,' said Zabillet. 'I'd forgotten how much I miss them since they left. The stories they tell are all the same as ours, people moving to live with relatives in other places to have more hands to work the land. And those are the lucky ones. Béatrice said that some of the villages around Neufchâteau are like ghost villages. That is what we have come to.'

'Michel hadn't heard about Jacquemin,' said Pierre.

'Oh!' said Zabillet, surprised. 'Well, it's hard to keep up with everything when so many dreadful things are happening. How sad it is to think of my father's land at Vouthon untended, covered in weeds, and the house beginning to fall down. He fought so hard for that land. Who would ever have thought that starting out such a large family, we would not have someone to see to that?' She shook her head bemused.

'Yvette has a child now,' said Pierre, 'according to Durand.'

'I'm glad about that,' said Zabillet slowly. 'It was such a sadness to them that no children were born. I don't blame her for finding a new husband even though so little time has passed. My poor Jacquemin.'

Zabillet started to weep again. It was more than two years now since her eldest son had died. No-one knew what had happened. He had gone one day to Grand to find a thatcher, the one they had always used in Febrécourt having gone away, and had never returned. Days later his body had been found in the forest, a long way off the path, half-eaten by wolves and vultures. Had his heart failed, or an écorcheur cut him down, or had he been attacked by wolves? There was no way of knowing.

Sometimes he haunted Zabillet's dreams, or had done until the terrible sores appearing on Jacques' body had taken over all her waking and sleeping thoughts. He would be running through the forest, a small boy calling her name. At his back a terrible danger; if only she could see what it was, she could surely do something about it. And always she would awake in dread and screaming, as she failed to see what it was that was about to pounce on him.

The walk of a horse coming along the lane broke through the muted sounds in the house, and Zabillet leapt to the door, and out into the yard.

'Goodnight, Zabillet,' a voice called. 'I'm going back to Coussey now. It has been a sad day for us all. God be with you.'

'Goodbye, Martin, goodbye,' she replied. 'Thank you so much for coming today.'

'Do come along and see us sometime,' he said. 'Hauviette would like to show you her new baby. We need to comfort each other in these times.'

He passed by, and Zabillet turned back into the house. Her face was flat.

'Maman,' said Pierre gently. 'You know that couldn't possibly be Petit-Jean.'

'I keep hoping,' she said rubbing her eyes. 'Maybe he won't come.'

'Even if word had got through that Papa was so ill, he couldn't have got here from Normandy yet.'

'If only I knew he would come,' said Zabillet, weeping again. 'I sent him away, Pierre. He probably thinks I never want to see him again.'

Zabillet had not seen Petit-Jean since that day when she had heard of his visits to Orléans and to the King to tell of the woman claiming to be Jehanne. She still felt shocked that he had tried to profit from it, saddened by his trampling so indifferently on Jehanne's memory. Yet was he not still her son, whom she loved no matter what he did, and was she not still his mother? And surely he would wish to honour his father's death, or did he no longer care, had he cut all family obligations and feelings from his heart?

'I don't know whether he will come,' said Pierre, guessing at her thoughts and unspoken questions. 'But if he doesn't it is only because he can't leave the campaign at the moment. And perhaps he knows from seeing others die of this terrible illness, that he could not have got here in time to be with Papa.' He paused for a moment and sighed. 'I would like to see him myself. All I can remember is his shouts from the gate of Compiègne. 'Pierrelot! Jehanette!' Again and again, as we were being captured. He was just a boy. We both were, really.'

'I'm sure he longs to see you too,' said Zabillet. 'He was so shaken that he had not been with you both at that time. He would rather have spent years in prison than be the one who was free. But after he shamed her memory, he probably wonders if you want to see him again.'

'Oh I do, I do. We have so much to talk about, things that we share about Jehanette that no-one else knows. I've sent several messages, but you know he won't come anywhere near Orléans or the King, so I can't see how I'm going to meet him. Perhaps if he doesn't come here to Domremy, I'll go and find him.'

'That would be good,' said Zabillet. 'I wish you would if you can travel safely. Nothing can change what he did, but we can put it behind us, for I know he's sorry and shamed. There's only you and me and him now, Pierre. I don't want there to be any bad feeling.'

She looked into the flames searchingly, as if she might see him come riding through into her arms.

'I think you said he's turned out to be a fine soldier, from what you've heard,' she said after a while.

'He always was,' said Pierre. 'Much better than me. He was brave, you know, and he took pleasure in fighting well. I never cared for it much, I just stuck close to Jehanette and hoped for the best. But he was learning every day how to use his weapons better, and control his horse. He was always trying to be better than Jehanette, you know.' Pierre laughed.

'I can imagine it,' she said. 'She was just his sister, and yet there she was leading the army.'

'It wasn't just that,' said Pierre, 'though that took some getting used to, I can tell you. It was also that she seemed to come into her own in battle; you should see how she handled her horse, even in her heavy armour. She took to it straight away. Most of us hated armour, and got out of it as soon as the day's fighting was over. But she wore it lightly. And it didn't matter if she was carrying her sword or that great banner, she was completely at ease in all the noise and chaos. She knew somehow what it would be best for everyone to do, where they should focus the attack. And she commanded them! She was amazing. At first, you wouldn't believe that she had even less training in all of this than us. But Petit-Jean soon caught up with her, as far as weapon skill is concerned, anyway. He was too careless with his own safety for my liking, but that was what made him so good.'

'You say he stays in the company of La Hire?'

'Yes, and others from that time. Their style suits him, completely foolhardy, and loyal to the King, though they hate his court and don't like to be near him. They always loved Jehanne, you know; they believed in her completely, and shared her impatience at all the delays made by the King. I'm glad he's with them, though they can be very cruel at times. They've always stuck by the King and France, even over the long years when it seemed quite pointless.'

There was a pause. 'I don't know much about a soldier's life. But Petit-Jean told me how hard it is when there's no actual campaign on. I always thought the écorcheurs were a different type of soldier, choosing to terrorise the villages. But from what he said, that's more or less what they all do when the King isn't actually paying them for some battle or campaign. I hope he is not violent to the people of the villages.'

'Well, that's how it has always been, though not all of them are so brutal. Some just take what they need, hopefully that is how Petit-Jean is.' said Pierre. 'But that's why I'm asking the King if I can give up soldiering. I've no stomach for it since I came out of prison, Maman. If it hadn't been for Jehanne, I would never have chosen to be a soldier. But at least at the moment they're doing something real, trying to free Normandy from the English. It will happen eventually, you know. Since the King made peace with Burgundy, the English seem to have accepted they'll never rule over all of France. They're just hanging on to those places they have been occupying the longest. But in time, France will be for the French, just as Jehanette predicted.'

'We never thought it would take so long, did we?' said Zabillet, shaking her head. 'How happy and confident we were after Orléans. So long ago now. Sometimes I wonder if there will be a France left when this is all over; it's become so wretched.'

Zabillet paused. She also wondered if she would have any family left by that time, but she was afraid to put such thoughts into words.

'I think we should have a bit of supper, don't you? I couldn't eat much today, but Tante Marguerite gave me some of the left-over food. We still have many friends.'

Zabillet and Pierre chewed slowly on their food. Although they had felt hungry, when it came to it they had little appetite. The dark house, which had often seemed so cheery with the bright fire and flickering lights, members of the family occupying themselves in the few ways they could on a cold winter evening before going early to bed, seemed gloomy, empty. As soon as they stopped talking, Zabillet's thoughts returned to Jacques. All their lives they had worked to make a living for themselves and their children on this land which seemed so harsh in winter, so light and fertile in the summer. And now it was all gone. Not just gone now, with Jacques' death, but slowly, slowly over many years. She could see nothing but poverty and loneliness ahead.

'Maman, what are you thinking about?' said Pierre.

'My thoughts are all confused and gloomy. In fact, I wouldn't even call them thoughts.'

'It's very soon to mention this, but you know I have to start back to Orléans in a day or so. I don't want to leave you on your own here. I want you come with me.'

'Come with you?' repeated Zabillet slowly. 'Come with you? To Orléans, do you mean? To stay?'

'You know Jeanne would love to have you. She is a long way from home there too, and she misses her country people. And it would help her with the children to have you. You would be very welcome.'

'But Pierre, from what you've said, you only have a little house there. Surely you don't want to add an old woman to your household?'

'That is just what we do want,' said Pierre. 'And tomorrow, Jeanne will tell you that for herself. And I'm hoping things are going to change. The King seems to have some sympathy for me. He knows that both Jeanne's family and ourselves used every penny to raise my ransom, and that the debt we took on is going to be hard to pay off. I've told him I don't want to fight any more, and one of his advisers said to me the other day that he might help me with some money. If he does, I shall buy a little farm nearby. Do come. Perhaps it would not be so different from Domremy.'

'Does the King do this for you because of Jehanne?'

'I'm sure that must be so. There could be no other reason, for in truth I have done little otherwise to impress him.'

'That is something then, that is something. He has done little enough.' Zabillet stopped. If the King had decided to do something for Pierre, that was good. She must not spoil it by expressing her great bitterness against him. How he had done nothing to save Jehanette or ever given any sign of sorrow at her death. Or stated publicly that the English had done a terrible wrong in declaring her a heretic and burning her at the stake. Nor had he honoured her in any way whatsoever, or acknowledged that he owed his very Crown to her.

'Would you not think of coming back to Lorraine, if you had a little money to make a new start? After all, Jeanne is a long way from home in Orléans.'

'We've talked about it,' said Pierre. 'I don't know, so much has happened. Me going away with Jehanette and being in prison was such a break from what we thought our lives would be like. At first, I assumed that if the King released me, we would come and live here, but we've come to love Orléans. We both feel we can't come back. We have to make our own lives in a different way. I don't know, it's hard to explain.'

'I understand that,' said Zabillet. 'I didn't think you would. It isn't much of a life here anyway, now. Further to the south must be safer, more prosperous.'

'Well, you know everyone who lives off the land is struggling. But yes, it is safer there. I can't promise you much, except you will be with us and we'll do what we can to make you happy.'

Zabillet stretched for his hand. 'You are kind, Pierrelot. You always were, and I love you for it. You must go back to your Jeanne now. It's getting late and her father will be wondering where you are. I shan't come with you when you leave, there's not enough time, and I have things I must see to here. But before you go, I'll give you my answer, I promise you that.'

Pierre smiled broadly and took her in his arms as he prepared to go. 'I'm so glad you haven't said 'no',' he said, rocking her gently. 'You call me kind, but there's a great deal of self-interest in this offer, you know. But you think about it, I know it's a long way to go, a big uprooting. And you know if you do decide to stay here in Domremy, I'll do whatever I can to make sure you're comfortable, so you mustn't worry about that. But I really hope you will come.'

'Thank you for being here these last few days,' said Zabillet. 'It meant everything to your father that you were with him at the last. Horrible though it was.' She shuddered at the memory of his suffering, of the once strong body that wasted away so quickly, rotting as though it were already dead.

'It was a terrible end for him when he was always so in charge of everything. We must remember him as he was before the sickness came. Now I must go. Jeanne and I will be over in the morning. Sleep well.'

2

Zabillet dampened down the fire for the night and sat back watching it burn low. She pulled a warm shawl around her shoulders and tucked a blanket over her knees. She had the long hours of the night to get through.

It was pointless going to bed. She knew that from long experience of grief. As soon as she lay down, her mind would become full of pictures and thoughts, driving sleep away and leaving her frightened and anxious. It was a dream-state, a distorted world, where thoughts of this grief triggered memories of that. These memories were heightened, bringing images of long-forgotten incidents, total irrelevancies that nevertheless took on meaning. What had seemed to be so, was shown to be different. After such a night she would wake low, sad, burdened, no longer sure if her day-time memory served her well.

At least she had learned to avoid that. It was better to stay up by the fire, not to seek rest in sleep when there was none, and cope with the long night hours by thinking and dozing, sometimes getting up to make a drink or do some small task that presented itself. She would drag herself around exhausted the next day, until at some point her weariness would become so extreme that a few hours of oblivion might follow.

Do you get used to grief? Zabillet wondered. Can loss be so

frequent and so profound that you actually get used to it? Well, she had seen that over the years, where one terrible misfortune after another had struck a family, eventually leaving just one behind. She had seen that one become so dull in their feelings that they began to move untouched through their daily life, unable to respond to kindness or beauty or even more misfortune. Zabillet dreaded that, though she recognized it as a cover for unsupportable pain. There was some attraction in it.

She sighed deeply, the long-drawn out exhalation dissolving into sobs. Cathérine, Jehanette, Jacquemin – three children dead. Three children whose presence would not accompany her into her old age, who had no changing days or griefs or losses of their own to pre-occupy her thoughts, whose children were mere ghosts of what would never be.

And now Jacques. Gone. Sometimes she felt that it was only in the last few years she had grown to love him; after she'd begun to stand up to him. Jehanne's departure had given her the strength and even the right to insist that he respect her thoughts. And he had responded. The man whom she loved, but who could be impetuous, angry and sometimes cruel, had learnt too. He had let the boys go to be with Jehanne and taken great pride in all of them. And after her death, he had faced down any who started to voice any doubt. And now he would not be here sharing this tough old age they had begun. How could that be, that she was left all alone?

Zabillet woke with a start. She had slept for a while, and as the reality of the day just gone broke on her, she felt a sharp anger with him for dying, just like that. She shook her head sharply, and got up to poke a little life into the almost dead fire, and pour herself a drink of water from the pitcher. She wasn't going to do that, blame him, be bitter. At least even if you never actually got used to grief, she thought, you could learn to side-step some of the cunning tricks it played on your thoughts.

She moved around the room for a while, straightening the bench where Pierre had sat a few hours earlier, piling together their dirty pots, covering up the remains of the food they had not eaten. She opened the door and stood looking out at dark Domremy. Black. There was no moon, and cloud threatening rain or even snow masked the stars. The murmur of the river brushing by the reeds was all that broke the deep silence of the countryside. It was bitterly cold.

Refreshed a little, Zabillet sat again and set herself the task of thinking about Pierre's offer. She found her thoughts difficult to control, because she could not imagine a city like Orléans, or what might life there be like.

She had always loved to be at home. She hadn't left it very often. Apart from occasional visits to her family, she had only spent those few days away at Neufchâteau when they had all had to leave the village, and of course when she had made her pilgrimage to le Puy. She had spent her childhood in a village on top of the hills, and the rest of her life in Domremy below. How could she know if she could be happy in another place, so far away?

What would it be like to wake up and not hear the Meuse moving endlessly along its river bed? Not to have the river just a stone's throw from the house for water, for washing. Not to look out across the valley and see the sun rise each morning, nor its fiery ball sink behind the house at night. Not to hear the bells ring across the villages, or the cows' murmurs as they meandered home at night for milking. Not to have the cheery greeting of people whose lives had butted against each other for decades, with the freedom that gives to help and be helped.

Zabillet wept. She was starting another grieving, losing her home. For although she thought about all those aspects of life as if she could not leave them, she was already doing so. She was beginning a litany of farewells to all of those things about Domremy which were as dear and familiar as life itself.

For in truth, what choices did she have? Of course, there were people in Domremy as well as Pierre who would make sure she did not starve. She couldn't work the fields, and there wasn't anyone else to do it for her, but she could still plant a few vegetables and tend some animals. And she could spin wool to sell. She would manage somehow.

But she didn't want to be a burden on the village. They had so little, though they might gladly share with her what they had. She was old. She could only expect to have times of illness and increasing frailty. And she would be alone. She knew that as she became less able, people would visit and help her out of charity. She didn't know if Petit-Jean would come, and even Pierre could only make such a long journey occasionally.

She could only see sadness, loneliness and struggle. At least in Orléans she might be useful as long as she could, contributing something to Pierre's household, and knowing her grandchildren properly. And if it wasn't Domremy, well there would still be things to enjoy. There would still be birds and sky and sun, even if they filled a different sort of space. And of course, they knew of Jehanne there. Not the bright little child or determined young girl of Domremy, but the leader, the hot-headed warrior, the saviour of their city. Maybe their memories could provide some warmth in her dull old age.

I will go, she decided. Once I know that is what his Jeanne truly wants, I'll tell Pierre that I shall come in the spring. And maybe by that time that wretched King, who owes us so much, may have granted him some money and we can live in the countryside.

CONVERSATIONS

Zabillet talks with Our Lady in Domremy

Dear Holy Mother, how strange it feels for this to be the last time that I shall kneel before you. We have talked so many, many times. Or I have talked rather, and you have regarded me with your kind compassionate eyes and listened, your knowing mouth always on the point of responding.

I have had to imagine your responses. But Zabillet, you would say, your anger is unseemly. Or, that is not a very kind way to think of this or that person, and certainly not of the King. And although sometimes you must have been shocked at my thoughts, you have not shown me, so that now and then I have felt ashamed that it is only in this most holy of places that I have been able to express such wickedness. You have accepted it all in loving silence. You have been a comfort and a challenge across all the years of joy and trouble in my life. And if sometimes I felt there was too much to bear, injustices which no-one appeared to care about, hardship which no-one could or would alleviate, well, you have borne it with me.

Holy Mother, you are everywhere, and yet I dread to leave you. I have knelt before you in many places, and yet here, at home in Domremy, you are closest and most familiar to me. And so I feel that you are one of these many dear people I must part from, although I know that even now, at this moment, you are also in some little church in Orléans where I shall find you and speak with you again. And also in what Pierre describes as that enormous, grand cathedral where my Jehanette prayed, and celebrated. Perhaps there I shall find a little of her spirit and of her bravery, and be the stronger for it.

I shall very likely never see these good people of Domremy again; people who have accompanied me every step of great stretches of my life. Kind Jean Morel, always ready to help and advise, and wise Béatrice with her healthful herbs and potions, though of course she herself is now gone to live elsewhere. Tante Marguerite, best of all good neighbours, willing to share the worries of everyday. And Jean Colin, who has always remained in my heart as a son, though long re-married after my poor Cathérine's death. I could go on, about this person and that one, so many to weep with in farewell.

And the graves too. The graves are hard to leave, a short row of them where I have been able to sit and feel again with my family. How shall I leave them? And yet they left me. They did not wish it I know, and dear Durand has said he will come and tend them from time to time. One grave is not there, of course. It is astonishing yet, though year on year has passed, that there is no grave anywhere for my Jehanette. They say the last remnants of her burnt body were thrown into the river, as if they were of no consequence to any one. Some river which does not come by here. We shall never find her or lay her lovingly to rest.

Dear Holy Mother, can an old woman, wracked with pain and loss, find peace in a new place? Must I say goodbye to all that is familiar, to this dear village bonded to its lazy flowing river and sloping fields and hills? Well, it must be so, for I have nothing. No strength to work the land, or money to pay someone else to, or family to do it for me. So maybe I can be of some use to Pierrelot and his children, and earn my keep thus.

One day, Petit-Jean may come and find me gone. Oh I have told everyone, if he comes tell him how much I want to see him and may he travel on and find me safe in Orléans. Perhaps it will not be so, for Pierre has said as soon as he is able he will go and find him and bring him to me. I crave for that day to be soon. Surely he will come when he knows that we want to put all of that behind us.

We are all ready to go. The cart is loaded, and at first light my travelling companions will be here, and we shall leave. Watch over us.

Farewell Domremy.

Celebrations

1441 – 1456

SPRING 1441

Orléans

1

Zabillet stood in the sheltered porch way of the cathedral watching the city's guards and soldiers trying to create order, whilst the little girl jumped on and off the stone steps, never straying far. Still more used to village than town life, there seemed to be more people in the square and streets around than she could have imagined living in one place. They seemed to be pouring in, townsmen and women joined by their neighbours from the countryside until the streets were hardly able to contain them. And occasionally there would be a fearful shouting as the soldiers roughly pushed the people back to allow the horses through, as captains, commanders and lords arrived, and went into the cathedral behind her.

But despite the shouting and hollering, it was a joyous occasion. Zabillet noticed that people had dressed festively in colourful clothes and hats, and some waved small pieces of cloth on the end of sticks in the green and crimson colours of Orléans. She knew she could turn into the darkness of the cathedral and wait in that quieter space for Pierre and his family to arrive, but she wanted to look at all these people, for they had congregated in Orléans for one reason only this day – to celebrate the deliverance of their city from the English, and remember with great joy her daughter's role in that liberation.

How Zabillet had looked forward to this. It was almost a year now since she had come to Orléans. She felt that she had come to a safe place, especially when to great fanfares the Lord of the city, Duke Charles d'Orléans, had come home that winter after his long, long imprisonment in England. She had learnt that those villages on the eastern border of the kingdom, like Domremy, were regarded as healthy and thriving compared to the poor villages to the centre and north of the country, which had not population enough left to maintain their peasant life, or peace to tend their fields. Nevertheless, it was only when she arrived in Orléans and felt the good spirits of the people, and saw how busily they were still re-building their city and its suburbs after the damage of the siege, and to house the flood of people coming in almost daily, that she realized how dour and hard life in Domremy had become.

But of course, her situation was far from ordinary. She had not been allowed to be like other refugees come into the city from the wasted countryside. The people of Orléans had given her a wonderful welcome. Those who had known Jehanne, hearing that her mother had come to live in the town, came to visit her, welcomed her warmly, wanted to share their memories with her. They insisted on taking her to this or that place where Jehanne had been; where she had stood on the bridge to shout her defiant message to the English captain Glassidas (whose name was always accompanied by snorts of contempt); the gate which she had forced the revered Messire de Gaucourt to open for her so she could go out and fight, despite the French captains having told him on no account to do so, and from where she fought all day to secure victory; the cathedral, before which Zabillet now stood, where she had headed immediately after that victory, and heard mass after mass. Even after all this time, her name was always joyously on their lips.

There was healing for Zabillet in their attitude. For them, Jehanne was a hero, a miracle-worker, the saviour of their city and their way of life. They were unequivocal; she would never be anything else. They had known the English, oh yes, they had lived under their cruelty for months, their city bombarded, the people reduced to starvation, dependent on supplies being brought in. The capture and trial of Jehanne and the scandalous extinction of her young life were just more examples, the most tragic, of their evil and their opposition to all things good and godly. They knew the English, and they knew their Jehanne, and there would never be a moment's doubt in their minds as to who was the hero and who the evil-doer.

A large group of priests came up the steps towards the porch of the cathedral, and Zabillet pulled the little girl closer to her out of their way. She bent to kiss her head as she pressed her to her side. What a strange and wonderful gift the child was. The previous summer, Pierre had gone to find Petit-Jean, and returned with this unexpected companion. She was Petit-Jean's daughter.

'It's unbelievable,' Pierre had said, laughing as he handed her down to Zabillet from where she was perched before him on his horse. 'Petit-Jean asks us to look after her. Guillaumette, this is your Grand-maman who I have told you about.'

The child hooked herself around Zabillet, and had never strayed far from her since.

'I found Petit-Jean in Pontoise, in a tense battle with the English,' Pierre had recounted to her that evening, as he and Jeanne and Zabillet sat in their little yard enjoying the last of the evening sun. 'I hardly recognized him! Instead of a scrawny youth, he was a big, strong soldier. At first he would not talk, except of everyday practicalities about the Normandy campaign, though I could see that he was happy to see me. He knew Papa was dead, of course, and that you had come to Orléans. Finally, it was only after a great deal to drink that we began to talk properly.'

Pierre fell silent for a moment. 'Once we began, we seemed to talk for days. We told each other everything. It was hard work at first because do you know, we have never really talked together?

We were just excited boys when we went off with Jehanne, and all our talk then was squabbling, or grandiose gestures about our skills at fighting. And our lives have been so different since then. I expect he hardly recognized me either. I learnt that he has had to put aside many painful things, and now he has become a great soldier and indispensable to the campaign. It hasn't been easy for him.

'I couldn't believe it when I heard he'd got married! I don't know when exactly, a few years ago, and then there was this child, Guillaumette. I don't think Petit-Jean ever knew this woman or the child particularly well; he was away so much, and his thoughts more on soldiering than home life. But apparently a year or so ago she died, maybe from the same illness as Papa, I'm not sure. Guillaumette was taken in by a sister of his dead wife, but Petit-Jean wasn't happy. He felt she didn't really care for the child and was always asking him for more money. So I said she could come and live with us. We went to fetch her, and here she is!'

Zabillet smiled. 'You are filling your tiny house with waifs and strays, Pierre. First me and now Guillaumette.'

Still she had not dared to ask Pierre the question most prominent in her mind.

'He will come, Maman,' said Pierre, not waiting for it to be spoken. 'He will come and see us here in Orléans, when he can. He wants to put it all behind him as you do.'

2

'Isabelle, Isabelle!' Zabillet could hear someone calling her. It still shocked her that many of the people of Orléans found her country name too strange or over-familiar. She spotted Charlotte Boucher struggling to make her way towards her through the dense crowd, waving her arms.

'Here I am,' she responded unnecessarily. The little girl shouted, 'Charlotte, Charlotte, here we are, over here,' waving from the top of the cathedral steps.

'Isabelle! Guillaumette! Hello! How glad I am to find you,' she shouted over the intervening heads of the few who still remained between them. A lad whom Zabillet recognized as one of the family servants struggled to keep up with her. He was meant to see that the young woman came to no harm, though she herself mocked the idea that she needed any protection. She liked to be independent; like Jehanne, she always added.

And it was true that Charlotte was more independent than most of the young women Zabillet knew, even in Orléans. She bore little resemblance to the similar-aged girls of Domremy. She was bright and expected much of life, and in fact worked alongside her father in the City Treasury. Eventually of course, she would marry and run her own household, and find other ways to satisfy her curiosity, intelligence and ambition.

'It's because I knew Jehanne,' she had explained when they first met; a meeting which Charlotte had sought out as soon as she heard Zabillet was in Orléans. 'I was only a little girl at the time, maybe the same age as your Guillaumette there. Jehanne stayed with us during the whole time she was saving the city from the English. She slept in my bed, and she told me about Domremy and her life there, and about you and her father, Jacques. Oh, it was such an exciting time. I never knew anyone so full of energy, so sure of what she was doing. So impetuous and foolhardy too – that's what my father kept saying anyway. He's very sensible, you know, and everything moved much too fast for him when Jehanne was around. I decided I was going to be like her, Isabelle. I was going to join her as soon as I was old enough, and fight alongside her. It didn't work out like that, unfortunately. Though my father is glad, I'm sure, for my sake if not for France's.'

Zabillet had looked at the proud young woman sitting by her, and felt again the grief of losing her own daughter. Charlotte was only a little older than Jehanne would have been when she died.

In the course of that meeting, Charlotte had shown Zabillet a hat which Jehanne had given to her one day during her stay in

Orléans, and it was that hat which she now held anxiously before Zabillet as they stood in the porch of the cathedral.

'You don't mind, do you?' asked Charlotte. 'If I wear this?' It was a man's hat, the sort that might be worn by a young knight when he was not in armour. 'In honour of Jehanne on her celebration day?' Zabillet smiled. It would look a little odd with Charlotte's plain long dress and the cape she had thrown over her shoulders against the wind. 'I wanted to wear man's dress like she always did, but alas Father forbade it.'

Zabillet took the hat from her and kissed it, as she had the first time it had been shown to her. 'Of course I don't mind, Charlotte. It's yours anyway to do as you wish, as Jehanne would have wanted you to, but actually I find it an honour that you would like to wear it on this day.' She hugged Charlotte and kissed her. 'Look at this amazing crowd,' she waved a hand about. 'It can't be true that they have all come to remember Jehanne, can it?'

'They have,' said Charlotte. 'Just as they have every year for ages. Oh, I can't remember how long exactly, several years anyway. To celebrate the liberation of the city, which she accomplished. May I stay with you?'

'Of course,' smiled Zabillet, and Guillaumette took Charlotte's hand and swung it delightedly. 'I would love to have you by me. I expect Pierre and Jeanne will arrive soon, in time for the mass. Then I don't quite know what will happen.'

'Oh, it's going to be wonderful this year,' said Charlotte. 'Now that Duke Charles is back, he will head up the procession with the Bastard at his side. It will be the biggest ever, I'm sure.'

'They're brothers, aren't they?' asked Zabillet.

'They are, at least they had the same father. It was the Bastard that defended the city alongside Jehanne, whilst Duke Charles was in prison.'

'And was he in prison all that time, until now?'

'He was. He was taken prisoner by the English at Agincourt—oh, I don't know when. I wasn't even born then. And he was held in England all those years until last summer.'

'My goodness.' Zabillet was startled. Although she had been aware of Charles being fêted on his return to Orléans a few months previously, she had not really understood his story. 'Nearly all his young life in an English prison. How dreadful.' And yet he had come home at last.

'Jehanne used to love him, you know,' said Charlotte.

'I thought you said he was in prison at that time?'

'He was. She never knew him. There were lots of stories about what a wonderful Lord he was, and how handsome. He still is, you'll see, though his hair is quite white. And as well as a great fighter, he was a poet too. Jehanne used to tell me all of the things she had heard about him, and of course Papa, who as City Treasurer was trying to raise his ransom, had been to England and seen him in prison. And she was enraged that the English were attacking his city when they had got him in prison, and everyone was trying to raise the money to free him.'

'I suppose even a Duke's ransom is hard to raise,' murmured Zabillet, thinking of Pierre.

'She used to say to me, "Don't worry, Charlotte, when we've kicked the English out and got the King crowned, we'll get your Duke back." Oh look Isabelle, there's Pierre and the baby. It must be nearly time for the mass to begin. Come on, Guillaumette, let's go in.'

The huge cathedral was full of people standing in the nave waiting for the mass to begin. But Zabillet and Pierre and those with them were led to the front where seats were set out for the dignitaries of the town. Zabillet looked at Pierre fearfully. Surely a mistake had been made. But he smiled reassuringly and put his arm around her.

'This is where they want us to sit,' he said. 'You are famous today, Maman; we all are.'

There was hardly time to recognize that nervous knot in her stomach before the fanfares began and everyone stood peering around to see the procession. The bishop of Orléans and his priests led the way, then a herald carrying the standard of Jehanne, followed by the Duke of Orléans and the Bastard, their knights and squires, most in light armour. Then came the town's leaders, amongst them Charlotte's father Jacques Boucher, who had accommodated Jehanne and ensured she had everything she needed, and others whom Zabillet had not seen before. Scores of them.

They all took their places, the herald standing by the altar holding the standard. Zabillet remembered Jacques telling her that at the coronation in Reims, Jehanne had stood by the King holding her banner. And it was beautiful, as Petit-Jean had said. The way the herald had arranged it, she could see the world being held by the angels, and the beginnings of what she knew were the words 'Jhesus Maria', which stretched into the tail. Zabillet had learnt that Jehanne had designed the banner herself and had it made for her as she prepared for her campaign in Orléans. She had noticed that when people talked of Jehanne, they nearly always mentioned the standard, how she liked to hold it herself to lead the soldiers, and use it to rally and encourage them. She could understand that now.

Every prayer, every word said, showed Zabillet that the people of Orléans felt they owed their very existence to her Jehanette. To them, she had performed a miracle, making the English feel hopeless and defeated where before they had been strong and defiant, inspiring the Orléannais and their companion French soldiers to courage and victory. The whole tenor of the mass was to thank God for sending Jehanne to them to save them.

Zabillet found herself weeping. *I never knew I had a daughter who would be powerful in the world,* she thought, *and sometimes I find it hard to recognize my little girl who sat and span with me, and chatted through the long afternoons, in this miraculously-inspiring leader whom they praise continuously, and who actually celebrated her victory in this very place.* She was conscious again of being just a poor country woman in her best but still homespun clothes. Unlike the smart-hatted women sitting near her with their knight-husbands or city aldermen, she had only her peasant cap to pull over her thin, grey hair. She knew that the few teeth she had were black and her hands rough and calloused from a life of hard, manual work. She had no money for better, but even if she had, she would not know where to begin.

When she had mentioned some of this to Jeanne Baudin a few days ago, chatting as they were about their life in Orléans and the many differences from Domremy, Jeanne had said that she would ask Pierre if they could both have a finer dress for the summer. 'But you know, Zabillet,' she had said. 'One of the reasons people want to see you and meet with you, is to understand a bit more about where Jehanne came from. They love to see you as a countrywoman. Believe me, they would be very disappointed if you became a smart town lady.'

Zabillet had laughed uproariously. 'I shall certainly never become that! Nor would I want to.' But the best that they had been able to manage in the time was a new shawl, which Zabillet pulled closely around her, partly against the cold of the cathedral, partly to ensure her old blouse was better covered.

As the mass ended, there were prayers that the suffering of France would soon be ended, that cities still in the occupation of the English should experience the freedom that they did in Orléans, that God would give the King and all his Lords and commanders the strength and the will to push the English out of the country once and for all. It was what Jehanne had promised, and everyone cheered.

The bishops, priests, lords, civic dignitaries began to file out. Pierre was able to look around now, and tell Zabillet of others who had known Jehanne who were here. There was the Duke d'Alençon and La Hire, her squire Jean d'Aulon and her page Louis de Coutes. All had loved her.

'When the procession is over,' he said. 'We will see if we can get a chance to talk to them,' he said.

'You are going to get the chance right now,' said Charlotte laughing at them both. 'You are all coming to the reception laid on by the city in honour of Jehanne and also because this is the first time our Duke Charles has been here at this time. Come on!' She twirled Jehanne's hat round her finger, and perched it on her head.

Zabillet held on hard to Guillaumette for comfort and safety, although the timid little girl would have been surprised to know this. The meal reminded her of the celebratory supper she had taken with Robert de Baudricourt at Vaucouleurs when they had first heard of Jehanne's success at Orléans. But grander, oh very much more grand. She had never seen anything so rich as the huge hall with its beautiful dark wood panelling and many coats of arms. And the tables, covered in fine linen and silver bowls and plates, enormous dishes of fruit and flowers down the centre, great pitchers of wine and ale.

Zabillet turned to Charlotte nervously, who was pointing out where they were to sit. She realized now that the young woman had been selected, or had selected herself, to be her guide for the day. She appreciated the fact that the table that had been set aside for her and her family was a place of honour, but one set slightly away from the Duke's table, where the knights and city leaders would sit. If she did not wish to, she need talk to no-one except Charlotte and her family.

But what Zabillet had not realized, because she had never thought of it, was that of course Pierre knew many of these people, had fought alongside them, and celebrated victory with them in the time before his and Jehanne's capture. She saw this son of hers anew – she had missed so many of his years as a young man, firstly when he had been away with Jehanne on campaign, then the long years of his imprisonment. She saw again that the kind boy had turned into a highly-regarded man; still young, but marked by a painful past and a lost dead sister whom he had felt responsible for in the same way that his brother did.

She remembered that Pierre along with Petit-Jean had often been in Orléans with Jehanne; not just part of the deliverance of the city that they were celebrating today, but on many other days in the months afterwards when they would come back together, sometimes for a feast in her honour, sometimes just to spend a few days with these people who loved her, away from the complexities of the King's court, with which she had no patience. And although Pierre had lived in the city for over a year, this was the first formal occasion on which the city leaders had the chance to meet with him. Some of those who had fought with Jehanne had not seen Pierre since he and Jehanne had been captured before Compiègne, and they wanted to speak with him about all that had happened, despite the many years that had gone by since.

Although Zabillet greeted warmly all these people pressing round her, delighted to meet the mother of Jehanne, she did not join in their conversation. Although they experienced the greatest sorrow that Jehanne had died, been murdered as they said, they were more interested in discussing with Pierre the possible reasons for the King's lack of action, and the clever, cruel determination of the English to have her dead in one way or the other. And of course, much else had happened in the dozen or so years since which they discussed endlessly.

Zabillet did not want to join in these arguments, which were so old to her. She had talked them out in her mind and with others so many times in the years since Jehanne's imprisonment and death. She had long since stopped trying to make sense of it all. No, today was about remembering her when she was alive, vibrant, and achieving impossible feats, and though Zabillet was realising that she could not do that, perhaps would never be able to do it, without great pain, she knew she did not want to give time to those other considerations today.

But she did appreciate it when someone who had known

Jehanne took the time to come and sit quietly with her for a little while and tell her things about her. One such was Jean d'Aulon, Jehanne's squire, who was surprised and pleased to discover that Zabillet's companion was Charlotte Bucher.

'Well, little Charlotte!' he said. 'You have grown from a cheeky little girl into a beautiful young woman. Do you remember me?'

'Mm,' said Charlotte mischievously. 'I think you are the man who received a box on the ears from Jehanne for sleeping.'

Jean d'Aulon roared with laughter. 'The very same, Charlotte,' he said, 'the very same. She was angry that day, wasn't she? I've never put armour on anyone so quickly in my life. I think you had to help too! And poor old Louis, he had to go and saddle her horse in ten seconds flat.'

'Yes, and she jumped on her horse virtually half-dressed. And there was such a brouhaha because she hadn't got her banner. I remember rushing into the room and giving it to poor Louis as he came flying in.'

'Then he handed it to her out of the window, didn't he?'

'That's right,' said Charlotte. 'And she was off like a shot. What was that all about?'

'She thought the Bastard and the others had started to fight the English without her. As they had. You know she was struggling to be fully recognized by them at the beginning, Isabelle? Hardly surprising, given no young woman had ever been in the thick of military planning before! Well, we were all having a nap during the afternoon, sure that nothing was going to happen, when she started up saying her Counsel had told her the fighting had begun. And she was right, of course, as always.' He smiled warmly. 'How did she know these things? That day we took the Bastille de St Loup and it was the start of the victory.'

'Was she often angry?' asked Zabillet.

'No! Yes!' responded Jean. 'She was always something – angry, impatient, frustrated. But you know, when she was in a battle she was in total control, absolutely sure and confident. I've never served with anyone so knowledgeable about battle and weapons and what to do for the best. She was brilliant, inspired! And yet when she was injured she cried just like the little girl she was, in pain and fear. It never made her give up, though, not for an instant. The only time she was truly quiet was when she would go and pray, in church, on the battlefield, perhaps somewhere with Pasquerel. That's where it all came from, for her.'

'You've forgotten what fun she was,' said Charlotte. 'She used to make me laugh so much with her comments about people. Especially important ones.'

'Oh yes. That was her peasant heritage. Never respect position!'

Order was being called. It was time for the procession to begin around the town, and people were starting to leave the hall. Zabillet would not let Jean kiss her hand as he wished, but she drew him close and kissed him.

'Thank you for being with her,' she said. 'Even at the time of her capture. I know that you also had to spend time in prison before your ransom was raised. And thank you for telling me these wonderful things about her. I hope whenever you're in Orléans, you will come to see me if you can spare the time. Her life was so short, and yet there are so many things I still don't know about her.'

'Pierre,' said Zabillet. 'I'm too tired for this procession. I would have liked to walk with you behind Jehanne's standard and go across the bridge to the Tourelles to celebrate her victory, but I don't think I can.'

'Are you all right?' asked Pierre anxiously. 'None of us need go; we can just walk home with you instead.'

'No, no, I want you to go. I'm fine. You know I hadn't expected that grand dinner and talking to all those people. It seems to have tired me out. If you want me to take the baby then Jeanne and you can be free to go. What about you, Guillaumette, do you want to walk with your uncle Pierre?'

It was a rhetorical question really. The little girl was most unlikely to leave her side. She shook her head and held on to Zabillet's hand.

'All right, if you're sure,' said Pierre. 'We'll come and find you at home when it's all finished.' He bent and kissed her, and Jeanne handed over the baby, who was sleeping on her shoulder. Suddenly, he gripped her arms. 'So many memories, Maman…'

It was this which had really worn Zabillet out. It was always exhausting, for every celebration brought with it waves of anger, sadness and regret, reminded her of her love for Jehanne, the pain of her loss. And today there had been incidents told about Jehanne's life which she had not known of before, and which she wanted to think about.

'Come on, my sweet,' she said to Guillaumette. 'Let's go home.'

CONVERSATIONS

Zabillet talks with the Chronicler in Orléans

The people of Orléans have made sure that Jehanne will never be forgotten or dishonoured. You can be proud indeed to be one of them, and here you are commissioned to set down not what she did at Orléans, about which so much has already been written and said, but what her family was like, and what she was like as a girl – well, she was always a girl, wasn't she, so young still when burned at the stake? About nineteen, I think, though you know in Domremy we never took notice of the years, and there was no book or anything to write down when our children were born. But that was roughly her age, too young, much too young, to face prison and trial all alone. Never mind that terrible death.

Sometimes I rage at her death still, though far more years than I can count have gone by. But when the rage dies down, as it must if we are not to become mad from anger at the injustice of it, I have this great sadness that she had to bear it alone. To be so very alone at such a time, to know that nowhere in all that crowd of watching, shouting people is one friend who really knows you and cares about what is happening, to not know whether any family or friends are even aware that the flames are licking at your feet, and that you are going to have to bear immeasurable pain alone. How hard that is! It's not really that I think, if only I had been there, I could have stopped it. I'm not foolish enough to believe that. It is, if only I had been there, even if I couldn't do anything about it, I could have offered some comfort just by sharing those last moments with her. She was brave beyond measure to face it alone, with the courage which we know she showed to the very end.

How did it happen, how could it happen? I know the people of Orléans also felt sad and angry about it, as well as many others across the whole country. And from what I have heard since I came here, many shared my outrage that the King did nothing to help her. But you at least were determined that she should not be forgotten, even in the worst days when France seemed to be lost despite what Jehanne had done. You kept her alive by your remembrance of her every year in this city, celebrating how she defeated the English besiegers. You were determined that the great push she made to free France from the English should not be diminished or forgotten, and tried to keep to the forefront of the King's mind the need to finish off what had been started.

I will not speak of the long years of the King's inactivity, both in forgetting Jehanette and sometimes it seemed in forgetting France. You know all of that. It never sat well with me to feel and believe the King was wrong, for the King must always be more than a man; he is appointed by God and is therefore not to be doubted – that is what I always believed up until that time. And of course, Jehanne believed in him completely. Oh, I know from what people have told me that she often became very impatient with him, but everything she did was to strengthen his position and to win back France. So it troubled me, not just that he had abandoned her so completely, but also that I felt so bitter against one who should inspire all our loyalty.

So I cannot tell you how happy I felt when finally, after so many awful years, he did manage to sustain a campaign against the English, and take back Rouen, the place of my poor Jehanette's suffering. No sooner done than he initiated a query about her trial, and I have to give him credit for that. Well, you know the story, how it immediately became clear that there was no evidence that she was a heretic, that the trial had not concerned itself with justice at all, but only with finding a way to put an end to her. It was a wonderful day, when those things which we had so long suspected, became public, announced. A sad day, of course, because sometimes your mind does a funny trick, and you actually think that by being found innocent, she might re-appear.

Nothing can bring her back. I have to keep saying that to myself, even now. Unlike even your Duke Charles, twenty-five years in prison in England they say, but finally restored to his family and city. There will be no such restoration for my Jehanne, no matter what happens. She was denied the right to continue to fight for France, perhaps in time to marry and have a household and children. To be a daughter and a sister and a member of whatever community she chose. And we were denied, well, so very many things, when we no longer had her in our lives.

But despite that unspeakable pain, I felt such joy when Guillaume Bouillé concluded his brief enquiry by saying that she should never have been branded a heretic, that the evidence had not been there. Of course, we all knew she was no heretic. She had complete faith and confidence in God, always, all through her childhood. Everyone in Domremy knew that she had a special relationship with the King of Heaven, as she apparently named him, even though it was only later that we heard that she felt she was specifically instructed in her tasks. And it is obvious that you of Orléans knew the same thing. Many of you who were with her on those days when she fought against the English have told me of her devoutness, of the time she spent in prayer, of her certainty that she was told what to do.

Did they choose the judgment of heresy because they knew that was a certain way to humiliate her? By turning something which guided and comforted her every day into a false belief, a glamour, an illusion, they dug away at the very essence of her. Did they make her doubt herself? I can only hope not, for then her end would have been anguished indeed. But now, to have her name cleared of that gross insult 'heretic' has become more important than anything else in my life.

But of course, nothing is ever so straightforward. Despite the findings of Guillaume Bouillé, as eminent a churchman as can be found, it seems that only the Pope can undo the verdict, and cleanse her name of that taint. And so we have waited. And waited. But now, at last, the Pope's legate has suggested that my sons and I might initiate a re-trial. Let it be so. How honoured I would be to do that. How wonderful, when I did so little when my Jehanette was alive, to help to restore her innocence now

You demur when I say that I did little for Jehanne when she was alive, and you pay me great respect by that. Too much respect. We don't know all that was said at her trial yet, but I have heard enough to know that she refused time and again to try and save herself by telling untruths, or evading questions to deceive her judges. I can only honour her by trying to apply those same standards to myself. I must always remember that I gave her no encouragement and support to go to the aid of the Dauphin, as he was then, and of France. She knew that she must find a way to leave without her father and I knowing, that we would do everything to stop her, because as I now understand it, we were too stuck in our traditional life to see what might be possible. However I berate myself, I cannot see how it could have been otherwise, so unimaginable was what she apparently called her 'mission'. But I never saw her again after that. Jacques and some of the villagers saw her at Reims of course, but I was never to see her bright face or hold her in my arms again, except in my dreams.

And in my memories of course. I'm going on, aren't I, in the morose way of an old, disappointed woman? You wanted to know about her childhood. Let me try and recall for you the first time I took Jehanne up to Bermont, the little hermitage a short walk from our home, when we were all happy despite the war.

It was a Saturday, I expect, because even in our hard-working lives there was a pattern in the week, and on that afternoon none but essential tasks were done. Of course, in a household of four children and numerous animals, it was difficult to get to that place of relative leisure. Often it seemed however hard I worked before the mid-day

216

meal – brushing out the house and laying down fresh hay for the animals, preparing meat and vegetables for the evening meal, clearing out after the chickens, gathering up the ashes from the insatiable fire – there was always more to do. Besides, I must be behind the children to help all the time: get the eggs in, Jehanne – no, not you Petit-Jean, you will only break them, you go and get wood for the fire. Come on, Cathérine, for of course that precious daughter was still with us then, get those clothes laid out on the stones to dry before the sun starts to go down. And Pierrelot, just run over to Tante Marguerite's, will you, and see if she can let us have a little bread. Tell her I'll bake tomorrow and give her a loaf back. I can hear my voice berating them for not getting the work done.

Every mother will tell you how exhausting it is keeping children at their jobs, for at any second each could be diverted by some more attractive idea. Everyday there was so much to do just to keep everyone warm and fed and clothed. But at last I could throw my good shawl over my shoulders, find Jehanne and go. She wasn't hard to find. This was the first time I had said she could come with me, and she had been perched on an old stump of wood at the back of the house for some time already, running in now and then to make sure I hadn't managed to slip out without her.

To get to Bermont, we had to walk away from the back of our house and the village, up the hill and along the edge of the woods. It was a long way for such a little girl, but we made our way slowly, stopping frequently to look down on the villages below along the valley, the patchwork of fields and the wide, curving river. How beautiful it was.

'Green, all green,' I remember Jehanne singing in her happy little child voice. The trees wore the rich tones of early summer, and the grassy verges, where the sun shone, were alight with purple and yellow flowers.

Eventually we emerged into a clearing in the trees, and on the flat top of the hill stood the chapel. 'Notre Dame de Bermont,' called Jehanne. 'Here we are at last.'

The tiny chapel lay squat and quiet in the forest clearing. As we entered, it seemed dark after the shady green of the trees, the small window spaces allowing only a little light into the grey interior. Jehanne held fast to my hand, and we walked slowly to the front where the Virgin stood, a few lighted candles brightening her homely, smiling face.

I remember taking a small white candle out of a fold in my dress and giving it to Jehanne, warning her to take care not to burn herself. Her eyes flashed in the darkness. She had never had a candle before. 'Me? Can I?'

Carefully she lit the candle from one of the others, and set it in the holder. We knelt in front of the statue.

'Look, Maman', she said. 'The baby Jesus has a little dove on his arm.'

I have never found such peace as in the dark coolness of that chapel. If I had known of the many troubles to come, I might have appreciated it more. Of course, it was here that I heard the details of her cruel death from Richard Moreau; perhaps I could not have borne to hear it anywhere else. But on that day, I remember the old priest and Jehanne murmuring at the base of the statue of St Thiébaut on the other side of the rough table that served as an altar, and her placing the flowers she had picked in a jug of water he brought for her.

Eventually I came to, and noticed that Jehanne was no longer in the chapel. I had no idea how much time had passed, and hurried out into the light. But there she was lying on the grass at the edge of the trees.

Her eyes were deep brown pools as she smiled up at me. 'Their faces were full of light,' she said, gazing upwards, and pointing vaguely at the trees.

I remember glancing up to where the sun was shedding its warm, late-afternoon rays through the branches of the tall trees around. The slight breeze caused the branches to move slightly, breaking up the beams of light in a leafy kaleidoscope. I asked her what she meant, whose faces.

'Oh, you know,' she replied vaguely getting to her feet and rushing off after a rabbit that was running through the grass.

That was Jehanne as a child. Do you think I should have known what would happen, from such small instances?

DECEMBER 1455

Paris

1

Zabillet walked slowly across the square in front of the cathedral. She felt guided and supported by the many men and women behind, who had come with her all the way from Orléans to Paris. 'We are here for Jehanne,' they shouted. 'We are here for justice,' shouted others, whilst others simply chanted 'Jehanne, La Pucelle'.

As they crossed the square bystanders, attracted by the celebratory happiness of the small crowd came over, and attached themselves, joining in the chants.

Zabillet looked at her two sons, one on each side of her, and pushed her arms more securely through theirs. They looked down at her and smiled; Petit-Jean, wiry, slender, strong in his captain's clothes; Pierre, big and broad, a calm happiness in his eyes. 'Even in Paris they love her,' he said, 'though it is so long ago, and they never knew her here.'

'They know she tried to free Paris,' said Petit-Jean. 'And perhaps would have succeeded if the King hadn't called her and d'Alençon back. What a mistake he made that day.'

'They certainly suffered under the English,' replied Zabillet, remembering the stories of poverty and plague. 'But we must forget all that. We are going to do something important for our Jehanette today.'

She looked up at the huge façade of the cathedral, the great towers and rose window; the perfect enormity of it. 'Notre Dame,' she murmured. 'I am a long way from the little church of Domremy, or even of Orléans, yet Our Lady is just the same here as there.'

She saw that a small group of priests and lawyers were waiting for them in the porch, and began to move more purposefully towards them. She could not be said to be moving more quickly, for her limbs that were once so strong would no longer take her as fast or as far as she would like. She leant strongly on her sons.

But despite the frailty of her body, Zabillet felt a great strength and resolution within her. All the years, all her life she felt, she had sat at home and waited for things to happen. Waited for people to arrive and tell her what had happened. Relied on others to guess what would happen next. Depended on others to interpret events for her so she could try to understand them.

She had sat idly by whilst Jehanne came to understand her mission. She had resisted every sign of her being 'different'. She had let her go without having any idea of her desire, her need to leave. She had not gone after her. She had not … she had not … she had not.

She had learnt to forgive herself a little over the years. It was after all more than a matter of listing the shoulds, and should nots, the dones and not dones. But nevertheless on this day, she thought, I am going to do something for my poor dead daughter. Whole cycles of life have gone round since the English set the flames to her body, but today I am going to stand up and do something for my Jehanette.

A man detached himself from the small group and came towards her. She could see that he was smiling, and he used a wide hand-gesture towards the many people shouting and declaiming behind her.

'My goodness, Zabillet,' he said by way of greeting. 'Have you brought all the good folk of Orléans with you?' He took hold of her hands.

'Good day, dear Pierre Maugier,' she said. 'You know, these people have always supported Jehanne in life and in death. How would anyone keep them away? Or wish to? Now, what's going to happen?'

'Well, I think we shall have to wait for a while, they're not quite ready for us yet,' said the lawyer. 'And then we will go in, and you will be asked to state your reason for coming, and what you seek. You know what to say then, don't you?'

'I certainly do,' smiled Zabillet. 'I have rehearsed it in front of these boys here a hundred times.' She looked towards the dark shadow of the entrance to the church. 'That doesn't mean I'm not nervous, though.'

She felt the imposing façade of the building. What right did she have to go into such a place and make speeches?

'Maman, Maman!' chided Pierre. 'There is no need to fear.'

'No need at all,' said Pierre Maugier. 'You are only asking for justice for Jehanne, who was denied it so cruelly. And this retrial is wanted, you know, really wanted by the King and all his advisers. And the Pope himself. Nothing can go wrong today.'

'You're right,' said Zabillet laughing shakily. 'Sometimes I just wonder how a countrywoman like me can have any business with the King or the Pope.'

Petit-Jean shook her gently. 'Come on, don't think about them now. It's a big day, but it is for Jehanne. Don't worry.'

'You're right,' said Zabillet. 'I must remember that whatever I am facing today is absolutely nothing compared to what she faced. I'm just being foolish.'

'I tell you what,' said Pierre Maugier, looking at Pierre and Petit-Jean. 'If one of you would stay out here with the people, just so they know nothing is going to happen without them, then we can take your mother into the cathedral, and have a look round. Perhaps that will make it easier.'

'I'll stay,' said Pierre, looking at where his wife was standing patiently at the front of the crowd with their children and Guillaumette, all grown young men and women now. 'Most of the people here know me anyway, and they know they won't be missing anything if I'm out here. You go with Maman, Petit-Jean. It's better if she's able to sit down in there whilst we wait.'

Leaning heavily on Petit-Jean, Zabillet passed into the cool darkness of the cathedral. It is a whole world within a world, she thought, gazing up, up and out at the immense curved height of the arches; noticing within the silence the small sounds of the people who were here caring for this vast place, brushing, trimming candles, polishing metal and placing flowers; glimpsing the richness of the choir and the altar far ahead of her; blinking in the mauve light of the huge rich windows. But despite its enormous sombreness, she felt calmer now. The faint smell of incense and candles was well-known and comforting to her, the statues and pictures no different from those she had seen in so many churches.

The familiar act of dipping her fingers into the holy water, crossing herself and bowing deeply to the cross, calmed her further.

'Let's go into one of the side chapels,' she said to Petit-Jean. 'It will be easier to wait there.'

2

Zabillet sat in the candle-lit darkness of the chapel of Our Lady and prayed that she would be strong enough today to set things right for Jehanne. 'It has been so long,' she murmured in her prayers, 'so very long.'

Zabillet was not necessarily thinking of the long, long years since Jehanne had been burnt. Nor was she thinking of the years of grief and war and loss and poverty, not just for her and her family but for the whole of France; the endless years when it seemed as though Jehanne might never have been, her memory, deeds and achievements lost in the bitter stalemate between the French and the English. Neither side cared enough to win, it seemed, and certainly cared little about the suffering of the people. The King enjoyed the luxury of his court on the Loire whilst the people starved, and the English Lords' eyes were diverted towards problems in their own country. Then, slowly, it began to change. She didn't know how or why, but Normandy, which for the best part of a hundred years had been ruled by the English – and perhaps even the French expected it to remain that way – had begun to fall to the French captains; some of those same brave captains who had fought alongside Jehanne.

No, it was not really of those years of despair that she thought, sitting facing the statue of Our Lady in her own chapel within her vast cathedral, though they formed the background of her thoughts. It was more the strange and wonderful turn of events of the last few years, since the King had eventually entered Rouen, the capital of England in France, and freed it from decades of occupation. And this King, whom Zabillet had never forgiven for abandoning Jehanne to her English captors, and being at the very least complicit in her death although of course not directly responsible – this cowardly, procrastinating, neglectful King had suddenly appointed Guillaume Bouillé and said, 'I want to know how our Jehanne was judged to be a heretic.' And astonishingly, within only weeks, Duke Charles d'Orléans was calling to see Pierre to tell him that Guillaume had found that the trial had been falsely conducted in so many various ways that its verdict could not be considered just. 'Your sister's good name will surely be restored,' he said delightedly.

Justice. All at once, Zabillet found she had an unquenchable thirst for it. Now it was an idea that was coming alive within her, and it uncovered feelings that had been buried for many long years. The story began to unfold of the terrible manipulations of Jehanne's judges, of their brutal tricks and physical violence against her, and of how she bore it all with no advocate or friend. Zabillet wept at the terrible pity of her momentary relapse, when she denied the very essence of herself for fear of death, and then, at some point later, said, shouted into the silence "NO! I would rather die than deny myself and my Counsel". Her grief and courage as she faced the stacked up wood that was to burn her shook Zabillet to the core, as it did the many people who had loved her. And shook her, and shook her again as she heard of the cruelty of the learned scholarly priests towards a young girl all alone.

But that thirst for justice, so quickly roused, had to wait and wait, so long, to be slaked. It was a church trial, they said, so only the Pope can declare it null and void. And miraculously, the Pope did order another enquiry, meticulously carried out by Jean Brehal, his Inquisitor. And then the Pope died. Another year had gone by, and another. Until finally the new Pope gave permission for the events of this day.

But Zabillet had learnt that there was more to it than the desire to overturn an unjust decision against a young girl who had been the saviour of France. One day, sitting by her fire with Pierre and Petit-Jean, she had said, 'It does amaze me. Maybe I've been wrong to judge the King so harshly when he seems so determined to see the verdict on Jehanette overturned.'

Petit-Jean laughed bitterly, a laugh never far away when the King's name was mentioned. 'It's not for love of her, you can be sure of that.'

'Petit-Jean,' said Pierre reproachfully. 'Let's give the King a little credit. I'm sure he does want her name restored.'

'Oh I'm sure he does,' replied Petit-Jean. 'But you know as well as I do that he only wants what suits himself.'

'What are you two talking about?' said Zabillet. 'Surely the King has started this enquiry because he knows as well as you or me that there was nothing of the heretic about Jehanne.'

There was silence in the room.

'I think he does,' said Pierre at last. 'I'm sure he does. I suppose what Petit-Jean and I and a lot of her friends have been wondering is why, when in all these years he has never once mentioned her name, or ever allowed us to talk about her in his presence, he is now so intent on restoring her. We can only assume that now he's the powerful King of all of France, he wants to remember the young woman who had him crowned, and started it all.'

'What he means,' cut in Petit-Jean, 'is that it is not good for the King's success to be associated with someone who was declared a heretic, so he has decided it would be best if her name was cleared.'

Zabillet sat silently considering this. How they were all at the mercy of that incomprehensible concept, politics. After all, was it not politics which had marred and sought to prevent the fulfilment of Jehanne's clear vision? Was it not politics which had assured Jehanne's death from the moment she was captured? Was it not politics which had made the King turn his back on her and do nothing to prevent her death? Well, it was no wonder then if it was politics now which drove the King to clear her name. She struggled to her feet, and began to take plates and bowls from the table.

'I'm glad you have said this,' she said, 'because I had forgotten that what is right or wrong is not always the first consideration of these people. But I don't care. I'm too old to bother about any man's motives. If the right thing is done at last by our Jehanette, that is quite enough for me.'

3

Zabillet felt a tap on her shoulder. It was Pierre Maugier. 'It is time, Zabillet,' he said gently.

Removing her attention from the Holy Mother after a last plea for courage, Zabillet could hear different sounds in the body of the cathedral. The sounds of many people standing, waiting, chatting quietly.

'The Bishops are already there,' continued Pierre Maugier. 'They are waiting for you, Zabillet. You know what you have to do?'

Zabillet allowed him and Petit-Jean to help her to her feet. She nodded her head. 'Oh yes,' she said, nervous but smiling. 'I have been waiting for a very long time for the chance to ask them to set aside that foul judgment. Come on Petit-Jean, let us not keep these gentlemen waiting.'

Supported by Petit-Jean, she began to walk across the church towards where she could see the small group of brightly-dressed bishops standing with the more sober clerics, priests and lawyers.

As the crowd in the body of the church saw her, they began to cheer and shout, calling her name, or Jehanne's, or that of France. Surely there were far more people than the group of Orléannais who had travelled with her.

Pierre turned towards her, his warm excited smile supporting her just as she was beginning to feel overwhelmed. He reached out his hand and drew her forward. 'It is for Jehanne,' he whispered simply.

The Archbishop of Reims smiled at Zabillet and greeted her. He nodded to Pierre Maugier to indicate that he was ready to begin. In a huge, stentorian voice designed to be heard by everyone in that vast place, he asked Zabillet why she had come.

'Shall I start, Zabillet?' asked Pierre Maugier, straightening the roll of parchment in his hand. Zabillet nodded.

'I had a daughter …'

'I had a daughter …' repeated Zabillet. Her voice was little more than a whisper. The crowd started murmuring and pressing forward to hear. 'Sshh, sshh,' they said. The Orléannais men and women drew together, forming a protective barrier around the group.

'I had a daughter,' she said more loudly, 'born in marriage, who took the sacraments of baptism and confirmation. I raised her in the fear of God and respect for the traditions of the church as she grew up in the fields and pastures, and she went frequently to church and received the sacrament each month. Despite her youth, she gave herself up to fasting and prayer with great devotion and fervour, for the sufferings of the people were great at that time, and she sympathized with all her heart.'

'Yes, yes,' shouted several in the crowd. 'Jehanne! La Pucelle!' Louder and louder until the Archbishop raised his hand for silence.

'But..' prompted Pierre Maugier, loud above the noise of the many people in the nave of the cathedral, who were trying to move closer to hear Zabillet or at least see her.

'But,' repeated Zabillet in little more than a whisper.

'Quiet! Shh!' said the people. Silence fell across the crowd.

'Although she never thought or did anything to offend against the Faith, certain enemies betrayed her in a trial concerning that Faith, despite her disclaimers and appeals. Moreover, no aid was given to her innocence.' Zabillet's voice began to gain in strength, broken by sobs, expressing years of pain and indignation. Even the unusual, complicated words she had been schooled to use could not hide that outrage.

'It was a perfidious, violent and iniquitous trial without shadow of right. They condemned her in a damnable and criminal fashion and put her to death most cruelly by fire, for the damnation of their souls and with irreparable damage done to me and mine.'

She held up the hands of Pierre and Petit-Jean who stood at her side supporting her.

'We demand a just sentence to be delivered.'

Zabillet was aware of a great cheering breaking the silence behind her. People were waving their hats in the air, cursing the English, shouting Jehanne's name. They pressed forward again to show Zabillet their support and she, tears streaming down her face, began to turn towards them to thank them. But as she raised her hand, a wave of dizziness sent her lurching into Pierre who could only let her down gently to the ground. She fell into blackness.

Zabillet came to in the sacristy. She was lying on a bench and Guillaumette was smoothing her face and dampening her lips with a small wet cloth, whilst Petit-Jean waved his papers to create a little fresh air around her.

'Jehanne!' she said, starting up. 'Jehanne! I must...'

'Ssh,' said Pierre, who was standing looking anxiously down at her. 'We are all still here.'

The darkly-clad figure of Pierre Maugier came within her view.

'Just rest a few minutes. The Archbishop wants to make sure you are quite well before we continue.'

'Do you feel all right? Does it hurt anywhere?'

'No, I'm all right, thank you. It was just a bit overwhelming out there. I hadn't expected so many people.'

'Come,' said Pierre. 'Let me raise you up a little so you can drink some water. It was wonderful, wasn't it? So many people who never knew Jehanne, quite apart from our neighbours in Orléans. All shouting for her. And you said everything exactly as we'd planned.'

The two men raised their mother so she was sitting on the bench, and Guillaumette handed her a bowl of water to drink.

Pierre Maugier came back to Zabillet's side from where he had been talking to the Bishops at the other end of the sacristy.

'Zabillet,' he said. 'The Archbishop of Reims has confirmed that there are just one or two more things which need to be done today. They can be done here in the sacristy with just us, but then he would prefer to make an announcement in front of the people in the cathedral. Basically, he will announce the new trial. Are you strong enough, or would you prefer it all to take place in here?'

Zabillet raised herself to her feet, holding on to Guillaumette. 'Those good people of Orléans must hear this,' she said. 'It is for them just as much as for us. Also the people from Paris who I don't know, they want to hear that there will be justice for Jehanne too. Come, let us get any questions done with here, and then go back into the cathedral. I am fine. I would not wish to let anyone down. This is a great day.'

A few minutes later, as Zabillet slowly made her stiff way back to her place at the head of the nave, supported by her sons, the crowd fell silent. They had kept up a chant of Jehanne's name throughout their wait, but now they wanted to hear the answer to Zabillet's request.

Pierre Maugier briefly but eloquently made the request again, and the Bishops appeared to consider it briefly.

Then the Archbishop said, his voice resonating throughout the cathedral. 'His Holiness the Pope has appointed us to investigate your request to nullify the verdict of heresy against your daughter Jehanne. That we consent to do. The enquiry will start immediately. May God help us to find the truth.'

The Archbishop stepped forward and blessed Zabillet and her sons, and with a sweep of his arms included all the people standing there. They parted to allow her to go out, out of the cold, dark stone building into the bright winter light. As they pressed behind her, their chants began to ring out again. Zabillet stood for a moment in the doorway, feeling the pale sun on her face. She sighed deeply.

CONVERSATIONS

Zabillet talks with Our Lady at Sandillon

My heart is filled with joy. Justice, at last! Oh, I know it hasn't quite happened yet, and I have lived long enough to know that I mustn't assume that anything is certain until it becomes reality. But I don't see anything preventing the Pope's appointees from announcing the innocence of Jehanette in the next few days, and declaring the verdict of that evil court null and void. Rejoice with me! I know you must.

Dear Holy Mother, you ask me why it matters. Your eyes are calm and serene, untroubled by the verdict of any earthly court, challenging me also to be unconcerned. You may say "We know, you and I, that all the important things that Jehanne did were by the Will of Heaven, so why worry?" I find it difficult to think why it matters. You are right, in many ways it does not matter at all. She is dead. Nothing can change that. She has been, or will be, judged in heaven like the rest of us when that time comes. Why should it matter, how she came about her death? After all, young people are dying all the time, as did my poor Cathérine, so what is the difference?

I can only stumble towards thinking what those differences are. There is so much evil in this world, but we can choose how we behave. There is honour and dishonour. They chose to burn my Jehanne as a witch at the stake, and having concocted the evidence, twisted facts to present a 'truth', or enough 'truth' to lull people's worries, and justify an end that had been decided long before. They did not have to do that, and none of those clerics, her judges, had or found the strength to oppose it. But you are right, of course. No matter what is said, the ending can never be any different, and the judgment of heaven will always be the same. But here and now, for us, the truth can be allowed to unfold. That is worth something.

And then, it's something that anyone must do for the person they love, if the chance comes along. To do whatever can be done to restore their good name and expose the wrong-doing of those who made such harsh and unjust judgments. To turn around the balance of power, when the loved one was so powerless at that time. What would the world become if powerful people were not brought to account, shamed for their ill deeds? It would have pleased Jehanne, who hated the power of position. It is one of the things that the people of Orléans remember about her. She listened to them, and accomplished what she did for them for their own sake, not obeying the lords and captains necessarily. That is why they adore her.

You know, Holy Mother, how long a journey it has been to get here. I am told that her trial lasted little more than three months, though she was in prison a year before it started. Three months to try her, judge her to be a heretic, sentence her to death, trick her into believing she could yet live, burn her. Then untold years for justice to be done. A whole generation. Already Guillaumette is older than my Jehanne ever was.

It is important for the sake of her memory too, how she will be remembered. If this injustice always remains, then people who wish to do so will be able to doubt what she did, and why. But if the verdict of her twenty-five judges is overturned after a thorough retrial, by the Pope himself, no-one will be able to name her a heretic again.

I have learnt so much about the cruelty of men as her story has unfolded during these enquiries, unbelievable acts of heartlessness. And I have had to face the part of her story that had remained a mystery to me, and in some details still does, those few days between the sentence being read out at the Cemetery of St-Ouen, and her burning at the stake just days later.

I could understand when Richard Moreau told us that day at

Bermont how Jehanne could deny her Counsel and agree she was a heretic, although it grieved me greatly. A young girl, however strong, must be weakened after months in a small prison cell with mocking, jeering and abusive guards, and endless interrogations by clever hostile people who want little more than to catch her out. She had no friend or advocate and only you, Holy Mother, know how she retained her strength and clear vision during month after month of bleakness with no relief. I hope she felt your presence with her. And at that moment, humiliated, misunderstood, beaten down, faced with the reality of the wood stacked up in the executioner's cart ready to burn her young self alive, no-one could blame her for choosing life, even if it meant a life spent in prison.

You know, though I cannot, whether she truly doubted in that moment. Whether she was weakened in her belief by the hardship of the previous year, and whether her public statement denying her Counsel had become her inner conviction. I hope not. I hope with all my heart she did not enter that desolation where she doubted everything she had believed in until that time. I pray that it was a denial in words only, out of fear for her life. I believe it was. She was still but a young girl, despite all she had done.

Jacques always said that a terrible trick was then played on her. I resisted this idea for a long time, but the enquiry has proved him right. Heretics should be held in a church prison, and she should have been guarded by women. Her words after that terrible ordeal at St-Ouen show she believed this would be the case. Instead she was returned to the same prison cell in the castle and her old English soldier guards who had nothing but contempt for her, and the desire to be rid of her. Witnesses at the enquiry say she signed just a few words written on a paper at St-Ouen that day, not the long detailed statement that was found in the trial documents, and which she probably never saw – another trick by the evil Bishop Cauchon to justify his wrongdoing. And it was all a farce. Many overheard the English saying that despite what she had said and signed that day, she would certainly still die. Some way would be found, whether it had a semblance of justice or not.

Holy Mother, you teach us to bear whatever life has to offer. Would that I could follow the example of my poor Jehanette who it is said even in the moments before she was tied to the stake, forgave those who were perpetrating this dreadful deed. But I cannot forgive, do not ask it of me, it is pure anger that still courses through my veins when I consider the misery of her last few days, and the fire on her body.

The enquiries have not been able to establish exactly what happened in the short time before her death. We know she had been made to agree to wear women's clothes, but within days had resumed her hose and doublet. Some say the guards made sexual assaults on her, and she put on men's clothes to protect herself. Some say the guards took her dress away and only men's clothes were available when she had to get up out of bed. Whatever happened, that was the moment when she was finally ground down. She had renounced her beliefs for what? More misery and humiliation. She might as well die, putting her faith in God's mercy as she always had, and having his comfort.

Countless years of silence followed. And even then, it has taken six years to hold all the different enquiries, to declare her innocent. So long, although it appears the King and even the Pope wished for it. Two Popes. Never mind, the important thing is that we are almost there.

I thank you, Holy Mother, that I am still alive to hear it. That was my great fear, for you know how old and frail I've become. I who once harvested grain, thrashed the washing in the river to clean it, carried water daily, cured the great haunches of the pig, can now hardly dress myself. I have become totally dependent on Guillaumette and others for all household tasks, and spend a great deal of time dozing in the sun and rehearsing the stories of my family in my mind. And I know that my life is coming to an end, to its timely end, and if you should preserve me just a short while longer until her name is cleared, I shall be glad to go, and come to you.

My life has been long, too long perhaps. Nearly all of it has been filled with this terrible conflict between England and France. War has been my companion throughout my life, with the poverty, disruption and loss it brings. It is only now, as my life is ending, that the English have more or less left France, been forced to leave France, and we can begin the life that Jehanne wished for us so long ago. When she defeated the English at Orléans, we could never have guessed that a quarter of a century or more would be needed still to complete her work.

My life and that of my family has been entwined with the battle of our country for freedom in ways we could never have thought of. Loss, pain, poverty, fighting. Like every peasant family of course, but our difference was Jehanette. Who can say why she was born to us? Is it written, Holy Mother, or does it just happen?

MAY 1456

Justice

1

Zabillet sat quietly with Pierre in the shady courtyard of her little cottage at Sandillon. She had lived here for a couple of years now, having begun to long for the wide-open spaces of the countryside. She had loved to be in Orléans, staying with Pierre and his family first in their house, and then in the little château Duke Charles d'Orléans had given him just outside the city, and enjoyed the friendship of the many townspeople who had known and loved Jehanne. But as her joints began to stiffen and Pierre's household became more busy and noisy as the children grew, she began to crave the sight of trees and grass from her window, the sound of animals being herded into the fields and back home at night, the resonance of the church bell ringing the times of day across the quiet of the village, and long for the simple life of the peasant.

So Pierre had found this little cottage for her in a tiny village just a few miles from the city. It wasn't Domremy of course. The Loire, an enormously wide river at this point, filled with tufted islets, could not be heard from her house, although it was not far away, and there were no hills rising gently and then steeply behind and in front of her. The land was less harsh, pushing up crops in a way that seemed almost casual in comparison with the less fertile soil of home. And to her surprise, she had discovered that snow was rare here in the winter, and the summer sun shone brighter and longer and more constantly. But despite such differences, her neighbours were engaged with their land in just the same way as her friends in Domremy. Sowing seed, protecting growth, harvesting the products, tending the animals, spinning and weaving, using what they could and trading the rest. These had been happy years for Zabillet, eased by the presence of her two sons, and blessed by the devotion of Guillaumette, now a young woman who had only agreed to marry her husband on condition that he came to live in Zabillet's cottage, and allow her to continue to care for her.

Zabillet and Pierre were waiting for Petit-Jean. They had been waiting for him for days, and every morning Pierre had ridden over to sit with her and bring her such news as he had.

'I'll kill him if he's stopped off somewhere on the way,' growled Pierre impatiently.

Zabillet laughed. 'I don't think he'll do that,' she said. 'He'll come.'

Pierre muttered into his beard. She knew he was thinking of the many times Petit-Jean had let them down, pursued his own interests at the expense of theirs.

'He's not like he was,' she continued. 'Those times are past. I've grown proud of him since he became captain of Chartres. And now he's in old Robert de Baudricourt's position in Vaucouleurs! How wonderful to have someone in the family back in our old place. No, don't worry, Pierre, he'll not let us down again.'

'I still wish you had let me go,' said Pierre. His voice had the slightly sulky note of the teenager.

Zabillet laughed and put her hand on his arm. 'Could I have stopped you?' she said regarding his huge frame sitting there, his hair quite grey, but his muscles still finely tuned from working on his farm. She was silent a moment. 'I wanted Petit-Jean to go,' she continued. 'You have always been faithful to Jehanette. You've never spoken one word against her despite all those terrible years that you spent as a prisoner. Of course, you deserved to go if you wanted to. But it seemed good to me that it should be Petit-Jean.'

Zabillet fell silent. She was thinking of how he had suffered when Jehanne and Pierre had been captured, then the long years when she did not see him, did not know where he was. She did not like to think of his life during that time, how he had lived, who had suffered for it. And yet, when the King had at last been ready to fight again for his country, he had been there, an able, strong soldier fighting with the other captains to reclaim Normandy bit by bit, and finally be rewarded with the captaincy of Chartres. And Guillaumette of course had come out of those years.

'It was a long journey for him,' she said, thinking of when he had finally sought her out in Orléans. 'All through these last few years you have both worked so hard to clear Jehanette's name. Perhaps we should all have gone to Rouen, but I don't think I could make that journey now. No, I'm glad that Petit-Jean is there for us all.'

'I am too,' said Pierre. 'Don't take any notice of me. I'm happy for him to be there, I was pleased that he wanted to go so much, and it's true that it would have been difficult for me to go. It's just this waiting, I never was any good at that.'

'We've waited a long time, haven't we?' said Zabillet. 'But we're nearly there now. Who would have thought it? Guillaumette likes to keep track of these things, and she says it's six years since the King first enquired about how Jehanne came to be burnt at the stake, though we knew nothing of that at the time. Now it is almost over.'

'I do hope so,' said Pierre, suddenly shivering. 'Come on, Petit-Jean, put us out of our misery. I've learnt the hard way never to assume good news.'

She must have dozed off for a while, as when she came to the sun had moved a way across the yard. Pierre was teasing Guillaumette who was folding the clothes dried in the heat of the day. 'Isn't it amazing,' Zabillet said to him as he settled down beside her again, 'how everybody has remembered Jehanne? A whole generation has gone by since she died, and yet so many people wanted to go to the enquiry and tell them what they remember about her.'

'I was surprised. I could understand the Domremy people turning out when the enquiry moved there for a few days because they were so proud of Jehanette and of course they had all her childhood to recall. And from what I heard, they told it in great detail! But here in Orléans, well it's been unbelievable.'

Zabillet remembered those wintry days when the enquiry held its sessions in Orléans.

'I was glad to be there,' said Zabillet. 'Although it was so cold. They didn't know her for long, just a few days really when you think about it, but even through all the dark years after she died, when she was forgotten or disregarded by everyone else, they celebrated what she had done for their city. It was wonderful to hear what they said. The ordinary people especially.'

'Yes, they spoke as if she had delivered the city only yesterday,' said Pierre. 'I had much more hazy memories than them, you know. I was just a boy when I fought alongside Jehanne in those days. I'd never seen so many people, never mind soldiers and weapons.' He laughed.

'A true country lad!' said Zabillet smiling.

'It was total confusion. Horrible! I didn't like the fighting, you know, not like Petit-Jean. All I wanted to do was stick close to Jehanette and try to make sure she didn't get hurt, and then come back home as soon as possible. I didn't realize she was so very special, even then. She was just my little sister doing something foolhardy. I don't know what I'd have thought if I'd had any idea what would happen after that.'

'Foolhardy, yes she was that. But you know the people here believe she did something miraculous when she helped save their town. I mean more than just a lucky or well-fought battle with the strange circumstance of having a girl at its head. Though that in itself was as unusual as anything could possibly be! But those people who came to the enquiry thought it was more than that.'

'We had no idea in Domremy at that time quite how desperate the situation was for the French,' said Pierre. 'It's hard to remember now they've gone that the English were supremely confident, determined to make the country their own. The Treaty of Troyes had more or less given it to them, after all.' He spat his contempt into the ground.

'They had reason to be confident,' said Zabillet. 'You were still a boy when the old mad King signed France over to the English, and disinherited the poor Dauphin, as King Charles was then. How we hated him for that, though probably he had very little choice. The English had already won so many battles on French soil. And many people, even around Domremy, thought that was best. Even me. Jacques used to get so angry with me when I said I thought peace was worth anything, even the country being ruled by the English, I'm ashamed to say. But that's what I thought sometimes.'

'I can understand that. Life was falling apart, wasn't it? And suddenly up jumps our Jehanette from nowhere and starts to turn everything on its head. The English were so sure of themselves that if Orléans had fallen there's no doubt they would have pressed south with hardly any resistance, and that would have been it. How amazed they must have been to see our Jehanette all bright in armour waving her standard at the head of the army.' They laughed with delight.

'We'll never know, will we,' said Zabillet, wonder in her voice, 'how she came to do those things?'

'It was also her undoing, you know, as well as her success, because they became convinced she must be a witch and a sorceress.'

'It's been good during these last few months to hear what people have been saying to the enquiry. I'd thought she was quite forgotten except in Domremy – just another of those figures who does something amazing in the world and then is never heard of again. Only their family remembers them. But when I came to live in Orléans, I soon learned that people here had such belief in her. "Don't you worry, Isabelle," they would say, "we will get justice for Jehanne one day." And here we are, maybe that justice is almost here.'

'If Petit-Jean ever arrives,' said Pierre, but no longer angry, happy to wait. 'What was so wonderful about the witnesses was that it didn't matter if they were dukes or captains or ordinary people, they all had a similar view of her.'

'Yes, from all they said, Orléans had been a miserable place before she arrived. Everyone crowded into the city, dependent on the Bastard or the King sending in supplies, and seemingly no-one having the will to fight off the English stranglehold. Then she arrives and gives them great hope, and in a few days the English are routed and on the run.'

'What I like,' said Pierre, 'is how everyone says the English completely lost heart when we arrived, and Jehanne started telling people what she was going to do. The French army was able to march into Orléans under the nose of the English, and they did nothing. How could that be? The life was somehow transferred from the English to the French and the battle was won.'

'You're beginning to sound like the Orléannais at Jehanne's celebrations,' smiled Zabillet. 'She has become such a legend. "You know, she got an arrow in her shoulder, and she insisted they pull it out, though she was in great pain. It was in a hand's length, you know. Then she got up and routed the English." Or, "I remember when she entered Orléans first, at night, and a lantern caught her standard alight, and she just turned her horse to the wind, and it went out. She could do anything on a horse." So many stories.'

'Some more likely than others. Do you have a favourite?' asked Pierre.

'I've got so many wonderful pictures of her in my mind,' said Zabillet, 'nearly all given to me by these people who treasure their store of memories about her. I love what they tell me about how before the battle, she stood on the town end of the bridge and challenged the English captains Glassidas and Talbot in their tower at the other end. You know, told them to take the English army home, or she would send them packing. She was so brave, and she wanted to give them warning. Determined and fair. They just saw a girl of course, daring to shout at them across the river. They had no idea. I like that picture of her standing there, innocent, defiant, totally convinced that she had the right of it.'

'I remember that,' said Pierre. 'I was with her even though I'd no idea what was going on. She insisted on being taken seriously, but they just saw a girl and shouted insults back. It upset her, their language was so foul. I remember her crying. Not that it deterred her.'

'They recognized her power soon enough. In fact, they feared that power so much that they did everything to suppress it once they caught her. They weren't going to let her go, that's for sure.' Zabillet gave a deep sigh. 'They needn't have killed her so cruelly, though.'

Pierre stretched across and took her hand. 'Nothing can take that away, can it Maman? Not even if a thousand people came to the enquiry to honour her, and tell us more about her.'

2

The sun had begun to sink behind the trees opposite, gleaming soft and yellow through the branches, causing the light to fade, before Zabillet heard the sound she had been listening for all day, for several days, of a horse riding at a swift clip into the village.

'Pierrelot, it must be him,' she called to her son who was helping pass the time by getting water into the cottage. Zabillet hobbled towards the lane and there was the tall figure of Petit-Jean beginning to pull his horse up. He leapt off and casually threw the rope around the post, and turned toward her.

'Maman!' he said. 'I've ridden all day to get here.' He stretched out his hands in greeting, then ruefully held the small of his back. But no amount of dust or fatigue could hide the bright smile on his face. She put her arms around him and he bent to kiss her.

'Hello,' he said to Pierre who came and clapped him on the back by way of greeting.

'Is it done?' breathed Zabillet, looking up into his face.

'Yes,' said Petit-Jean. 'It's done. It was all fixed as we've known all along. In their words, they've declared her trial and its verdict null and without value or effect.'

'Without value or effect.' Zabillet repeated the strange words as if to grasp their meaning. 'Null. Do you mean it's as if the trial had never been? She is completely innocent?'

'Yes,' said Petit-Jean. 'They did not uphold one thing that was said against her.'

'So no-one believes that she's a heretic any more?'

'That's right. It's struck from the record. There's no longer any blot on her memory.'

Zabillet's face opened into a great smile. She held her hands up to the sky for a moment of thankfulness.

'Oh, my Jehanette,' she called into the night air. 'Do you know this? Justice has been done at last. You are free, we are all free, of that dreadful judgment.'

She put her arms around Pierre and Petit-Jean and held them close. 'Thank you,' she said. 'Thank you for everything you have done to make this happen. No girl had better brothers, that's for sure.' She was weeping now. 'Come, help me sit down. I shall want to hear all about it soon.'

As the men led her back to her seat by the cottage door her weeping grew noisier and she moaned as if the agony of years was being wrested from her. 'I'm sorry,' she said to them at last. 'You must forgive my tears. It has been such a long time! It is so wonderful what has happened, and now everyone knows for sure that Jehanne never turned her back on God or the church. It is a final defeat for the English who were so cruel to her, and for their

French supporters.' She wiped her eyes on her shawl, sobbing still.

'You sit here quietly,' said Pierre. 'I'll ask Guillaumette to set food out whilst Petit-Jean and I see to the horse. She'll be glad to see her father safe, and then he shall tell us all about it.'

'It was very solemn,' said Petit-Jean at last, sitting down with his mother and brother to eat. Guillaumette sat a little apart. She had never known Jehanne of course, but that hadn't stopped her from being part of this long wait. And she kept her usual watchful eye on Zabillet.

'We gathered in the great hall of the Archbishop's palace in Rouen. They said that was where the first sessions of Jehanne's trial were held. But this was a far happier occasion. The sun poured through the windows and people from Rouen packed the hall tight. I sat there with Pierre Maugier imagining how different it must have been then. The English had been ruling in Rouen for years, and who knows what the people felt, seeing young Jehanne and the hope of France put on trial by the English and their cruel French henchmen. Well, we know they didn't like it; otherwise the clerics wouldn't have had to hold all their sessions in the tower where she was imprisoned, or even in her cell, well away from the eyes of the public.

'But today it was full of ordinary people, townsfolk, tradesmen and country people from the villages around, all wanting to hear what had been found. The Archbishop of Reims sat with the two Bishops, and Jean Brehal was there, Maman, just like when we went to Notre-Dame in Paris. Pierre Maugier was with me of course, and our good lawyer, Guillaume. Some of the priests and clerics who'd been involved were there too – Martin Ladvenue for example, you know the one who pleaded for Jehanne to be allowed to make her confession on the day she was to die, and heard it. It was he who held the cross before her as she burnt. Everyone was waiting, expectant.'

'He was one of the few who recognised that Cauchon was intent on carrying out the Goddams' orders, rather than reaching a fair verdict,' said Pierre. 'Not that it made any difference.'

'Well, maybe there were more than we thought,' said Zabillet. 'That's one thing this enquiry has shown, lots of those judges weren't happy with what Cauchon was doing, and even voted against him several times. He took no notice.'

'Well,' said Pierre. 'Maybe they didn't try hard enough.'

'Let's not talk about them,' said Zabillet. 'Some of them were threatened, and one was even put in prison for opposing him. They were weak, perhaps; I don't know if we can forgive them. But carry on, Petit-Jean, none of that matters now.'

'Well, the Archbishop read out this statement. Such a clear strong voice, Maman, so certain. I don't know exactly what he said. Pierre Maugier has a copy of it all, and he said he would come and see us very soon and go through it with us in detail. But I remember his voice ringing round the hall – he said something like the trial and sentence were tainted with fraud and there were many errors of fact and law, and it was null and void. He said "Jehanne is washed clean of infamy". And the people cheered even though it was a court of law, and the ushers were furious.'

Zabillet smiled. 'Wonderful!' she said. 'Wonderful! He actually used those words, "null" and "washed clean"? Oh Pierre, Petit-Jean, is it not everything we hoped for?'

'That's not all,' said Petit-Jean. 'The Archbishop pointed to the clerk and said "Tear up the articles of accusation!" You know, the ones Cauchon had prepared with all his lies as a basis for her sentence. And the clerk stood up and tore these great sheets of parchment into shreds. It was dramatic.' Petit-Jean was silent for a moment whilst the others watched him closely. Tears fell down his cheeks, and he wiped them away slowly. 'That is how her name was washed clean.'

He pulled himself together slowly. 'But that wasn't the end of it. The Archbishop led us out of the great hall and a long procession formed as we walked to the Cemetery of St-Ouen. More people joined us all the time, and there was a huge crowd when we got there. All chanting her name and cheering for the King and the Bishops.'

'A bit like the old days,' said Pierre, a sad regretful smile on his face. 'Was it, Petit-Jean? Like the people were whenever Jehanne came along?'

'It was,' said Petit-Jean. 'It did remind me of when we used to go at the head of the army into those little towns after the battles. How the people would cheer. They all wanted to show their love for her, and for France. It was exactly the same. Anyway, when we got there, the Archbishop read his verdict all over again. It was the exact spot where they made our poor Jehanette agree she was a heretic, you know, to save her life.'

'My poor girl,' said Zabillet. 'What a terrible moment that must have been. I remember Richard Moreau telling your father and I about that day when he came to see us at Bermont. How the executioner had the wood for the stake stacked up where she could see it. It was nothing but another way to torture her.'

'It was both happy and solemn. Despite the cheering, the sadness was profound,' went on Petit-Jean. 'More so the next day, for the Archbishop led another procession from his palace to the Old Market Place in the middle of the town. He stood in the exact same place where she was burnt, and he read the verdict again and preached a short sermon. The place was full, people were weeping rather than cheering. And then something happened which I hadn't been told about. The city aldermen had had a cross made, a huge wooden one, and it was carried out and put up in that place where she was burned. And the Bishop of Paris, I think it was, said that it was to remain there in memory of her forever, and be a place to pray for the salvation of her soul and of others. It was beautiful.'

The three sat in silence, the cottage now dark and lit only by the light from the fire. Zabillet got up and kissed Petit-Jean and Pierre. 'Thank you, Petit-Jean,' she said. 'Thank you both. It is done. The most powerful in the land have agreed that she was innocent and cruelly used. The fact that anyone ever thought otherwise doesn't matter now. That is the most important thing, though nothing can bring her back to us.'

Zabillet sat on by the fire. At her slightest call, Guillaumette would come through and help her to bed, but she wasn't ready yet. She could hear her two sons in the next room talking quietly, no doubt going over details she was too tired to hear just now. How strange that was, and how reassuring; she could not say when last both Pierre and Petit-Jean had stayed with her. Their deep voices and occasional laughter gave her a sense of safety, a sense of family when she had come to look on hers as so fractured. Tomorrow she must ask Pierre to send for Jeanne and the children and grandchildren. They would never forget all those who were lost to them, but that did not mean they had nothing to celebrate.

She thought of Domremy, and hoped that her friends there, friends of Jehanne even after all these years, would hear the news soon. How they would rejoice and, no doubt celebrate, even if there was little village life left compared to earlier times. For a moment she longed to be there, to share this wonderful day with those people, to see the familiar houses, fields and church. Never mind, there would be celebrations here too, and she would be happy to be part of them.

She could not help tears falling as of their own volition, but there was a strange, unknown peace in her heart. There were few days she had not wept for Jehanne over the years, all the many years since she had lost her. Many different kinds of tears there had been, full of anger or compassion or self-pity; even hatred sometimes, bitter with the English, with the French, with the King, with fate, even with God himself. Sometimes it had seemed as if the picture in her mind of the flames eating at her daughter's body would never fade, would always continue to sear her heart.

If time had brought any healing over those many long years, it had been a superficial healing. A healing brought solely by the passage of time, not by any acceptance. The process of the enquiry had uncovered those old wounds and caused new outbreaks of anger and bitterness. She could see how shockingly Jehanne had been treated, not just in the unspeakable manner of her death, but in the filth of her prison and its warders, in her friendlessness throughout a gruelling, senseless trial, in treachery and betrayal.

But now, gazing into the fire which had been her constant companion for good and ill throughout her long life, she felt completely at peace. Peace swept over and through her like a warm cleansing breeze on a hot summer day. It was a sweetness flowing through her veins like the most fragrant of honey. It was the scent of evening flowers, clearing the mind after a hard day, rooting out worry and fatigue. She nodded gently, smiling.